Begonia Brown:

A Philadelphia Story

Begonia Brown:

A Philadelphia Story

Julia Press Simmons

www.urbanbooks.net

Urban Books, LLC
300 Farmingdale Road, NY-Route 109
Farmingdale, NY 11735

ISBN 13: 978-1-64556-660-1

First Mass Market Printing November 2024
First Trade Paperback Printing June 2024
Printed in the United States of America

10 9 8 7 6 5 4 3 2 1

Distributed by Kensington Publishing Corp.
Submit Orders to:
Customer Service
400 Hahn Road
Westminster, MD 21157-4627
Phone: 1-800-733-3000
Fax: 1-800-659-2436

We were named for the flowers in Grandma's garden—begonias, violets, and daisies—and much like those flowers, we were showered with a love that rivaled sunrays. We knew nothing of pain, or sorrow, or just how cruel the world could be, until the day God saw fit to call Grandma home. Her heart stopped two weeks after Daisy was born. My mother smoked us homeless two weeks after that. Now, with Grandma gone and Mommy on a constant crack high, it's up to me to keep our little family together, and you best believe I'll stop at nothing to do just that. My name is Begonia Brown. I am an 18-year-old hustler, and this is my story.

BEGONIA BROWN

For my son

Prologue

Holy Trinity Shelter for Women and Children

February 19, 1995

Moonlight slid through the grimy, crud-smeared window of the bedroom that the shelter provided. Begonia felt as though the walls were closing in on her because their room was filled with crap. When the sheriff kicked them out, her mother stuffed a twin bed, two cots, a crib, and everything they could carry from their grandmother's house into the nine-by-twelve-foot room the shelter provided.

And it was hot, hell-fire hot.

She couldn't sleep. Sleep was not an option. Her baby sister was screaming like somebody was killing her. The heat was oppressive, and a funky mix of mold and stale mop water was in the air.

Begonia rolled off her cot and walked over to the window just as Daisy let out a blood-curdling scream.

"Oh my God, Vy. What is wrong with her?"

Violet sat up and cradled Daisy in her arms. "I don't know."

Begonia tried to open the window, but it was painted shut. "Well, give her the pacifier."

"She doesn't want the damn pacifier."

"Well, what does she want?"

"She wants some milk."

"Give her some milk then. Shit."

Violet rolled her eyes. "Don't you think I would give her milk if I had some milk?"

Begonia squinted at the clock on the wall above Violet's head. "It is two o'clock in the morning, Vy. I'm tired. Where's Mommy?"

"She's in the basement playing cards with Mrs. Carla."

"Well, that's just great." Begonia slid her slippers from under the cot and pulled a t-shirt over her bra.

"Where are you going, Bee?"

"I'm going to get the baby some fucking milk."

Violet looked her up and down. "Dressed like that? You better put some clothes on."

"What? I got on boxers. They're practically shorts." Begonia headed to the bedroom door.

"Bee, how are you going to get milk when the kitchen is locked?"

Begonia walked over to Violet and snatched a bobby pin from the bun on her head. Her jet-black hair fell past her shoulders.

"Oww, girl, what'd ya do that for?"

"I'm going to pick the lock."

The hallway was almost as hot as the bedroom. Begonia fanned herself with her hand and pulled at the collar of her shirt but did not receive any relief from the heat. *I know it's cold outside and all, but damn, this is a bit much.* She closed the door quietly and tiptoed down the length of the stark white hall.

The mop water smell was worse out here, she noted. She peeked down the stairs, trying to see if Peter, the security guard, was at his desk. *No Peter*, she thought as she started down. She clung to the wall, avoiding the rickety banister and squeaky steps.

Once at the kitchen door, she dropped to one knee and peered at the lock. Bending the bobby pin back with her teeth, she inserted it into the lock.

"Awwwww, come on," she whispered. "This shit always works on TV." She curled the other half of the bobby pin into the lock, jiggled it around a bit, turned the handle, and almost fell on her face when the door sprang open.

"Hot damn." Begonia eased the door closed and flicked the light switch on. She took a step toward the pantry and paused. "Don't be a dickhead, Bee." She reached back and flicked the light back off. "Now, first things first." She smiled. "Milk for the baby and then snacks for the big sisters."

There was no formula in the pantry, so she got whole milk out of the refrigerator. She didn't hear the kitchen door open.

"What are you doing in here?" Peter hollered.

Startled, Begonia dropped the gallon of milk on the floor. The top came off, and the milk gushed out over her feet.

"My, m–my si–sister wa–was hungry."

Peter rushed Begonia and grabbed her arm. "How did you get in here?"

"The door was open."

"No, it wasn't," Peter said, twisting her arm backward. "I checked it on my last rounds." He bent her arm back until it touched the counter. "You're a little liar."

Begonia screamed. Tears sprang from her eyes. The pain was blinding. "I'm not lying. I swear the door was open."

Peter's voice rose a couple of octaves as he mocked her. "I'm not lying, I swear." He pressed himself against her and squeezed her arm until her hand went numb. "You're not lying?"

"Noooo," Begonia sobbed. "Please." She grabbed his forearm with her free hand. "You're hurting mc."

"Shut up." He licked his lips and pressed against her until the edge of the counter bit into her back. "Was the door open?"

"Yesss," she sobbed.

"Or did you open it?" He banged her arm against the counter.

"Noooo, please, God." Her breaths were coming hard and fast. Tears slid into her ears. It hurt so bad she thought she might vomit. "Please . . ."

Peter dangled the bobby pin she forgot to remove from the door in front of her face. "Then explain this."

Begonia could hardly see; her eyes were blinded by her tears. She blinked the tears away and moaned when she saw the bobby pin in his hand. Fear vibrated through her entire body. "I'm sorry."

"What?"

"I'm so–so–rry–y. My sister was hu–hungry. She wo–wouldn't st–st–stop crying."

"Shut the fuck up, you little thief. Do you know what we do with thieves here?"

Begonia froze. Her eyes grew to the size of saucers. "No, I'm sorry. Please don't put us out. We don't have anywhere to go."

"Oh, I'm not going to put you out, sweetheart." He ran his free hand up her side and squeezed her waist until she hollered out.

"Shut the fuck up. This is what we do to little thieves here at Holy Trinity."

Begonia went wild. She pummeled his face and back with her free hand. "Stop, God. What are you doing?" Begonia screamed.

Peter grabbed a wad of paper napkins off the counter and stuffed them in her mouth. He pinned both of her arms above her head and held them securely with one of his hands.

Begonia's eyes threatened to bulge out of their sockets. Her tears flowed like a river. She tried to scream with all of her might; however, nothing but murmured gurgles escaped through the gag in her mouth. She bucked wildly, sobbing into the napkins. Peter struck Begonia in the face three times, bloodying her mouth and nose. The third time knocked her out cold. He grabbed the gallon of milk off the floor and doused it on her face.

Begonia woke up choking and sputtering. Her thighs and groin were on fire. She rolled over on her side and threw up on the floor.

Peter laughed. He backed out the door, fastening his pants. "Clean this shit up. Oh, yeah. If you tell anybody, I'll make sure you and your pathetic little family are tossed out in the cold."

Begonia slid off the counter and squatted in the milk on the floor. She hugged her knees and let the reality of what had happened wash over her.

The door opened, and Peter stuck his head back in. "I said clean it up, not sit in it."

Begonia jumped up and grabbed the mop from the corner. It took her fifteen minutes to clean it up. She stood in the corner of the kitchen, clutching the sponge she used to wipe her blood off the counter.

"Move, Bee, come on. Move!" She forced herself to stop crying and then had to force herself to take one step after the other. Begonia threw the sponge in the trash on her way out and stood in the hallway, confused. Taking two steps in the direction of the stairs, she shook her head, swallowed hard, and went the other way. The thought of crossing by Peter's desk made her heart crawl into her throat.

I want my mommy, she thought sadly. *I just want my mommy.* The tears threatened to come back, but Begonia shook them off. Limping, she walked down to the basement. She wanted her mother to hold her. She knew that if she told her what happened, she would know what to do.

The basement was pitch-black. Begonia flipped the switch, but nothing happened. "Mommy?" she called, but no one answered. The steps were old and rotted, so Begonia took her time going down them.

"Mommy? Mrs. Carla?" Her voice shook, and she stopped to take a deep breath. "Mommy, are you down here?"

Begonia reached for the light cord that she knew hung in the center of the room. She yanked on the cord and could not believe her eyes. Her mother and two other women were sitting in a semi-circle sucking on glass pipes.

"Momma," Begonia whispered.

Her mother didn't open her eyes. Peter rose from the corner. Begonia hadn't even noticed he was down there. He placed a couple small chips of rock in Doreen's pipe.

"Mooomma," Begonia said louder this time. Her mom opened her eyes briefly, took a deep draw on the pipe, closed her eyes, and began to rock back and forth.

Peter smiled at Begonia, and something broke inside of her. Fear turned into fury. Shame morphed into betrayal. She rolled her eyes at her mother, switched off the light, turned on her heels, and left. She decided at that very moment that she was leaving Holy Trinity. She didn't know how. She didn't know when. All she knew was that she was getting her family out of the shelter as soon as she could get enough cash. She didn't care if she had to rob every-motherfucking-body in Holy Trinity, including the priest.

Part One

Begonia

Chapter 1

2 years later . . .

Breaking and entering just doesn't pay like it used to! Begonia cupped her left breast and fingered the small knot she'd stored there. She started to dig in her bra, take it out, and then paused. *No matter how many times you count the money, dumb ass, it's not going to add up to more than fifty bucks, which ain't even gonna stretch to cover food for the week.* She jammed her hands in her pockets and walked into the middle of the street to look for the bus.

Where the fuck is the bus? She sighed and decided to walk up a few more blocks. Cecil B. Moore Avenue looked like a ghost town. Begonia half expected to see tumbleweeds rolling across the empty lots. Now and then, she would look over her shoulder for a bus, but there was none in sight. She sped up her pace. The stars began to disappear, and the night sky was a tad bit lighter. Begonia checked her watch and resisted the urge to finger the money again.

Breaking into that house was a boneheaded move, Begonia, especially when you spent a month casing the house beside it. But instinct had clouded her better judgment when she spotted the owners of the neighboring house pull from their driveway, leaving a first-floor window open. She'd learned to always take the path of least resistance, and when you couple that with an open window that was partially concealed by a ragtag carport—easy money.

The fucking house was polluted with books. It had nothing in the way of small, portable electronics. The second floor was even worse. The lady of the house had a thing for cheap-ass costume jewelry. She sucked her teeth at the memory. The night would have been a complete bust if not for the fifty bucks she scored from the suit jacket strewn across a chair.

Begonia trudged up the bridge that led to her neighborhood. She checked her watch and sighed. There was still enough time for her to stretch out before school. The streetlights winked out as she turned onto her block. She looked up at the abandoned building she called home and hesitated only a moment before going inside.

Home sweet home.

She scrunched up her nose as she walked into the house. It stunk of cat piss. She and Violet had ripped up the carpet and scrubbed the floors for hours, but the smell of kitty pee was ever-present—saturated throughout the walls and the second-hand furniture.

Well, you get what you pay for.

Begonia kicked off her shoes and nudged them into the corner of the vestibule. Toys and clothes were scattered all over the floor, so she nixed the idea of lying down. She worked her shoulders before walking through the living room, picking up this and that.

She found her younger sister, Violet, huddled by the lamp on the dining room floor, surrounded by books. They had hooked the electricity up themselves but only managed to get juice on the first floor.

Begonia smiled down at her. *The girl must have been born with a book on the end of her nose.* Violet would be 16 years old in two weeks, and although Begonia was only a year older, she did her best to shield Violet from the evil in the world. She vowed to do something special for her birthday.

Somehow, Vy, someway!

Bending over to switch off the lamp, she shook Violet awake. "Vy, wake up and go on up to our room."

Violet stretched and rubbed her eyes. "Bee, Daisy hasn't eaten anything."

"What do you mean she hasn't eaten? I left you guys some beans and franks."

"I know, but they were gone by the time we got home."

Begonia didn't hear anything else that was said. She shot up the stairs and rushed to the room she shared with her sisters. Daisy was in her crib, slick with sweat.

Her voice cracked out like lightning. "Violet, get me her damn glucagon shots." She cradled Daisy in her arms, crooning softly, "Come on, baby. Wake up now." Begonia smoothed back her hair and braced Daisy against her shoulder. Then she tore the top drawer of the dresser out, looking for Daisy's glucometer. "Come on now, sweetie, wake up!"

Violet burst into the room, breathless. "This is it," she said, handing Begonia the needle and what looked like an empty vial.

"What do you mean this is it? I just filled her prescription." Begonia fought down the lump in her throat. Daisy moaned against her neck.

That's it, girl. Wake up! You're a fighter!

Violet began to cry. "I looked all over the kitchen, Bee. That's all there is."

"Forget it, Vy. Just find her machine, *okay*? I have to check her sugar before I give her this."

Violet wiped her eyes and began taking things out of the drawer. Begonia snatched the curtain away from the window to give her some more light.

"It's not in here, Bee."

"What do you mean it's not in there?" Begonia ripped the remaining drawers from the dresser. "Look for it!" she screamed.

She laid Daisy in her crib and filled the small needle up with glucagon. *Two fucking units.* She flicked the air bubbles out of the needle as best she could, careful to squirt out only a tiny bit.

This is it, baby girl. This is the last of it. Begonia unzipped her sleeper and pulled out one chubby thigh.

"What are you doing?"

"What does it look like I'm doing?"

"But you didn't test her sugar."

Begonia rolled her shoulders and pinched the soft skin of Daisy's inner thigh.

"Noooooooo!" Violet screamed. She jumped up from the floor and snatched Daisy out of the crib. "Remember what the doctor said. He said never to give it to her without knowing her level first." Violet cradled Daisy on her shoulder. "You remember, don't you?" she asked between sobs. "Don't you?"

Fuck!

"All right, Vy." Begonia laid the needle down in the crib. She held her hands out for the baby. "She needs something, though. Take her pacifier downstairs and put some peanut butter on it."

"Okay," Violet said. She handed Begonia the baby, took the pacifier out of the crib, and ran back downstairs.

Begonia's back stiffened, and pain bloomed at the base of her neck. She placed Daisy in her crib just as red dots began to flash before her—a sure sign of her blood pressure rising. She squeezed her eyes against the pain and stuck her head out of the bedroom door because Violet was hollering something from downstairs.

"What?"

"I said we don't have any peanut butter."

"Then put some syrup on it, Vy. Some sugar or something."

Sunlight shone through the shade-less window and lit the faded wallpaper of their bedroom. Begonia looked down at her little sister and swallowed hard. She scooped her out of the crib and hugged her tightly.

God, help me!

Begonia kissed Daisy on her forehead before silently reciting the only prayer she knew.

Our Father that art in Heaven, hallowed be thy name.

She rolled up Daisy's t-shirt.

Give us this day our daily bread.

She picked up the needle from the crib and plunged it into Daisy's stomach.

And forgive us our sins, as we forgive those who sin against us.

Daisy's screams rocked the tiny room.

"That's my girl. That's what I want to hear."

Violet rushed up the stairs armed with a pacifier dripping with syrup. "Oh my God, Bee. What's wrong with her? What did you do?"

Begonia took the pacifier from Violet and gave it to Daisy, whose big brown eyes were open now and glossed over with tears. Daisy clamped down on the pacifier like a vise, and Begonia smiled. She walked over to Violet and wiped her tears.

"It's okay, Vy. Just look at her now. I had to do it." She handed Daisy to Violet, dug money out of her bra, and handed Violet twenty bucks.

"I want you to get you something to eat before you go to school. Take Daisy over to Ms. Lenora's house and tell her that I will be there in a little while to take Daisy to the doctor."

Violet's eyes narrowed at her sister. "You're not coming to school?"

"No, Vy. I have to tend to Daisy. She needs more stuff."

Violet nuzzled her chin against Daisy's cheek and was relieved when Daisy tried to grab one of her earrings.

"I want ea-wings, Vywet," Daisy said softly. She slid the pacifier to the side of her mouth so that she could talk around it.

Begonia leaned over and kissed Daisy's cheek. "I'll get you some earrings just like Violet's, okay? I'll get you anything you want, 'cause you're my baby girl."

Daisy touched Begonia's face and gave her a big, gap-tooth smile. She took her pacifier out for Begonia to kiss her, and Begonia smacked a sloppy kiss on her, which made her squeal with laughter.

"Look, Violet, go on to school without me, 'cause I have to take care of a few things. I promise I won't miss any more days, okay?"

"All right."

"Atta girl." Begonia smiled at her sisters and wiped her sweaty palms on her jeans. The smile fell off her face abruptly. "Where's your mother?"

Violet nodded her head toward the hall. "She's in her room with Uncle Dave."

Begonia cracked her neck and headed toward the back room. "Violet, we don't have an uncle Dave."

Violet poked her head into the hallway. "What are you going to do, Bee?"

Begonia paused at her mother's door and looked over her shoulder. "Don't worry about what I'm going to do. Do what I told you to do."

Chapter 2

Violet headed downstairs to do what she was told. *I feel just like one of those Ethiopian kids with the flies buzzing all around them,* she thought. Her stomach growled as she dressed Daisy and continued to growl after she dropped her off at Ms. Lenora's house.

She headed straight to the diner.

Oh my God, she thought as hunger pangs tore through her stomach. She had to bite her bottom lip to keep from hollering out. The cramps stopped her in her tracks. *Why in the hell does it have to hurt so bad?* she thought. She dropped her book bag on the pavement, clutched her stomach, and pressed her cheek against the hot metal of the mailbox on the corner of 29th and Oxford. *Feed the Children should make a stop at 31st Street with one of those food trucks before they go over to Africa, for real.*

An elderly woman pushing a rickety old shopping cart paused beside Violet. "Are you all right, child?"

"I'm fine, ma'am." Violet forced a smile. "I just had a little pain in my stomach, that's all. It's gone now."

The older woman frowned. "Are you sure, honey? I live right up the street there, and I could call somebody for you if you'd like."

Violet instantly thought of Kyle. She knew his number by heart, and he had told her to call him if she ever needed anything. *I wonder what would happen if Kyle came to pick me up*. Violet rolled her eyes. *Begonia would kill me, that's what would happen. I would die before I had a chance to turn sixteen,* she thought.

Violet smiled at the older woman. "No, you don't have to do that." She picked up her book bag. "I'm going to the diner across the street. I'll be fine." She hurried across the street and checked her watch. *Damn, it's 7:30 already*. She hesitated a moment before going inside. *I'm already late for homeroom. If I turn around now, I'll make it to first period on time*. Her stomach rumbled loudly.

"Well, I guess that settles that." She chuckled and entered the diner.

Mr. Jim and Ms. Kelly were arguing over the small black and white TV behind the counter. Mr. Jim slapped his hand down on the countertop. "I want to watch the news."

"I know that, dumb ass. I'm turning it to the news."

"Well, watcha turnin' it for? It was already on the news."

"I only watch Channel 10 News, and you know that."

"All's I know is that I'm going to crack yo fo'head if you touch that TV 'gain."

Ms. Kelly turned from the TV and stuck her head in Mr. Jim's face. "Go 'head and crack it, Jim. I dare ya. I double dog dare ya to lay one hand on me. I betcha it'll be the last damn thing you do with that hand."

Mr. Jim leaned back from the counter. "Girl, move ya big ol' head from in front of the TV. Ain't nobody playing with you."

Violet shook her head and laid her book bag down on the table at the first booth. Ms. Kelly looked up at her and smiled. Then she looked at the clock on the wall.

"Shouldn't you be in school, baby?"

"Yes, ma'am. I'm going to go straight there after I eat."

"Does Begonia know that you're here?"

Begonia is not my mother, she thought. "Yes, she's the one who told me to come here."

"All right, baby, but don't be trying to hang around. Eat your food then carry yourself on up to school."

"Yes, ma'am."

"How's your mother doing?"

"She's still cracked out."

"Now that's just ugly, Violet. Your mother is sick, so don't be talking 'bout her like that. A simple 'she's doing good,' or 'she's doing the same' would do."

Mr. Jim took a sip of his coffee. "The little girl ain't lying, Kelly. You know Doreen's cracked out."

"Shut up, Jim, and mind ya own business." She turned to Violet. "You heard what I said, didn't ya?"

"Yes, ma'am."

"All right." She took the hand towel from her shoulder and started to wipe off the counter. "Now, what can I get you to eat?"

Violet looked up at the menus on the wall. "I'll have three pancakes, two eggs scrambled with cheese, sausage, bacon, scrapple, wheat toast, and a corn muffin."

Ms. Kelly chuckled. "Is that it? You sure you don't want any grits and hash browns with all that?"

Violet smiled. "No, but I do want some milk." She flopped down in the booth.

"Jim, did you hear what that little girl just ordered?"

Mr. Jim looked over his shoulder at Violet. "I sure did. She must have a tapeworm or something."

Violet stared out of the window and pretended not to hear their comments. Getting a regular meal was becoming harder and harder for them. She was tired of acting like everything was OK. She was tired of Begonia acting like she had everything under control, but most of all, she was tired of being worried and scared all the time.

Her mind drifted to Kyle again. Shakiyya had told her not to mess with him. She said that he was dangerous. But Violet just couldn't figure how someone so sweet could be dangerous at all. *I mean, I know he sells dope, but half the boys around the way do that.* Violet smirked. *There is nothing else for them to do.*

Violet shook all thoughts of Kyle out of her head. She watched as a young girl swung her toddler up into her arms. The baby was giggling and squealing with joy. Violet smiled, thinking of Daisy. *God, please let her be okay!* A lone tear worked its way down Violet's cheek, and she wiped it away quickly, looking around to make sure no one noticed. She wondered what Kyle was doing. It was too early for him to be posted on the block.

Ms. Kelly put a plate of food in front of Violet, and she dug into it before it hit the table. Violet stuffed a sausage in her mouth, and Ms. Kelly chuckled.

"It ain't going anywhere, girl. Take your time."

Violet couldn't even hear her. Heaven was spread out before her in the form of buttermilk pancakes and a mountain of scrambled eggs. She swallowed her first few bites whole, trying to sate the hollow in her gut.

Chapter 3

Begonia opened her mother's door, and the smell of crack cocaine smacked her in the face. Her nostrils flared, and her eyes watered. No matter how many times she smelled it, she could never get used to the stench of freebase. "Uncle Dave" was lying face down on the piss-stained mattress that their mother had dragged in from the trash. He was surrounded by crushed beer cans, little empty baggies of cocaine, and cut-off straws. Begonia ignored him. She turned her attention to her mother, who was sitting on a silver fold-out chair in a serious drug-induced stupor.

She looks like something from a horror movie, Begonia thought. Her skin was ashy and gray, her long black hair was matted and nappy, and her eyes were beginning to sink into her skull. Naked from the waist down, Begonia's mother cradled a glass pipe in her lap, and her head lolled to the side while drool slithered from her chin to her shoulder.

They're having a fucking party, she thought.

Begonia hopped over the mattress, ripped the pipe from her mother's hand, and chucked it across the room. "Wake the hell up!" Begonia screamed.

Her mother didn't budge. Begonia grabbed her shirt and yanked her up from the chair. "Momma, Momma, wake up!" She shook her mother so hard that her head snapped back, and drool rolled into her nose.

Doreen choked, sputtered, and opened her eyes. She cringed at the look on Begonia's face. "What's the matter, baby?"

"I ain't your baby, you trifling piece of shit. I want you to tell me how much you got for Daisy's medicine."

Doreen's eyes almost popped out of her head, and Begonia flung her back into the chair.

"I want you to tell me what kind of woman sells her two-year-old baby's diabetic supplies. Huh, Momma? Can you tell me that?"

"Baby, I didn't touch–"

Begonia smacked her mother so hard that her hand stung. Doreen raised her hand to her face and cradled her cheek in disbelief. Her eyes were wide and full of fear. The shock of the blow burned away some of her high. She took a deep breath as her eyes filled with tears.

"Begonia, I swear I didn't touch–"

Begonia raised her hand to strike her again, but Dave caught her wrist and twisted it behind her back. She rammed her elbow into his stomach and then swung around to punch him square in his jaw.

Dave grunted and fell back against the wall. His bloodshot eyes registered shock and alarm. Begonia dug a switchblade out of her back pocket and stuck it between Dave's legs.

"Whoa, shawty, what the fuck are you doing?"

Begonia pressed the blade against his nuts. "Put your hands on me again, slick, and I'll cut your balls off quicker than you can say sorry."

Dave recognized the truth in the statement by the hate in her eyes.

"Noooo!" Doreen screamed. She stretched out her arms toward Begonia but stayed glued to the seat. "Please, don't hurt him, Bee."

Begonia's jaw clenched. *I know this bitch didn't just scream out for him.*

Dave looked down at Begonia as if she'd grown horns. "Look, you need to calm down, shawty, for real." He held his hands up and stood on his tippy toes, trying to distance himself from the blade in Begonia's hand. "Look, put the knife away. I'm out of here." He looked over at Doreen, who was trying to curl up into a ball on the chair. "There is something the fuck wrong with your daughter, yo. I don't have to put up with this shit."

"You damn right there is something wrong with me. I got a thing about no-good, cracked-out, limp-dick motherfuckers in my house." Begonia backed up a few paces to allow him to leave, but she kept her blade visible. Dave eased down, grabbed his shirt, and high-tailed it out of there.

"Baby," Doreen whimpered. "You have to believe me. I would never sell Daisy's medicine."

Begonia closed her eyes in an attempt to shut out the pain. Her heart rose into her throat. She turned to her mother and opened her mouth to say something, but nothing would come out. Her mother eyed the knife in her hand, so Begonia slipped it into her back pocket.

"You have twenty minutes to get your shit and get out."

"What?" Doreen dropped her feet from the chair.

"Momma, I'm only going to say this one more time. I'm giving you twenty minutes. Get out or get thrown out."

"But I don't have anywhere to go."

"You should have thought about that before you sold my sister's meds."

Chapter 4

Syrup dripped down Violet's chin. She scrubbed it away with the back of her hand and stuffed another sausage in her mouth. *Oh my God. This is so good,* she thought. *I bet this is what sex feels like.*

Ms. Kelly looked over at Violet and frowned. "Slow down, baby. That food ain't goin' nowhere."

Violet took a big gulp of milk and smiled, too happy to be ashamed. "I know, Ms. Kelly. It's just sooooo good." She squeezed ketchup over her eggs and folded a piece of bacon into her mouth.

Mr. Jim ducked under the counter and pulled out a bag of plastic to-go containers. "Leave the little girl alone, Kelly."

"Shut up, Jim."

Violet ignored them, determined to clean each plate of food in front of her. She scooped up a heaping spoonful of eggs, rolled her eyes in pure pleasure, savored the flavor, and then stuffed more eggs in her mouth. She knew she looked a mess with butter and ketchup running down her chin, but she couldn't help it. Violet didn't know when the last time was that she ate so well. *You need to stop acting like a pig,* she thought as she reached for the napkin to wipe her mouth.

The door chime sounded, and Violet turned around in time to see Kyle and two of his boys stroll in. His friends went to the counter to order, but Kyle headed straight toward her.

"What's up, young'n?" Kyle asked, smiling.

Violet choked on her eggs.

"Yo, you a'ight, shawty?" Kyle moved in to pat her back.

Violet coughed once and unthinkingly reached for her milk, knocking it onto the table. Her eyes watered, and she clawed at her chest. She tried to stand up but was caught by the table and only managed to send two of her plates skittering to the floor.

Ms. Kelly turned from the TV at the sound. "Oh my God, Jim, she's choking."

"Move, boy!" Mr. Jim yelled. He hopped over the counter and snatched her from the booth and jerked her toward him.

"Come on, baby," he said, repeating the Heimlich. "Let it out."

Her eggs shot across the room.

"Daaaaaaamn," the young boy by the counter said. "That's some nasty shit right there."

"I know, right?" said his friend. "Make a nigga lose his appetite."

Violet doubled over, gagging while Mr. Jim rubbed her back.

"That's it, baby. Let it all out."

She coughed and spilled her breakfast onto the floor.

Ms. Kelly slapped her rag down on the counter. "Why in the hell are you staring at her? Order or get the hell out."

"How the fuck can somebody eat after seeing that shit?"

"If you're not eating, then you're leaving. Now, get gone."

Violet stood up and locked eyes with Kyle. The look of pity on his face was too much for her to bear. She turned on her heels and ran to the bathroom.

Chapter 5

Begonia stood in the bedroom that she shared with her sisters and waited for her mother to leave. She walked over to the window and stared down at the backyard. The leaves were beginning to turn a yellowish brown and fall to the dirt below. Her mind was racing, and her breaths were coming hard and fast. *Calm down, Bee,* she thought as she placed her head against the window. Her heart pounded against her chest. *You are going to give yourself a fucking heart attack.*

She could see her mother dragging bags down the hall out of the corner of her eye. She turned from the window and looked at her. Doreen paused at the door and returned Begonia's stare. She opened her mouth to say something, and Begonia shook her head in warning.

"We don't have anything else to say to each other."

Doreen nodded sadly, dragged her bags down the stairs, and left. Begonia waited ten minutes to make sure that her mother was gone, and then she walked down to Mrs. Lenora's house to pick up Daisy.

The sounds of Curtis Mayfield's "Pusher Man" drifted out of Mrs. Lenora's front door. Begonia tried the doorknob before knocking.

"Who is it?"

"It's me."

"You got a name, me?"

Begonia smiled and leaned against the door jamb. "You know, Mrs. Lenora, I can come in if I want to."

Mrs. Lenora's laughter rolled out in waves. She turned the radio down and opened the door. "That's not anything to be proud of, little girl."

"And why not?" she asked as she walked into the house and kissed Mrs. Lenora on the cheek. "I'm good at it."

"Just because you're good at something, ya little thief, doesn't mean you are supposed to do it. Look at Earl," she said, kicking her sleeping husband's feet off the coffee table. "He's real good at getting drunk as all hell, but should he do it every night?"

Earl didn't move a muscle. His soft snores turned into a loud rumble, and Mrs. Lenora shook her head.

"The baby's upstairs with Shakiyya, Bee. She hasn't settled down since Violet dropped her off."

Begonia hollered upstairs for Shakiyya to bring her down. "She's not feeling too well, Mrs. Lenora. I'm gonna take her straight to the doctor."

"Um huh, Violet told me what happened. Ain't nothin' you own gonna be safe with ya momma fiendin' the way she do."

"Violet needs to keep her mouth closed about what goes on in our house."

"Oh, hush up. It ain't like I'm a stranger. I asked her what was wrong with the baby, and she told me. You know how I worry about you girls."

Shakiyya came down with Daisy, who stopped crying as soon as she spotted Begonia. Her smile split her face in two.

"Beeeeeeeee! I don't want to lay down. I not tired."

Begonia laughed and kissed her nose. "Who said you were tired?" She picked up the baby bag in the corner and bent over to kiss Mrs. Lenora's cheek again.

Daisy pointed her finger at Shakiyya. "Her said I was tired, and I said I wasn't."

Begonia took a step toward Shykiyya. "Do you want me to smack her, Daisy?"

Daisy laughed and nodded her head.

Shakiyya put her hands up, and she and Begonia started play fighting. Daisy squealed with laughter.

"Stop that now," Mrs. Lenora said, laughing. "Y'all too big to be doing that stuff in my house."

Begonia put her hands down and picked up Daisy. "You lucky, big head. I was just about to warm your butt up."

Shakiyya headed back upstairs. "Whatever, chicken head. I whooped your butt in the second grade, and I can do it again."

Begonia smiled up at Shakiyya. "We all have dreams, ya know." She winked at Mrs. Lenora as she walked to the front door. "You don't have to worry about us. We'll be just fine." She left the house before Mrs. Lenora could say anything further.

Daisy was asleep by the time they reached the clinic. She snored softly against Begonia's neck. *You're getting heavier by the day, little girl. Sheesh!* Begonia shifted Daisy's weight to her other shoulder and shook out her arm. She opened the door to the clinic and sighed. *What the fuck? Is everybody and their momma up in here?* The place was packed. There wasn't an empty seat in sight, and people were lined up against the walls. Begonia had to fight the urge to turn around and leave. She walked up to the counter to sign in and bumped into a little boy racing through the aisle.

"Damn, bitch, can't you see nothin'?"

"Excuse you?" Begonia looked down at the little thug in training. She could feel her blood pressure rising.

"You heard me. Open up your eyes and look where the fuck you're going."

A young woman dressed in a royal blue catsuit with a tacky gold belt grabbed the little boy by the collar. "What the hell is wrong with you, Isaiah? You can't go around talking to people like that." She shook the little boy so hard his teeth chattered. "Tell her sorry."

"I ain't telling her shit. She should watch where she's going."

Catwoman jerked the little boy off of his feet and got into his face. "Boy, I'm not going to tell you again. I said, tell her sorry!"

Begonia sidestepped the sad little scene. "It's okay, miss. He doesn't have to tell me anything." She was no longer mad at the little boy. She hated it when people hemmed up their kids in public. She continued to walk up to the counter and signed Daisy's name on the walk-in list.

Crack!

Begonia spun around to see the little boy laid out on the floor. He was holding his cheek, and his eyes brimmed with tears.

"You ain't no man, Isaiah. You're a little boy. Call me a bitch again."

Isaiah bit his bottom lip and turned to face Begonia. Their eyes locked, and Begonia felt all of his hurt right down to her toes.

"Come on, Isaiah. I'm waiting. Call me a bitch one more time, and I promise that I'll beat the shit out of you right here, right now."

The entire clinic was quiet as they watched the scene unfold. You could hear a pin drop. Isaiah's face burned red, and the tears he fought so hard to keep in dripped down on his face and landed on the dingy collar of his shirt. In an instant, he was on his feet and at the door.

"Fuck you," he said to Catwoman. "Fuck all of you." He hit the street running.

"Good. Shit, I didn't want you here no way." Catwoman switched her stank ass toward the back of the clinic and grabbed a magazine off the rack. She scanned the room. "What the fuck are y'all looking at?"

Nothing, Begonia thought, *absolutely nothing.* She walked to the back of the clinic and leaned against the wall. *Some people should never be allowed to have kids.*

Begonia nuzzled Daisy and held her tight. *What in the hell are we going to tell them, baby girl? We sure as hell can't tell them the truth. Can't just walk up there and say, "Ur, rrmm, my momma exchanged my sister's meds for crack, and is it any way possible you could hook us up with a new prescription?"*

Begonia leaned up against the wall and shifted Daisy's weight again. She rolled her eyes at the dude sitting in the seat nearest her. *I thought men were supposed to give up their seats to women with babies in their arms.*

She shook out her arm and noticed that it was wet. She wiped it on her jeans and frowned. She held Daisy up to see if her diaper soaked through because the Lord knew how hard it was trying to potty train her. "Come on, Daisy. You are to say *potty* when you have to go." She rubbed Daisy's back to wake her and noticed that her entire outfit was wet. Daisy's head rolled down, lifeless.

"Oh my God," Begonia shouted, shaking her sister. "Daisy, wake up, baby!" Begonia ran over to the counter. "We need to see a doctor now!"

The receptionist at the desk sucked her teeth and covered the receiver with her hand. "What you need to do is wait your turn. All of these people were here before you." With that, the receptionist turned back to the computer.

Begonia snatched the phone out of the girl's hand and slammed it on the floor. "You better get a doctor out here right the fuck now, or so help me God, I am going to beat the bullshit out of you."

The girl pushed her chair back from the counter and started to scream at the top of her lungs. "Security! Joe, I need someone out here ASAP."

"What the fuck we need out here is a doctor."

A big, burly man dressed in a blue and black uniform burst from behind the double doors. "What the hell is going on out here?"

"This chick is crazy."

"Ma'am, I'm going to have to ask you to leave."

Begonia held Daisy out to the security officer. "Look at her. Just look at her. Get me a doctor, damn."

An Indian man came from the back with a white lab coat on. "What is the problem out here?"

"Are you a doctor?"

"Ma'am, now, I asked you nicely." The security officer stepped in between Begonia and the counter. "If you don't leave, I'm going to call the cops."

Begonia ignored him. She craned her neck toward the doctor. "Please sir, my baby passed out. Help me!"

The officer grabbed Begonia by the shoulders.

"Get the fuck off of me."

"Aye, you dude, get off of her. She just needs help."

"Sir, please sit back in your seat. We have the situation under control."

"What the fuck do you have in control, rent-a-cop?" a woman shouted from across the room.

"I need a doctor!" Begonia screamed, and the entire clinic fell silent. Begonia could feel the blood rushing to her temples as her head began to pound.

The man in the lab coat came from around the counter and took Daisy from her. He checked her pulse and called for a nurse. He turned to the receptionist.

"Get the blue crash cart."

Begonia sighed. The nurse was asking her questions, but she couldn't hear her over the sound of her own heartbeat. The security guard still had his hand on her shoulder. She turned to face him. "I told you to take your hands off me."

"How old is she, ma'am?" the nurse asked again. "Ma'am?"

Begonia kneed the security officer in the nuts, and he went down like a ton of bricks.

The clinic erupted in laughter. "Daaaaaaaaaamn!" someone hollered from the background. "That's what the fuck you get, you fat fuck."

Begonia turned to the nurse, who was staring at her wide-eyed with her mouth hanging open. "Her name is Daisy Brown, and she's two years old." Begonia stepped over the security guard and headed to the back of the clinic to find her sister.

Chapter 6

Violet leaned against the bathroom door and exhaled slowly. Her eyes misted with tears, so she quickly held her head up to the ceiling. "You are not going to cry." She took in a shuddering breath. "You are not going to cry." She squeezed her eyes tight against the tears. *Oh my God,* she thought, *Oh my God. Did I have to puke in front of him?* Tears slid down her face despite her best efforts.

"I am such a fucking dick!" She put her head down and looked at her reflection in the tiny mirror above the sink. She pushed the plunger down in the sink. "All I needed to do was piss myself to make the picture complete." She turned on the water. "I know what he's thinking. He's thinking about what everyone thinks. Violet Brown is a retard with a cracked-out mother and a no-good thief for a sister."

Violet splashed water on her face until her shirt was saturated, and long strands of her ebony hair clung to her cheeks. She blindly reached for the paper towel dispenser and cranked it until the towel pooled on the floor by her feet. She gathered the paper towel, pressing some to her face and the rest down her shirt. She nearly jumped out of her skin when she heard a knock at the door.

"You okay in there?" Ms. Kelly asked.

Violet didn't answer. She continued to mop up her face. She took the paper towels out of her shirt and placed them on the floor so that they could sop up the water she splashed there.

Ms. Kelly knocked harder. "Violet, are you okay?"

If you call suicidal okay, then I'm just peachy, she thought snidely. "I'm okay, Ms. Kelly."

"All right now. Mr. Jim cleaned up the mess, and those little assholes left. You don't have to worry about them. You come on out here so that you can get to school, ya hear?"

"Yes, ma'am. I'll be out in a minute." Violet leaned against the bathroom stall, relieved. *At least I don't have to face him.* She bent over to retrieve all the paper towels from the floor and placed them in the trash. She smoothed her hair back up into a ponytail, took one last deep breath, and left the bathroom.

Kyle was sitting in the back booth. He stood up when he spotted Violet.

Oh my God. Violet wanted to turn on her heels and run back into the bathroom, but her feet wouldn't move.

Kyle walked over to Violet. "You all right, shawty?

Violet nodded slightly. She picked up her book bag and walked over to the counter to pay her tab. She dug in her pocket, pulled out the crumpled twenty, and tried to hand it to Ms. Kisha.

Kyle grabbed her arm. "Aw, hell naw, shawty. Hold up. I got this." He pulled a fat knot of twenty-dollar bills from his pocket. "What kind of man would I be if I let you pay for a meal you didn't eat?" He smirked. "I mean look, ma. I think the floor got more of that grub than you."

Violet put her head down in shame.

"Aww, come on now, ma. Don't look like that. I was just playing with you." Kyle grabbed her chin and tilted her face up to his. A single tear worked its way down her cheek. He frowned slightly and wiped the tear away. Lightning worked its way down Violet's spine. Kyle then pulled her close and gave her a hug. His shirt was soft and smooth as silk. It smelled sweet and tart like incense. He rubbed her back, and she melted against him. His heart beat at a steady, rhythmic pace, and every other noise in the diner faded into the background.

Kyle handed Ms. Kelly the money. "Keep the change."

Ms. Kelly sucked her teeth, snatched the money from Kyle, and rang up the check. She leaned over the counter and tapped Violet on the shoulder.

"Shouldn't you be getting on up to school?"

"Yes, ma'am."

"Well, get going then."

Violet pulled away from Kyle and shouldered her bag. She started for the door, but Kyle grabbed her hand. Ms. Kelly handed Kyle his change.

"Come on now, ma. I told you to keep it."

"I heard what you said, boy, but I don't need, nor do I want, any of yo' money."

"It's like that, Ms. Kelly?"

Ms. Kelly laid his change down on the table. "It has always been like that, Kyle." She looked down at his grip on Violet's arm. "You need to let that little girl go on up to school. You are way too old to be fooling around with her anyway. She's just a baby."

Violet blushed and tried to free herself from Kyle's hold, but he tightened his grip a little.

"Calm down, Ms. Kelly. I'm going to give her a ride to school. That's all." He turned to face Violet. "My car's outside. You want a lift?"

Violet smiled and nodded shyly.

Ms. Kelly sucked her teeth. "She can walk just fine."

"I really could use the ride, Ms. Kelly," Violet said, walking fast to the door. "I am really late." She hurried out the door, not waiting for Ms. Kelly to respond.

Excitement ran down Violet's spine as she approached Kyle's black Beamer. It had been seven years since she'd ridden in a car. Her grandfather had a huge Lincoln Town Car, and he would drive them to church on Sunday mornings.

Violet ran her hand lightly over the hood of the car while Kyle opened the passenger door for her. Once he got in the car and turned the key in the ignition, the sound from his speaker system nearly burst her eardrums. "Damn, Kyle!" Violet screamed. She placed her hands over her ears and shrank back into the seat.

Kyle laughed and turned down the sound.

"Jesus, I bet you any amount of money that the niggas all the way up in South Philly can hear that shit."

"That's them Bose right there, shawty. You don't know nothing 'bout that right there."

"I know that you're going to lose your hearing if you don't stop driving around like that." Violet put her seatbelt on as Kyle pulled away from the curb.

"What, you don't trust me, sweetheart?"

"Why you say that?"

Kyle reached over and tugged on her seatbelt. "I'm saying you all strapped in and shit—all buckled up for safety and whatnot."

Violet looked confused. "What do you mean? Aren't you supposed to wear your seatbelt?"

"Oh, that's right." Kyle laughed. "You're the good girl. Ms. Goody Two Shoes and shit." He brushed the back of his hand against Violet's cheek, and she jerked her head away. "You always do the right thing."

"You don't know me, Kyle. You don't know what I do or don't do."

Kyle turned onto Ridge Avenue and parked right in front of Strawberry Mansion High. "A'ight, shawty, wicha bad self, tell me what it is that you do and do not do."

"I do whatever the hell I want to do." Violet was pissed. She was tired of everyone thinking she was an angel just because she didn't cut the hell up like her sister. Her arms were folded tightly across her chest. *I should have walked to school,* she thought.

Kyle turned off the ignition. "Let me find out you running things. You a boss, huh?" He leaned back and pulled a pack of Newports out of his pocket. He lit a cigarette and smiled. "Let me find the fuck out. Little miss boss . . ." He pulled hard on his cigarette and let the smoke curl out of his nose. "Okay, Miss Boss, you better get inside that school before your sister kicks your li'l ass."

"Begonia won't be kicking nobody's ass." Violet snatched her book bag off the floor and fumbled with the car door handle. She hit the buttons above the ashtray but only managed to roll the window up and down.

Kyle chuckled. He reached over and touched Violet's shoulder. "Calm down, shawty. I'm just teasing you, damn. Lean back and let me get the door for you, 'cause you trying to tear my shit up." He leaned over her and opened the door. His cologne drifted up into Violet's nose, and the tickle between her legs grew to a full-fledged itch.

The door popped open smoothly, but Kyle lingered over Violet. He turned to face her. "See, you need to stop actin' all rowdy. I was just teasing you." He looked into her big brown eyes and let his gaze fall onto her lips.

Violet could hardly think with him in her face. Her entire body was on fire. "Well, I didn't think it was funny," she breathed.

He brought his face so close to hers that she could taste his breath—an intoxicating mix of nicotine and spearmint. "You didn't think it was funny, huh?"

Violet shook her head no, not trusting herself enough to speak. He was so close.

"Well . . ." Kyle said, brushing his lips against hers. "I thought it was funny as shit." He sucked her bottom lip into his mouth and grazed it with his teeth.

Violet didn't even think. She couldn't. All she could do was react. Her arms slid around Kyle's shoulders, and her tongue snaked in his mouth before she could stop herself. She threw her soul into the kiss.

Kyle leaned back against the window and shook his head. "Damn, girl."

Violet let out a nervous laugh.

"You better get on up in that school before you get yourself into some trouble."

Violet licked her lips and closed her eyes. She took a deep breath and turned to face Kyle. "I don't want to go to school today."

"Word?"

Violet nodded.

A slow smile spread across Kyle's face. He gripped the steering wheel and rocked his legs back forth. "I don't know about that, shawty."

"I'm not going to school today, Kyle. Either I'm going home, or I'm going with you."

Kyle started the car.

Chapter 7

The doctor's instructions played over and over in Begonia's head. She needed to get Daisy's meds, but she wasn't sure if she had enough money for them. Daisy walked beside Begonia at a snail's pace, chattering endlessly. Begonia swooped Daisy up into her arms. *Maybe I could go boosting at the mall.* She shook her head. *Now that's just stupid, Bee. Who in the hell are you going to get to buy that shit? The first of the month has come and gone, and all of those welfare checks are just as good as spent.*

Daisy was singing the Barney song by the time they arrived at Mrs. Lenora's house. The door was open, so Begonia walked right in. As usual, the place was filled with the smell of good food and nice music. Mrs. Lenora stood at the sink, washing dishes. Daisy wiggled and kicked so that Begonia could set her down. As soon as her feet hit the floor, she took off running. She crashed into the back of Mrs. Lenora's legs, hugging her ample thighs. Begonia just smiled.

"Oh my goodness, who is this child grabbin' on me? Do I know you, little girl?"

"I'm Daisy."

"Daisies are flowers."

"Nuh-uhn, Daisy is me."

Mrs. Lenora bent over and started tickling her. "Flowers, I said. Daisies are flowers." Daisy let out a string of giggles that rang around the house like silver bells. Mrs. Lenora caught her up in a bear hug. "I'm so glad you're feeling better, honey."

Begonia walked into the kitchen and sat down at the table. She folded her hands in her lap and stared at the floor.

"What did the doctor say?"

"He said she would be fine and wrote me a prescription for a new machine and supplies."

"Well, that's good then. Real good." She nuzzled Daisy's neck and kissed her on the cheek.

Begonia closed her eyes and took a deep breath. She wasn't accustomed to swallowing her pride.

Mrs. Lenora put Daisy down and swatted her playfully on the bottom. "Go on up to the playroom, honey, while I talk to Bee. Shakiyya's upstairs."

"Okay, Aunt Nora."

Mrs. Lenora pulled up a chair and sat down heavily. "What's the matter, girl? What did the doctor really say? Is that baby gonna be okay?"

"Un-huh," Begonia said, nodding her head. "She's fine, Mrs. Lenora, really. . . . It's just . . ." Begonia put her head down and swallowed hard. She hugged herself and rocked back and forth.

Mrs. Lenora leaned forward and rubbed her arm. "It's okay, child. Tell me what's wrong."

Begonia turned away from the concern in her eyes. She looked toward the front door. "I don't have enough for her medicine," she said softly. "Her meds will come up to about two hundred and fifty dollars, and all I have is thirty bucks." Begonia rested her elbow on the table, brought her hands up to her head, and started to massage her temples vigorously. "I could probably hustle the money up in a couple of days, but the doctor said she would need it by tomorrow. He gave me enough for today." Begonia bit her bottom lip and forced herself to look Mrs. Lenora in the eyes. "I need to borrow three hundred bucks until next week. I swear I'll give back to you the moment I get it."

Mrs. Lenora sat back in her chair and exhaled slowly. "Aw, baby, I'm so sorry. I don't have it. If you could wait until Friday, I'm sure Mr. Earl could give it to you. That's when he gets paid."

"That's okay," Begonia said, standing up from the table. "I'll get the money." She jammed her hands in her pockets and walked backward to the door. "Violet will be by later to pick her up. Page me if you have any problems. The nurse put a crash pack of goodies in her little book bag, so if she starts to sweat or looks funny, give her some of that stuff. It's only like peanut butter and graham crackers and stuff."

"Well, just wait a minute, Bee. Don't go. Let's put our heads together. There's got to be somebody that we could get this money from."

Begonia grabbed the door handle and turned away. Her hands trembled slightly as she opened the door. "Don't worry about it. I'll get the money."

"What are you gonna do, honey?"

"I'm going to do what I do best." Begonia closed the door gently behind her. She raced down the steps and into the street. A light breeze lifted her hair off her shoulders. Begonia bit her lip and looked around wildly. Her hands were clenched at her sides, her head throbbed, and her stomach tied itself into tight knots.

She spun around twice, not knowing exactly where to go. Shaking, she forced herself to be still. She looked down the block toward Mr. Johnson's house, and her skin began to crawl. She walked toward his house as if she were walking through water—every step heavy and measured. *How many times did you promise yourself that you weren't going to do this?* she thought, irritated.

As she climbed Mr. Johnson's porch steps, her blood turned into ice. The cold calm that came over her every time she shoplifted or broke into a house washed over her. She rang his doorbell and leaned on the rail, completely frozen. The tiniest voice inside her heart wished that he wouldn't answer. Begonia locked that wish away. She stored it with the other bullshit wishes that made her long for a normal life and a mother who loved her more than a crack pipe.

The door opened, and Begonia found herself face to face with a middle-class, middle-weight, middle-aged, pathetic old pervert. She cracked her neck and floated right past him into the living room. *I wonder if I could just get the cash and go,* she thought as she walked to the couch. *Naw, he's not having that.* Begonia noticed that his dick was hard and poking through his pants by the time she sat down.

He sat on the chair across from her with a sickening look on his face. Rubbing his erection through his pants, he cocked his head to the side and arched his eyebrow. "So, how much do you need?"

Begonia undid the buttons of her shirt, exposing the black lace-front bra that she stole from Victoria's Secret. "I need five hundred dollars."

His breath was coming hard and fast. He unzipped his pants and loosened his belt. "I don't think I have that much."

Begonia let her shirt fall open. She leaned back and crossed her legs. "Then I don't think this is going to happen, you trifling fat fuck."

"Oh, it's going to happen." He wiped the drool from his mouth and dug in his pocket. He pulled out a wad of cash and counted out three hundreds and ten twenties. She watched as he smirked and put the rest of the money in his pocket. He slipped his pants down and let them fall to his ankles.

Begonia slid off the couch onto the floor and crawled over to him. She kneeled between his thighs, and when he reached in the drawer of his nightstand for a condom, she headbutted him in his groin and took all the money from his pocket.

He hollered out in pain, grabbing his crotch. Begonia jumped out of the way as he doubled over.

"You stupid little thief, come here. I'm going to whoop your ass."

"I doubt if that's going to happen," Begonia said softly. She walked swiftly to the door, averting her eyes from the mirror hanging in the vestibule. She knew she couldn't face herself. Her heart hung heavy at the base of her stomach. *Well, at least I have the money for Daisy's meds*, she thought.

"Fuck!" Mr. Johnson screamed. He fumbled with his pants, gathered himself, and limped to the door.

Begonia smirked and skipped down his steps.

"You little fucking thief. You better give me my money, you little cunt, or I swear—"

"You swear what? Huh, Mr. Johnson, what exactly are you going to do? Call the cops?" She let out a bitter laugh and turned to walk down the street. "I'll bet they would love to hear how I got it."

The smell of Mr. Johnson still burned the inside of her nostrils. She rubbed her nose.

I need a drink. . . .

Chapter 8

"A'ight, shawty," Kyle said while speeding up Roosevelt Boulevard. "I am going to make sure that your very first day of being a bad ass is special."

Violet chuckled. "I didn't say I was a bad ass, Kyle. You trippin'."

"Trippin', my ass. You gots to be a bad ass, skippin' school and givin' out those kisses like you do."

"Oh, shut up," Violet said, although she couldn't help but to blush. She'd never had this kind of attention before, and she didn't quite know how to respond.

"Now look at you, gettin' all bossy with me. No, I won't shut up, bad ass. I'm grown." Kyle turned onto 5th Street and parked the car. "I got to drop off this bundle right quick. Do you want to go catch a movie or something?"

Violet's eyes lit up like diamonds, and her smile spread wide across her face. "Are you serious?"

"As a heart attack, shawty. I think the early movie starts at eleven o'clock. We could catch that and be back before school lets out."

He pulled a bundle out from under the seat, hopped out of the car, and ran up the steps of what Violet assumed to be a crack house. *Shit, that looks like my house*, she thought. The house was painted a rusty brown with black trim. The first floor windows were boarded up, and the second floor windows were encased in bars.

Violet watched as Kyle pressed the intercom beside the doorbell. A few moments later, the big oak door swung open, and Kyle disappeared inside. Violet began to feel the smallest twinge of regret, but she shook it off. *God, Vy, all you're doing is missing one little day of school,* she thought, *and you are acting like a little punk. Shit, Begonia does this every day.*

Violet turned her attention to the people on the street. She loved watching people, wondering about their lives. It was like a watching a movie that was always on. She reached down the side of the door and fingered the CDs that sat in the pocket. A man walked by in the middle of the street, pushing a shopping cart full of junk. A car whizzed by and nearly ran him off the road. His cart tipped over, and all sorts of things started rolling out. Violet resisted the urge to go and help him. *What would Kyle think if he came out and saw me knee deep in trash*? she thought. She flicked the CDs so hard that they spilled out onto the floor of the car.

"Oh, shit." She leaned over to retrieve them, reaching her hand under her seat as far as she could. Her fingers grazed against the hard, cold steel of a handgun, and she snatched them back as if she'd been burnt.

She clutched her fingers to her chest, because now they were itching to hold the gun. The car door opened, and Violet jumped. She turned to face Kyle wide eyed, with her shirt balled up in her hands.

"What the fuck is wrong with you, ma?" Kyle rubbed his face with his hands and shook his head. "Look, shawty, I knew this was a bad idea. Let me take you back to school, and maybe we could kick it some other time."

"No, I don't want to go back to school."

"Then why you look like I'm about to rape you or something?"

Violet sucked her teeth. "Because you have a gun under the seat."

Kyle took a good look at her and then looked down at the seat. He noticed his CDs all over the floor. "What, you searchin' my shit now?"

"No, I'm not searchin' your shit. I dropped your dumb-ass CDs all over the floor, and I was trying to pick them up." She released her shirt and crossed her arms under her breasts. "You know what? Just go 'head and take me to school. I didn't want to see no movie no way!"

Kyle laughed. "I'm just fucking with you, ma. Damn, learn to take a joke, Ms. Bad Ass." Kyle started up the car and pulled off. Violet kept her arms crossed tightly and kept her eyes trained on the window. They rode in silence for about five minutes.

"Look, ma. You know what I do, how I get mines. Niggas out here try to test you left and right."

"So, if somebody tries to test you, then what? Are you gonna blow them away?"

"Blow them away. Are you serious?" Kyle chuckled. "You watch too much TV, for real." He laughed even harder but stopped when he realized she didn't find it funny. He cut his eyes at her and reached over to pull her arms down. "Violet, for real, I keep that gun for show. If niggas know you're packin' heat, they are less likely to try some dumb shit, that's all. I never pulled a gun out on a nigga a day in my life. I swear my hands up to God."

Violet sighed. She let her hands fall onto her lap. "It just, you know, makes me nervous."

Kyle ran his hand down her arm and linked his fingers through hers. "Carrying a weapon is a part of what I do. It's not any different from when a cop carries his."

Violet looked at Kyle as if he'd lost his mind.

"Okay, maybe it's a little different."

"You don't say?" Violet stared down at their laced fingers. She liked the way his light skin looked against her darker tone. She smiled as Kyle rubbed his thumb across the back of her hand.

She cleared her throat. "Can I see it?"

"What do you mean, *can I see it*?"

"You know." Violet smiled shyly. "I want to hold it. I never have seen a gun in living color before."

Kyle pulled into the Franklin Mills Mall parking lot. "Well, today is not the day, kid." He got out of the car and opened the car door for her. They walked hand in hand to the mall. "That's not a toy below that seat, little girl. That's a nickel-plated Glock 9, better known as the Fat Lady. Best believe when she starts singing, the game is over."

Violet wasn't paying any attention to Kyle. She was more interested in the bright lights of the mall.

"What movie would you like to see, shawty?"

"I don't even care." She shrugged her shoulders. "Anything."

He let her window shop while he bought the tickets, and he waved her over once he was done.

"What are we going to see?"

"I thought you didn't care."

"Come on, tell me."

Kyle laughed. "You want some popcorn, shawty?"

"No, I'm good. I want to know what we are watching."

"I bought two tickets for . . . um . . . " He held the tickets up to his eyes, pretending to read them.

"Will you just tell me?"

"A'ight, bad ass, we are going to see *Liar Liar*. It's the third theater to your left."

Violet snatched her hand away from his and took off running. Once in the theater, she headed straight for the seats all the way in the back, dead center. That's where she and her sister used to sit when they were younger.

The theater was deserted. Violet looked up at Kyle when he came to join her. "I think we're going to have this place all to ourselves." She bounced slightly up and down in the chair, barely able to contain her excitement.

Kyle smiled. "I hope so." He slid into the seat beside her and trailed his fingers down her back. Violet shivered under his touch, which made him instantly hard.

She turned to look into his eyes, and the heat she found there shot straight through her and started to pulsate between her legs. He pulled her in for a kiss, and as soon as their lips met, she let out a breathless moan.

They kissed for an eternity, neither one of them noticing when the lights dimmed or the movie started.

Guilt started to needle at Kyle, so he eased out of the kiss. "We missin' the movie, shawty."

Violet smiled and sat forward in the seat, her big and bright brown eyes shining in the darkness. "This is going to be good," she whispered excitedly.

Kyle grunted in agreement, the guilt twisting in his gut.

Chapter 9

A horn sounded, and Begonia almost wet herself. Her whole body jerked, and she turned toward the mind rattling sound, clutching her chest. Her breaths came out in short, ragged bursts.

"Oh my God." She was face to face with a shiny black Lincoln Navigator driven by an asshole and his three whole-ass friends. Begonia went from zero to pissed in 6.5 seconds. She hated Rodney.

"Get the fuck out of the street, little girl."

Begonia rolled her eyes. "Don't you have unborn babies to kill and single mothers to string out?"

The guys in the car started laughing. Rodney patted his friend's chest. "Watch this, son." He looked Begonia up and down. "Oh yeah, shawty, how is your mom?"

Begonia walked quickly out of the street. "I don't have a mother."

The Navigator rolled away slowly. "Yes, you do, shawty. That's my best customer."

Begonia stood stark still and let the humiliation wash over her. *I'm tired*, she thought. *I'm so fucking tired of this bullshit; I don't know what to do.* She closed her eyes and took deep breaths.

"Begonia."

She heard her name being called, but she didn't open her eyes. *I just want to lay down and go to sleep until 1998, because this damn sure isn't my year.*

"Begonia! I know you can hear me."

Begonia opened her eyes. "The whole fucking neighborhood can hear you, Portia." She walked toward the speakeasy's steps, where Portia was sitting with her legs cocked open.

"Well, why didn't you answer me?"

"Because I was thinking." Begonia sat down on the steps right below Portia.

"Thinking, my ass. I know you aren't trippin' over Rodney and his bullshit-ass crew."

Begonia looked up at Portia. "Ain't nobody trippin' over Rodney. And why don't you close your damn legs?"

Portia sucked her teeth. "A bitch has to let her kitty cat breathe sometimes."

"Do you have to air your ass out while I'm sitting right here?"

Portia crossed her legs. "You lucky I like your crazy ass."

"Yeah, well, I love you too. Can I get a drink?"

Portia leaned back on the porch and hollered into the house. "Hey, Peanut!"

"What?" came a deep voice out of the living room window.

Portia nudged Begonia with her foot. "What you sippin' on?

"Shit, anything strong," Begonia grunted.

"Peanut, get Bee a fifth of Bacardi."

"A'ight." The blinds rattled down, and Peanut came outside with a brown paper bag. He stood there for a minute, waiting.

Portia sucked her teeth. "A'ight, dayum, Peanut, go inside! Don't you see grown folk trying to talk?" She snatched the bag out of his hand and laughed.

"Shut up, Portia! You are only a couple of years older than me."

"Ain't it a shame that no one can tell?" said Portia as Peanut turned to go in the house.

"Fuck you, Portia."

She laughed again. "You're my brother, and that's nasty." She waited until he went inside before she handed Begonia the bottle. Begonia reached into her bra to get Portia some money, but Portia stopped her.

"Don't insult me, sis. I saw you come out of Mr. Johnson's house. I know how hard you just worked for that stash."

Begonia took a swig off of her bottle. She wiped her mouth with the back of her hand. She would have slapped the bullshit out of anyone else minding her business, but Portia was cool.

"Bee, for real, you need to stop fucking with that sicko." She grabbed the bag from Begonia and took a long draw herself. "Shit, as pretty as you are, you could make some real paper with these wannabe ballers."

Begonia had a flashback of her head between Mr. Johnson's legs, and she grabbed the bottle back, took two big gulps, trying to ignore the bite of the liquor.

Portia snatched the bottle from her and twisted the lid on it. "Slow down, killa. Damn!"

Begonia shook her head. The buzz was kicking hot and heavy. "I couldn't do this shit full- time, Portia. I don't even know how you can. It's fucking disgusting. When I was a little girl, I never said I was going to grow up to be a prostitute. Shit's just not in the cards for me, ya know?"

Portia got up and dusted off her tight blue jeans. She walked down the steps and stood directly in front of Begonia. "Look, ain't nobody said it was a dream job, but fucking niggas for cash will help you and your family out. You wouldn't have to live in a hellhole and suck shriveled- up-ass dicks for spare change."

Begonia rose to her feet real slow as she stepped into Portia's face. "Watch how you walking, family. We cool and all, but if you keep talking reckless, you're gonna end this relationship real quick."

Portia smirked. "Bitch, please. You ain't endin' shit. We will just be some lumped-up bitches out here, rolling around in the street." Portia arched an eyebrow and stepped closer to Begonia. "Anytime you wanna break bad, Bee, just say the word. We can tussle real quick and smoke some herb right afterwards."

The girls stood there staring at each other for a few seconds. Then Begonia just burst out laughing and grabbed the bottle off the steps. “I’m not fucking wit’ you, yo. You ’bout the only broad I know just as crazy as me!”

Portia hugged Begonia around her neck and whispered in her ear. “Bullshit ain’t nothing, Bee. You are my girl, and you say the word, I’ll lace you up with a baller who can make all your problems melt away.”

Begonia hugged her back because she needed to. She held on tight when Portia tried to pull away. “Listen, baby girl, I know you love me, but my body is no longa for sale.”

Begonia kissed Portia on the cheek and walked off toward the park. She took another swig off the bottle, swishing it inside her mouth before swallowing. She wanted to erase all the traces of Mr. Johnson away.

Walking across 33rd Street to the playground, she ignored the traffic lights. Horns again blared, but his time, Begonia wasn’t phased. *I could care less about a car right now*. She staggered a bit through the grass and gravel that surrounded the swing set. *Let me find out I’m tipsy*! she thought as she belched loudly and laughed. *Damn, do I got to be belching like a wino?*

Drinking the last bit of the Bacardi, she licked the rim of the bottle and tossed it into the trash. *I wonder if I could get a ride to Thriftway to fill Daisy’s prescriptions?*. Begonia sat down hard on the swing with her back facing the street, rocking backward so hard she almost fell on her head.

Reaching to grab the chains, she laughed. “Oh, yeah, I’m sauced!”

“You sure as hell are, and you smell like an alleyway!”

Begonia laughed. “Oh, that’s just Mr. Johnson’s nut sack, Portia. Nothing a little soap and water won’t wash off.”

“I’m not Portia, Bee.” Begonia swung around, causing the chains on the swing to grind and twist about each other.

“Oh, shit, Shanice. What’s up? Have a seat,” she said as she pointed to the swing beside her.

“I was just coming through to see if you’re okay because you haven’t been in school all week.”

“Well, damn, Shanice, it’s just Wednesday. I still have Thursday and Friday to redeem myself.”

“Shut up, Bee. I don’t know any other seventeen-year-old who talks like that.”

Begonia smiled. “That’s probably because I’m eighteen. They flunked me last year, remember?”

Shanice pushed off with her feet and let her swing blow in the breeze. She grabbed Begonia’s swing and pulled it over to her. “There’s not a huge difference between seventeen and eighteen, Bee. I thought you said you weren’t going over Mr. Johnson house no more. What’s the matter with you?”

Begonia laughed and leaned her head against the chains. “What isn’t the matter? Doreen sold

Daisy's meds and I needed money, so I went and got money."

Shanice let Begonia's swing go. "Why the fuck didn't you come to me? I'm sure me, Tab, and Lisa could have come up with something."

"That's sweet," Begonia said, kicking off again. "But I already took care of it."

Shanice scrunched up her face.

Begonia stopped her swing. "Look, Shani, don't judge me, homes, 'cause I don't judge you."

Shanice stopped her swing, too. "I'm not judging you, Bee. I just wish you didn't have to do that sort of shit."

Begonia looked down at her feet. "Yeah, I wish I didn't have to do it, either. Shanice, I just got done having this same conversation with Portia, and I really don't feel like having a repeat convo with you."

Shanice kicked out again. She pumped hard with her legs, letting her head fall back. Her chocolate curls bounced around wildly. "How's Daisy doing?"

"She's doing fine," Begonia said, pumping her legs to match Shanice's speed. "I got enough to fill her script and get a little bit of food."

Shanice looked at Begonia. "Give me the money and the script. Me and my mom will take care of it. I don't want you to be walking all over the place with bags of groceries in the middle of the night."

Begonia just shook her head. "A'ight, that's cool. Thanks."

"A'ight, cuz, so that's taken care of. Now tell me what's wrong with Violet."

"What the fuck are you talking about? There's nothing wrong with Violet." Begonia put her feet down to stop the swing.

Shanice followed Begonia's lead. "Well, I thought she had to be sick or something, too. She wasn't in school today, and that's not like her."

Begonia's head spun. "What do you mean she wasn't in school? I told her to go to school."

Shanice's eyes bulged out of her head. "Oh, shit, Bee, I thought you knew."

Begonia stood up. "I didn't know anything, but I bet you I'll find out." She dug in her bra and took out three hundred dollars. She handed Shanice the prescription from her pants pocket. "Her meds should be about two-fifty. Just get some basic shit from the supermarket, okay?"

Shanice crumpled the money and the script in her pants pocket. "What are you gonna do, Bee?"

"What do you think I'm going to do? Why the fuck does everybody keep asking me that? I'm gonna go find my sister," Begonia said, walking away from the park. "And when I find her, I'ma kick the living shit out of her," she said quietly under her breath.

Chapter 10

The credits rolled, and Kyle nuzzled. She laughed because it tickled.

"You smell good, shawty. What you got on?"

"I don't have on any perfume, Kyle. All you smelling is that hand soap from the diner."

"Well, that shit smells good. I'm going to buy you a case of it."

Violet jumped in the seat. "What time is it? I've got to get home."

"Calm down. It's only like one thirty."

Violet smiled. "I did really have a great time."

"Yeah, shawty, I seem to have that effect on girls. If you want a good time, call Kyle."

"What you mean, *girls*?" Violet's face fell. "How many girls do you be taking out?"

Kyle stood up and stretched. "Look at you getting all jealous and shit." He grabbed her chin and tilted her face up to his so that he could stare into her eyes. "It doesn't matter how many girls I take out."

Violet tried to pull her face away, but he held her still.

"Look at me, 'cause I'm serious. All that matter is that I am taking you out now. You and only you. Do you hear me? You belong to me now."

Violet's face burst into a smile. "Are you serious, Kyle? I mean, does that mean I'm your girlfriend?"

"Hell yeah, I'm serious. You best to believe you my shawty. I am gonna be the first and last dude you dealing with."

Violet leaped into Kyle's lap, and they both fell back into the movie chairs. Kyle's laughter echoed throughout the movie theater as Violet showered kisses all over his face.

"A'ight, shawty, calm down. You're gonna break my back."

Violet eased off of Kyle. "I'm sorry."

"It's okay, ma." He stood up and checked around his seat to make sure nothing slipped out of his pockets. Satisfied, he grabbed Violet's hand and started down the aisle.

"Well, what we gonna do now?"

"I don't know, Ms. Bad Ass. Let's go into the mall and see what sort of shit we can get into."

Violet could not get the ridiculous smile off her face.

"You a'ight, shawty?" he asked smugly.

"What are you talking about, boy? I'm fine." Violet tried unsuccessfully to straighten her face.

She pursed her lips and turned them up toward her nose.

Kyle burst out laughing, and Violet giggled. "What are you doing now?"

"I'm trying to stop smiling."

"Well, it looks like you're trying to take a shit."

"No, it doesn't!"

"Yes, it does. You look like you're on the toilet crapping."

Violet's face fell, and Kyle laughed harder. She snatched her hand away from his, but he grabbed her by the waist and kissed her. Sucking in her bottom lip, he gently grazed it with his teeth. Violet melted against him and lost herself in the kiss.

Kyle snaked his tongue into her mouth with such force that Violet went wild. She pressed herself into him and began clawing at his back. Kyle grabbed her belt loops and pushed her hips away from him. It took him a little more time to tear his mouth from hers. He shook his head to clear the fog.

"You're going to get yourself into trouble if you keep kissing me like that, shawty. Come on. Let's go down to City Blue so I can cop the new Jordans." He grabbed her hand, and her goofy little smile returned, although this time, he did not comment on it.

Violet was having the time of her life. The mall smelled like French fries and disinfectant. She stared at the people shopping and wondered if they were having as much fun as she was. *I can't believe I have a boyfriend.* She rubbed her thumb across the back of Kyle's hand just like he did hers earlier. *I bet Bee would die if she found out.* Violet frowned. *She'd probably kill me first!*

She followed Kyle into the back of City Blue, fingering the clothes as she went. She sat down hard on the bench that separated the men's and women's sneakers while Kyle went straight to the Nike wall. She pulled a strand of hair out of her ponytail and twirled it around in her fingers.

Kyle came over with three boxes and sat down beside her. "So, Ms. Bad Ass," Kyle said as he took off his shoes. "What's up with your peoples?"

"What do you mean? There's nothing up with them. Why you asking about them?"

"I'm asking because I'm asking, shit. I want to know."

Violet got up and walked over to a clothing rack. "I want to know why you're asking because I know you already know." She flipped through the shirts and slammed the hangers together. "I mean, it's not a secret my moms is on crack and my sister's a thief. Hell, everybody knows that." She turned to face him with her arms crossed tightly under her chest, waiting for him to say something, anything. Kyle shook his head at her and then waved a salesgirl over.

"Can I help you?" the young girl asked.

She is smiling way too hard.,Violet thought. *She better take her high yellow self somewhere.* She walked back over to Kyle, sat down beside him, put her head on his shoulder, and fingered his t-shirt.

He chuckled and handed the salesgirl the two shoes. "I'm going to need both of these in a size eleven. You can take them right to the counter." Kyle kissed Violet on her forehead. "I know what I heard about ya people, and I know what I see. But I wanted to hear it from your pretty little lips, okay? I'm going to be around a lot, and a nigga has to know what he's getting into, ya know? Come on. Let's go over to Express and get you a couple of outfits."

Violet jumped up and shouted, "Oh no, you can't get me any clothes."

Kyle's face darkened. "Why can't I? And lower ya fucking voice when you're talking to me, for real."

"I'm sorry for hollering. It's just that Begonia gets my clothes, and she would be mad if she saw me in something that she didn't get."

"Damn, shawty, Begonia is not your mother. She's only like a year or two older than you, so how can she tell you what to wear?"

"I know she's not my mother, and it's not like she lays my clothes out for me, Kyle, but as much of a bitch as she can be, I know she loves me. She would flip the fuck out if she knew I was going out with a boy."

Kyle paid for his sneakers. "First off, I'm not a boy. I'm a man. Second, how the fuck she's taking care of you and y'all posted up in an abandoned house and shit?"

Violet whipped her head around, making sure nobody heard that. One of the salesgirls laughed, and she shot her a look that could melt steel.

Kyle grabbed her chin and turned her face to his. "Look at me, shawty."

Violet looked up at him. "Can you lower your voice, Kyle? I'm not trying to have the world in my business."

Kyle tightened his grip on her chin a little bit. "I don't give a fuck about these girls in here, yo." He let her face go and took her hand. "Come on. I'm not going to buy you no clothes this time, but I need you to know that I'm not playing around when I say that you are my shawty now. *I* take care of you now. Do you understand me?"

Violet nodded her head. Something had changed in Kyle's voice. It wasn't easy and lighthearted anymore; it was thick, deep and firm. There was a dangerous glint in his eyes that both excited and frightened her.

"I'm going to take you down to Cellular One and get you a phone."

Violet opened her mouth to object, but the look in Kyle's eyes kept her silent.

"You need to be able to call me day or night." He half dragged her across the mall to the cell phone store. He stopped in front of the store and looked down at Violet. "You are mine. I will take care of you. Not Begonia, your mom, or anyone else." He pointed to his chest. "Do you understand me?"

Violet nodded slowly, and Kyle kissed her softly on the lips. At that moment, she could have sworn that her heart floated right out of her chest and into Kyle's back pocket. Her goofy smile was back, and this time, she didn't try to hide it.

Chapter 11

Begonia went home mad as a motherfucker, walking from 33rd and Diamond to 29th and Girard Avenue, and still couldn't find any traces of Violet. What she did find was another pint of Bacardi and a pack of Newports. She kicked off her shoes and went upstairs to find the extra extension cords. She trailed the cords from her bedroom to the living room and then plugged in the two lamps and the stereo. Slipping the Jodeci CD in, she pulled out paint and a brush and set up her easel.

Begonia undid her blouse and threw it across the couch. She stood before the easel and canvas barefoot in her bra and jeans.

"Don't talk, just listen . . ." Jodeci sang sweetly through the speakers. She cranked the volume up, cracked her knuckles, and swooped her hair into a bun. Lighting a cigarette, she puffed deeply and swayed to the music. She knocked back the Bacardi, enjoying the warm sensation it made in her chest. If the windows weren't boarded up, someone looking in would see Begonia standing in front of her canvas and think that she was at peace. However, Begonia was on fire. Her blood was boiling, her head was pounding, and she was praying to God that her sister was okay and on her way home so that she could beat the bullshit out of her.

"Okay, honey," Begonia said to the blank canvas. "Talk to me." She blew cigarette smoke out of her mouth, and it curled into her nostrils. As she plucked ashes on the floor, a picture began to form in her mind. It was the homeless woman she saw on the steam grate downtown. It was the woman's eyes that first drew Begonia's attention. They were the prettiest shade of blue. Bright and alert, they were in direct contrast to everything else Begonia could see about the lady. Her face was worn, wrinkled, and smeared with dirt. Her hair was dull and gray, stringy in some places and matted in others. She wore layer upon layer of tattered, dark-colored clothes. She held a black trash bag grasped tightly to her chest as if someone were going to walk by and take it away.

Begonia put her cigarette out on the door jamb and started painting. She mixed royal blue with white and began with the old woman's eyes. It didn't take long for Begonia to get lost in her artwork. The CD played the whole way out and started over twice before Begonia put her brush down. She backed up from the canvas and lit another cigarette just as Violet came in with the baby. She glanced at the clock on the wall: seven o'clock.

I know this bitch is crazy, Begonia thought.

Daisy was asleep on Violet's shoulder. "Hey, Bee," she said quietly. Her voice shook slightly, and Begonia nodded her head.

At least the bitch got good sense to be scared, Begonia thought as she took another swig of Bacardi and sat on the sofa.

Violet cleared her throat and put Daisy's book bag down by the door. She looked over at Begonia. "Mrs. Leonora said she been knocked out for about twenty minutes. She said she fed her dinner, gave her some medicine, and Daisy was out like a light." She stood there rubbing Daisy's back, waiting for Begonia to respond, but Begonia didn't say anything. She just stood there and puffed on her Newport.

Violet cleared her throat again. "I'm going to lay Daisy down and get these clothes off of her." She headed for the stairs.

Begonia took another drink. "When you're finished doing that, I think you should come back down here and tell me where in the hell you've been. Because I went to your friend's house, and you damn sure ain't been with her."

Violet went up the stairs quietly while Begonia opened the back door to let the night air help dry her painting. By the time she came back downstairs, Begonia was lighting yet another cigarette.

"Why in the hell are you chain smoking, Bee?"

Violet glanced around and saw a bunch of cigarette butts scattered all over the floor. She knew Begonia was pissed. *Bee can't stand shit on the floor*. She searched her head for a convincing lie.

Begonia walked over to the other couch to get her shirt, and she staggered a little, having to hold her hands out to gain her balance.

Violet wrinkled up her face and folded her arms. "You are drunk, Bee."

Begonia shook her head. "Don't play with me, Violet. Drunk or not drunk, I asked you a fucking question. Where were you? " Begonia shouted as she lifted her hands in the air. "Where were you all fucking day, Violet?"

"What do you mean all day? I was in school, then I went to the library."

Begonia slipped her shirt on. "You weren't the fuck in school, and your ass wasn't in the library, so try telling me something different, 'cause that's out," she said, crossing her arms, mimicking Violet's pose. "I mean, I'm going to whoop your ass whether you tell me where you were or not, but I would still like to know where you were."

Violet let her hands drop to her side, and she braced herself. "Your drunk ass ain't gonna whoop shit."

Begonia laughed. "Oh, so you bad now, huh? Come on then, sis. Show me how bad you are."

She took a step toward Violet, and Violet backed up a few paces. “Oh no, don’t back up. You bad, remember?” Begonia stepped closer to her sister and stuck her finger in her face. “Drunk or not, high or not, Violet, you ain’t seen a day you could whoop my ass. Please believe it.”

Violet pushed Begonia out of her face.

Begonia staggered back against the coffee table and saw red. “You little fucking bitch.” Begonia ran toward Violet and grabbed her by the shirt, swung her around, and slammed her against the wall. She slid her left hand around Violet’s neck and slapped the shit out of her with her right hand.

Tears rolled down Violet’s face.

“Oh, don’t cry now. You bad! You bad enough to skip school, you bad enough to lie to my face, and now you think you bad enough to whoop my ass. I don’t know where you were today, but I know you must have lost your mind there. I know that.”

Violet struggled to free herself from Begonia’s hold. She tore at Begonia’s shirt and tried to scratch her face, but Begonia was too fast for her. She whipped her head from left to right, avoiding Violet’s hands. Violet closed her eyes tight and started swinging blindly. One of her punches connected with Begonia’s jaw.

“You little bitch,” Begonia said as she caught Violet’s next swing mid air. She pulled her off the wall, swinging her around, twisted her arm behind her back, and pressed her face into the wall. Violet's sobs were loud and shook her entire body. Snot ran down her nose onto her lips.

Begonia steadied her weight to hold Violet still. "I don't know what the hell got into you, but today is not a good day to be fucking with me. I never hurt you before in my life, but I swear to God, I will break your arm off if you don't tell me where you were."

Violet's sobs subsided, although her tears continued to stream down her face.

Begonia swore. "Do you have any idea what I've been through today to get Daisy's meds? Do you have any fucking clue what I was doing while you were playing hooky?"

"Okay, Bee, you win. I didn't go to school. Are you happy? I skipped school, okay? Shit. You think you're the only one living this nightmare? Oh, I see, it's just your mom that's fucked up and just your sister that's sick. You asking me where I was today? Where was you yesterday? I was the one here listening to them have sex while our sister was crying for food. Mrs. Lenora wasn't home, and I didn't have anything to give her. Where were you, Bee? 'Cause I was here. When Daisy went to sleep with nothing to eat and started sweating, where were you? When Momma cursed me out when I asked her about our food, where were you?"

Begonia let Violet go. She backed away from her sister. “I’m sorry, Vy. I’m so sorry.”

Violet slid to the floor and shook out her arm. “No, I’m sorry, Bee, but you’re not in this by yourself, so chill.”

Begonia walked over to the counter and grabbed the bottle of Bacardi. She handed it to Violet, who hesitated only a moment before grabbing it and taking a few gulps.

Violet coughed and sputtered. “Oh, shit. How can you drink this?”

Begonia laughed and lit another cigarette. “You drink it slowly, genius.”

Violet took a slow sip, leaned back against the wall, and pulled her knees up to her chest. The bottle of Bacardi dangled loosely from her fingers. “We can’t keep living like this, Bee. It ain’t right.”

Begonia sat on the arm of the sofa. “It’s not going to be like this forever, Vy. Hell, all we can do is go up from here.”

Violet laughed. “I know that’s right. If this ain’t rock bottom, then I don’t know what is.”

Begonia smiled as she picked at the fabric from the couch that was poking out from between her legs.

There was a knock at the door, and both girls jumped. Violet sat up and slid the bottle behind her back. Begonia opened the door, and Shanice walked in, dripping wet.

"It's raining?" Begonia said, stepping back.

"You don't say!" Shanice said, wringing out her ponytail. She had several bags of groceries wrapped around her wrists, and they clinked with the motion. "Can you get this heavy shit?" She stuck out her arm, and Violet scrambled off the floor to help.

Begonia took the bag off Shanice's wrist. The handles left an angry red ring. Violet took the groceries into the kitchen.

Shanice waited till she was out of ear shot. "What the hell happened to her?"

Begonia snorted. "She'll live. Where's Daisy's meds?"

"Oh, yeah." She turned around. "It's in my backpack. Hurry up. My mom is waiting for me outside."

Begonia pulled Daisy's medicine out of the bag and zipped it back up.

"Gotta go," Shanice said, and she walked back out the door.

"A'ight, young'un, thank you," called Begonia. "Ay, yo, wait up."

Shanice turned around on the steps. "What?"

"That was more than fifty dollars' worth of groceries."

"Oh, you can thank Tabitha and Lisa for that. They seemed to think you could use a lot more." Shanice opened the passenger side door. "Begonia, don't kill your sister."

Chapter 12

Violet's tears returned when she entered the kitchen. She checked to see if the refrigerator was plugged into the surge protector that ran from a line upstairs before she put anything into it. She started to empty the bags, and her fingers shook. She didn't like lying to her sister, and she thought not telling the truth would be the same as lying.

Begonia came into the room, and Violet jumped. "You scared me," she said, stretching her neck into the living room. "Where's Shanice?"

"She had to bounce"

"Oh, okay," said Violet.

They spent the next few minutes in silence. Violet looked at Begonia. "I'm sorry, Bee. These last couple of days have just been too much." Violet wiped her eyes and leaned against the sink. Her voice was thick and shaky with her tears. "I can't keep on acting like this shit is okay, Bee, because it's not, and I'm not you."

Begonia leaned herself in the doorway, and Violet took her silence as permission to continue.

"Where's Mom? Did you guys fight? I saw that her room was empty when I went upstairs, and I was like, damn." She laughed a little and wiped her nose with the edge of her shirt. "That was it. I know she's gone, and I don't feel anything for her. I mean, what kind of woman does that? She doesn't care if we live or die! What the fuck, Begonia?" Violet's hands moved rapidly with every word. "You expect me to go to school and act like everything is okay. Then you gonna fight me because I don't tell you where I was. You leave outta here every day and don't go to school. You don't tell me where you're going or what you're doing."

Begonia pushed herself off the doorway and hopped up onto the counter. "Violet, I know you are nothing like me. We're like night and day. Why do you think I do all the shit that I do? You think I wanna do this? I know what people be saying about me." Begonia smiled. "And I don't want you to go through what I go through. You're an angel.

Violet shook her head. "I'm not an angel, Bee."

"Yes, you are, compared to me. And I want you to have everything your heart desires."

"Well, I desire a normal life and a normal fucking family."

"Well, shit, I can't give you that!" Begonia threw her hands up. "This is all I have. This and my word that it's not always going to be like this."

As if on cue, the lights flickered and then went out. Begonia let her hands fall down and slap against her sides. She laughed and shook her head. "This is unbelievable. Well, on that note, I have to go."

Violet could barely make out Begonia's form in the dark. "Where are you going?" She reached for Begonia, but she was already moving toward the front door.

"I've got to get outta here for a little while. You just think about what I told you."

"I've thought about it, Bee," Violet said softly under her breath. "But it's just not enough for me. Not anymore."

Violet climbed up the stairs and crawled into the bed with Daisy. She was used to the dark because their lights went out at least twice a week. She could walk through their house back to front five times without bumping into anything. She kissed Daisy on her forehead and smoothed her hair back from her face.

Violet pulled her cell phone from her book bag and called Kyle. "I'm done with this life."

Chapter 13

Smoke billowed through the kitchen as Begonia tried unsuccessfully to raise the window. "Come on, baby," she grunted. "Open up for Momma."

Violet entered the kitchen, coughing and waving her hands. "What in the hell?" She walked to the back door and jerked it open.

"Why didn't I think of that?" Begonia said, turning around. "Good morning, sunshine!"

Violet just stared. All of the pots and pans were dirty and piled up in the sink. The kitchen table was covered with all kinds of burnt, unrecognizable foods.

Begonia beamed. "I made breakfast."

"Have you lost your mind, Bee? I'm not eating that."

"What's wrong with it? I made all your favorites!" Begonia pointed from one mound of goo to the next. "That's scrambled eggs with cheese, and that's bacon and sausage. And look," she said while picking up a plate covered with hockey pucks. "Blueberry pancakes."

Violet laughed and hopped up onto the counter. "You are definitely tripping."

"What?" Begonia put the plate back on the table and lit a cigarette. "You said that you wanted a normal life. What could be more normal than someone cooking you breakfast before you go off to school?"

Daisy ran into the kitchen with her arms outstretched. "I wan' bacon, Bee."

Begonia picked her up kissed her on her cheek and handed her two very black strips of bacon off the table. Daisy stuffed one strip into her mouth, and Begonia kissed her again.

"You see, Violet? At least someone appreciates my cooking."

"What does she know? She eats boogies!" Violet said, laughing.

"I do not!"

Begonia looked as if she were shocked. She held Daisy away from her. "Do you eat boogies, munchkin?"

"No, no, no!" Daisy kicked her feet and shook her head in protest, giggling.

Begonia put Daisy down, being careful not to burn her with the cigarette. "Whatever, boogie eater. Go upstairs and get your washcloth and soap. I'ma get you washed up and dressed."

"Okay," Daisy said, jumping up and down. She stuffed another piece of bacon into her mouth and ran up the stairs.

Begonia finished her cigarette and flicked it out the back door. She turned around and looked at the food that was spread across the table. She placed her hands on her hips and sighed. "You ain't even gonna taste none of this good food?"

Violet rubbed her eyes and yawned. "Not even if I was starving and that was the only food left on the planet!"

Begonia sucked her teeth and picked up a burnt pancake. "You're crazy. This . . ." she said, flapping the pancake around in Violet's face, "is the truth!" Begonia took a big bite out of the pancake and paused. Her eyes began to water, and her nostrils flared.

Violet smiled. "How is it, Bee?"

The pancake crunched between Begonia's jaws. She pocketed a large piece of it in her cheek and coughed. "It's good."

"You're a mothafucking lie!"

Begonia tried to chew the pancake a few more times before giving up and spitting the remainder of it into the trash.

"All right," Begonia said, wiping off her mouth. "Maybe the pancakes are a little overcooked, but the rest of this shit is good."

Violet hopped off the counter. "For real, yo, you could leave this stuff out on the table all day and all night and won't no rats or roaches even touch it."

Begonia dusted off her hands on her pajama bottoms. Her face fell, and her bottom lip poked out, making her look more like a teenager, but she quickly recovered. Before Violet could blink, Begonia had fixed her face. The little girl was gone, replaced by the hard-faced young woman that Violet was used to seeing.

"Well, Vy, I tried," Begonia said softly. "You said you wanted a normal life, and I tried to give you one, but who the fuck was I kidding, huh?" She folded the tablecloth around all the food and dishes on the table and lifted it into the trash. "We wouldn't know what a normal life was if a fucking normal life jumped up and bit us in the ass." She stuffed the pile of dishes and burnt breakfast deeper into the trash can with her foot. "Now, if you'll excuse me, I'ma go upstairs and wash my baby sister, because she's still young enough to appreciate someone being nice to her."

Chapter 14

Violet walked a few paces behind Begonia after they dropped Daisy off at the sitter. Begonia was in a foul mood, and Violet didn't want to be bothered. *Getting all mad 'cause didn't nobody wanna eat her black, burnt- up biscuits for breakfast,* Violet thought as she waited at the stoplight longer then necessary just so she could put a little more distance between her and her sister.

Begonia looked back and rolled her eyes at Violet. "Will you come on?"

"I'm coming, Bee."

"Well, hurry the hell up. Unless you're planning on trying to skip off right in front of me."

Violet crossed the street as slowly as she could. She tucked her arms tightly under her chest. "Ain't nobody trying to skip school. God!"

A white Cadillac raced down the street and stopped two inches away from Violet. She jumped back, screaming. "Damn, watch where the fuck you going!"

The old man behind the wheel just nodded his head and gave her a gap-toothed smile.

"Learn how to fucking drive. You could have killed me!"

Begonia put her painting against the light pole and grabbed Violet out of the street.

"Come on, Vy. Get the hell outta the street before he runs you over for real this time."

"Get off me, Bee," Violet said, snatching her arm away.

"Okay," Begonia said, putting her hands up. "Shit, I was just trying to stop dude from running you over." Begonia frowned and bent over to pick up her painting. "Are you on your period, Vy?"

"I don't know why you even ask me something like that."

"Because," Begonia said, shrugging. "You're acting like a real bitch, and I don't know why. What's wrong with you?"

Violet stared at Begonia like she wasn't too bright.

Begonia rolled her eyes. "I mean besides all that."

Violet shrugged. "I'm just tired, Bee, that's all."

They were surrounded by other students as soon as they reached the school. Shanice snuck up behind Begonia and covered her eyes. "Guess who?"

"Get off me, Shani." Begonia laughed and swung around.

Shanice backed up, giggling. "Oh, is that your new painting? Let me see!" She grabbed for it, but Begonia held it away.

"No, this is for Ms. Blakely."

"Oh, I see," Shanice said. "Nobody but your baby can see it." Shanice waved absently at Violet before disappearing with Begonia into the crowd.

Violet frowned. *So much for all your fake-ass concern,* she thought.

Once inside the school, they were attacked by the non-teaching assistants with the metal detectors. It was a simple procedure, really. All students were supposed to open their book bags and hand them over to the school's police officers to be checked. Then the NTA would give you a once over with the wand to make sure no one was packing. It took no longer than three minutes if none of the students got out of line. However, Begonia almost always jumped clear over the line. Violet dropped her book bag and leaned against the banister as she watched her sister give her morning performance.

"What the hell are you looking for, Butt Gut? You are not going to find any snack cakes or cookies in my drawers." The kids on the stairwell laughed.

"My name isn't Butt Gut. It's Mrs. Harriet," she said, putting her finger in Begonia's face. "I swear, girl, if you call me out of my name one more time . . ."

"And what?" Begonia asked with a smile. Her eyes, however, remained cold as steel. "What are you going to do about it, Butt Gut?"

A boy from the bottom of the stairs hollered, "Begonia's crazy!"

"And you know this!" Begonia shouted back. She blew a kiss at the boy, snatched her book bag from one of the officers, and walked into the hallway. "The queen is here!" she shouted. The mantra was repeated by Shanice and another one of Begonia's cronies that Violet couldn't see.

Violet picked up her book bag and walked up the steps. Mrs. Harriet damn near growled when she approached her. She ripped Violet's book bag from her hands and threw it on the table.

"What?" Mrs. Harriet said harshly.

"What do you mean, *what*? I didn't even say anything!"

Mrs. Harriet didn't respond. She ran the wand over Violet's torso, and it started beeping rapidly once it moved over her stomach. Mrs. Harriet smirked and put the wand on the table and pushed Violet up against the wall.

"Oh my God!" Violet said. "It's just my belt buckle."

"Shut up." Mrs. Harriet squashed Violet's face down against the cinderblock and patted her down roughly. Violet had to hold her head up to keep the tears from falling. She grabbed her bag and walked into the school silently. She could still hear Begonia and her friends shouting that the queen was here. Violet wiped her eyes and put her head down. *Pretty soon, I'm not gonna have to pay for the queen's crimes.*

Chapter 15

Begonia strolled into her homeroom, bobbing her head with her hands held high in the air. She opened her mouth to make her usual announcements, but she was cut off by the teacher, Mr. Kinglsey.

"Yes, we know your majesty, the queen, is here. I think everybody in the school knows now." Mr. Kingsley sat on the edge of his desk and waved Begonia to her seat. "Can you please sit your royal butt down so I can finish taking attendance?"

The corners of Begonia's lips turned up into the slightest smile. She lowered her hands and slowly switched over to a desk in the front row. She licked her lips and sighed. "I'll sit anywhere you want me to, Mr. Kingsley." Her smile widened as her eyes roamed up and down her teacher's five-foot two-inch, stick-like frame.

"Spare me, Begonia, please." He glanced at the clock. "Its only eight o'clock, and homeroom only lasts for about fifteen minutes. I have a punching headache. The quicker you settle down, the quicker you can go torture the rest of the faculty." Mr. Kingsley grabbed his roll book off his desk and continued calling out names.

She kept the smile pasted on her face and snorted. *You're not the only one with a headache,* she thought. She resisted the urge to massage her own temples. *Come on, Bee, you can do this. You only have a few more hours of bullshit. Two forty-five will be here before you know it.* Begonia rolled her eyes. *You'll just have to go home and deal with a different load of bullshit.*

Staring out the window blankly, she let her fingers trail the names engraved in the desk by students long gone. Her thoughts turned to her sister. *I wonder what the fuck has gotten into Violet.*

A crumpled up piece of paper sailed past her nose, and a second one hit her in the head before she had a chance to react. "What the fuck?" Begonia said, slapping the desk. Three more crumpled up missiles hit her head, shoulder, and neck. She swung around and threw up her arms as a weak shield. The classroom filled with laughter. Then Begonia locked eyes with her best friend, T-Bone. His smile was as goofy as ever. His tall, lanky frame blanketed his desk, and his baseball cap partially covered his face. He was as real as they came.

T-Bone ripped a piece of paper out of his notebook, rolled it up in his hands, and then took aim. Mr. Kingsley was beside him in an instant.

"Throw another wad of paper in this class, Thomas."

"My name is T-Bone."

"I don't care what your name is. If you throw one more piece of paper in this classroom, you'll be in detention until graduation."

T-Bone threw the paper. Begonia swung out and missed. The ball socked her in the eye, and she burst out laughing. The bell rang, and the class made a speedy exit for the door.

Begonia walked over toward T-Bone, who draped one long arm over her shoulder. "T, you are such a punk," she said as she snaked her arm around his waist.

"If I'm a punk, how come you're gonna marry me and have all of my big-headed babies?"

Begonia giggled as they walked out of the classroom. "Ain't nobody marrying you, T-Bone.

Mr. Kingsley was at his desk, furiously scribbling something down on his pad. "Thomas," he yelled. "Thomas, get back here!"

Begonia and Thomas continued to walk down the hallway and were soon surrounded by a throng of students. T-Bone took his arms from around Begonia once they came to his locker.

He raised his voice and mocked Mr. Kingsley. "Thomas, Thomas, I said come back here!"

Begonia smiled. "You're an asshole."

The bell rang again, and the hallway thinned as students rushed to get to first period before they were locked out.

T-Bone leaned against the locker. "How come you missed my last game, Bee?"

"I was busy, T, damn! Come on, man. You know I would have been there if I could."

"Yeah, I know." He turned his cap to the back. "So, where's your new masterpiece? Shanice told me you brought a painting to school."

Begonia's face lit up like a sunrise. "It's in Ms. Blake's classroom."

"Well, are you going to let me see it?" T-Bone tilted his head and batted his eyes.

Begonia laughed. "That puppy dog shit does not work on me, homey!"

T-Bone straightened himself out. "It's not called puppy dog shit when you're a mac."

"Well, what the hell is it called then?"

T-Bone smiled. "I do believe it's called Mac Daddyism!"

"Whatever, yo, I have to get to class."

T-Bone looked at her strange, and then his eyes widened. Begonia could have sworn she saw a light bulb turn on over the top of his head, just like in the old cartoons.

"That's right!" he said, snapping his fingers and pointing at her. "Your first period is art class."

Begonia nodded her head slowly. "You know what? I think you're right!" She turned and started walking down the hall.

"Speaking of art class, hey, wait up. I'm coming with you."

"Go to your own class, T-Bone!" Begonia said, walking through the stairwell doors. Advanced art and science classes were held on the fourth floor. She took the stairs two at a time, and T-Bone matched her stride.

"I'm not showing it to anybody."

He stopped cold. "Not even me?"

Begonia laughed. "Nope, not even you."

T-Bone continued up the stairs. "That's cold, Bee, really cold."

Begonia sighed. She and T-Bone had been friends since kindergarten. If she was going to trust anyone outside of her sisters, he would be the first, with Shanice running a close second.

Begonia looked over her shoulder, and T was doing his best puppy dog impression again. "A'ight, come on, boy! Damn. But don't start your shit."

Rahim, the school's security guard, stuck his head into the stairwell and hollered up at him. "Aye, yo, Thomas, come here, man. You have to go to the dean's office.

T-Bone put on his best innocent look and pointed to his chest. "Why do I have to go to the dean's office?"

Rodney sucked his teeth. "Come on, man. You know why. You shouldn't have been trying to hold baseball practice in homeroom. Mr. Kingsley told the dean how you walked out when he was trying to give you detention."

Begonia laughed. "Run along, T-Bone, like a good little boy. I'll let you see my painting some other time."

"Fuck you, Bee!" T-Bone said on his way down the stairs.

"All you have to do is say when and where, and I'll fuck you cross-eyed."

He laughed.

"Come on. I don't have all day," Rahim said, leaning against the doorway. "Y'all kids got some nasty mouths, for real."

Begonia ran up the last flight of stairs and leaned over the railing. "Aw, don't be jealous, Rahim. You know my heart belongs to you." She ran to the end of the hallway and burst through the art room door. Running into the desk, she knocked a few paint supplies onto the floor. "Oh, shit," she said, stopping to clean up the mess.

"Ah, Begonia. Nice of you to grace us with your presence," Mrs. Blake said as she helped Begonia pick up the last couple of brushes and charcoal.

"I'm sorry I'm late, ma'am."

Mrs. Blake snorted. "You are many things, Begonia, but sorry isn't one of them.

Begonia smiled as she placed the small sketchpad back on the desk. She scanned the room for her painting but did not see it. She loved art class. It was the only place she really felt at home. The windows were draped with long, silky, multi-colored curtains that hung to the floor. The room was dotted with paintings and paint paraphernalia. The desks were replaced by five wooden islands with black marble tops and silver sinks.

"Your painting is back in my office," Mrs. Blake said, walking over to Sydney, who was painting the view from the window with breathtaking detail.

"What do you want to talk to me about?" Begonia asked.

Mrs. Blake held up her hand to cut Begonia off. She tapped Sydney lightly on the arm. "There should be more shadow around here at the base of the buildings, Sydney. You need to focus on where you want the lights to hit the scene."

Mrs. Blake indicted for Begonia to follow her with a wave of her hand. They walked into her office, where Begonia's painting was positioned on an easel beside her desk.

Begonia looked from her painting to Mrs. Blake and back again. "Well, what the hell is wrong with it?"

Mrs. Blake walked over to the painting and extended her hand toward it as if about to touch it, but did not. She withdrew her hand quickly and then placed her trembling fingers to her lips. When she finally turned to face Begonia, her eyes glistened with tears. She sighed heavily, and her voice came out in a soft whisper. "There's nothing wrong with it, Begonia. It's absolutely perfect, and I think . . ." She paused, placing her hand on her chest. "I think that you should enter it into this year's National Commission for the Arts Amateur Artist Competition." Mrs. Blake smiled and looked back at the painting. "I believe you could very well win a full scholarship to the college of your choice, dear."

Begonia opened her mouth, but nothing would come out.

Chapter 16

Mrs. Hawker called Violet's name four times before she responded. She laid her head down on her desk, and her face was tucked inside the crook of her arm to hide her tears. *I can't stand this school*, she thought.

"She can't hear you, Mrs. Hawker. She's sad," an evil girl called from the front of the room.

"Yeah, she was molested by Butt Gutt twenty minutes ago."

Violet's stomach clenched into a knot, and she squeezed her arms tighter around her head as if she wanted to disappear. *If Begonia would just act right for once, I wouldn't have to go through this.*

Mrs. Hawker called a few more names out of her roll book and made a couple of announcements before the bell sounded. Violet wiped her face on her sleeve, grabbed her book bag, and practically ran toward the door. Someone in the front row stuck their foot out in front of her. She tripped over it but did not fall. The laughter behind her felt like hundreds of little knives sticking in her back.

She turned when she reached the doorway and came face to face with Angela Mooney. She was the girl her sister beat the dog shit out of last year.

"You need to be careful, Violet. You almost fell on that pretty little face of yours."

Violet's bottom lip quivered, but she forced herself not to cry. "Leave me alone, Angela. I don't have time for your shit right now."

Angela stepped into her face. "Your eyes are red, Violet. Have you been smoking on your mommy's crack pipe?"

Violet opened her mouth to say something but was cut off by a pimply-faced girl who came to stand beside Angela. "If you keep picking on her, Angela, she's gonna run upstairs and get her sister."

Angela started to laugh, but Violet could tell that it was forced. Angela's eyes looked wide and frightened.

Pimple Face sneered. "You always get your sister to fight your battles, don't you, Violet?"

Violet stepped into Angela's face. Her eyes shifted back and forth rapidly. Violet snorted and laughed. "As a matter of fact, I do. And after I tell her you've been fucking with me, Angie, maybe she won't mind breaking your nose again." Violet turned to her pimple-faced friend. "Who knows? Maybe she'll have time to knock out a few more of your teeth."

Pimple Face jumped at her, but Angela held her back. Violet shouldered her bag and walked out the door. She needed to wash her face, but she saw a few of her classmates walk into the girls' bathroom, so she decided to use the bathroom on another floor. Violet didn't notice the group of girls that followed her into the stairwell.

Chapter 17

Begonia carried the painting out into the classroom. She set it on the easel beside her desk. She looked over her shoulder at Mrs. Blake. "You really think it's that good?"

"Oh, shit," Sidney said. She and a few more of Begonia's classmates got up to look at the painting.

Sidney knocked Begonia on the shoulder so hard she almost fell out of the chair. "Did you do that, Bee?"

"Yeah, Sid. You like it?"

"Are you friggin' kidding me? It's friggin' amazing!"

"I couldn't have put it any better." Mrs. Blake smiled and patted Begonia on the shoulder. "We are going to submit Begonia's painting into the NCAA'S annual competition."

"All right, now!" said a girl from the back of the classroom. They all started laughing and talking at once.

"Hold on," Begonia said, rising from her stool. She hopped up on the desk so that she could face the class. “Hold on,” she said, holding her hands up. “I didn’t agree to do it yet.” Her serious tone was marred by the bright smile on her face. “Okay, Mrs. Blake, tell me what’s up. What do I have to do?”

“Well, first you’ll need to get a permission slip signed.”

“That’s easy,” Begonia cut in. ” “I can forge that today.”

The class laughed, but Mrs. Blake went on like she didn’t hear her. “Then there are regional, state, and national competitions.”

Begonia couldn’t tell if the prickly sensation forming in the pit of her stomach was excitement or fear. She eyed her painting warily. She could no longer hear what Mrs. Blake was saying. Her eyes were locked on the eyes of the old homeless woman in the painting. *Look at what beauty, stress, rum, and cigarettes can make.*

Chapter 18

Violet paused in front of Begonia's art class. She raised her hand to knock on the door, then thought better of it. She ran inside the girls' bathroom instead. Throwing her book bag in the corner, she gripped the sides of the sink and stared at her reflection. "Why the fuck do you have to be so weak, Vy? Damn." She wiped the tears from her eyes and turned on the water. *Kyle will be here in a couple more hours. You can make till then, can't you?*

The bathroom door banged open. Violet whirled around and faced three girls from around the way. She recognized the tallest girl as Kyle's sister, Kisha. She looked a lot like him, except her features were smaller and more girly. The second girl was cute, if a little on the chubby side. Violet recognized her from the basketball courts. The third and biggest girl looked like the crack of someone's ass. Neither of the girls looked like they were there to make friends with Violet.

Ass Face spoke first. "What were you doing at the mall with Kyle the other day?"

Kyle's name sounds ridiculous coming out of her ugly-ass mouth, Violet thought. She switched off the water and started backing up toward the door. She recognized a trap when she saw one, and she didn't want to add getting jumped in the bathroom to an already fucked up day. "I was minding my damn business," Violet said, trying to back out of the bathroom door. She looked longingly at her book bag lying on the floor by the stalls, but she wasn't going to risk grabbing it.

"I'm going to need you to stay away from my man," said the chubby one.

"Your man?" Violet asked.

"Yes, her man," Kisha said. "They've been going together for a year now."

"Well, he wasn't your man last—"

The ugly girl smacked the last word right out of Violet's mouth. Violet stumbled across the bathroom. *Well, so much for getting out of here*, she thought. Her back slammed against the stall. Before she had a chance to react, pain sliced across her other cheek. She couldn't tell which girl had thrown the punch. She didn't need to.

Violet went off. She started flailing her arms wildly, not caring who she hit or where she hit them, until Kisha hit her so hard that she was stunned and fell back against the sink, clutching her breast. The air flew out of her like someone had stuck a vacuum cleaner in her mouth.

She blinked hard, trying to get her bearings. The chubby one was saying something to her again, but Violet couldn't hear her. She could barely think. She saw the ugly girl trying to hit her out of the corner of her eyes. Then all she could hear was Begonia's voice in her head. *Whenever you are getting jumped, Vy, all you have to do is grab one person out of the crowd and fuck them up.*

Violet ducked ugmo's swing, grabbed her by the hair, and yanked her to the ground. Both of the other girls were raining punches and kicks down on Violet, but she couldn't feel them. Her heart was beating faster than it ever had in her life. *Now I know why Begonia likes to fight so much*, she thought as she tried to bang ugmo's head into the marble floor. *I feel fucking great!*

Chapter 19

Everyone gathered around Begonia, excited that someone from their class may actually win a national art competition. But Begonia didn't know what to think, because the prickling feeling at the base of her stomach was starting to turn into a stabbing sensation. She couldn't focus. Everyone's voices started to mesh together into some weird kind of buzzing noise. Big, bad Begonia was scared out of her mind.

Mrs. Blake waved a hand in front of Begonia's face to get her attention. "Are you listening to me, sweetheart? Just think of how proud your mother would be sitting there in the front row."

"What makes you think my mom would be there?"

"Your mother has to accompany you, Begonia. If not you mother, then another legal guardian must be with you. It is in the guidelines."

Well, that did it.

Begonia blinked to clear her head. "I'm not entering no competition."

"What?" Mrs. Blake looked as if Begonia had spat straight in her face.

"You heard me," Begonia said, hopping off the desk. "I'm not entering my piece of shit painting into no stupid competition." She pushed past her startled classmates. "I have to pee."

Begonia stormed out of the classroom, walked into the bathroom, and stopped cold. She couldn't believe her eyes. Her baby sister was rolling around on the floor, beating the shit out of a girl that looked like a gremlin. Begonia leaned against a stall and enjoyed the show until one of the other girls tried to kick Violet.

Begonia stepped over them and put her hands into the chubby girl's face. "Try to kick my sister again and see what I'll do to you."

Violet looked up at the sound of Begonia's voice. She pinned the girl down and tried to put her knee in her chest like she'd seen and felt Begonia do before, but it didn't work. Ugmo flipped Violet off of her with such force that Violet's butt bounced on the marble.

Begonia laughed at Violet's flop but straightened her face quickly. "What the fuck is going on here?" Begonia asked while dusting Violet's clothes off and trying to fix her hair.

"Nothing," Violet said, slapping Begonia's hands away.

"Yeah, that looked like a whole bunch of nothing." She rolled her eyes at Violet and turned her attention to the three girls who were trying to kill her.

"Why don't you mind your business, Bee? I can take care of myself."

"Please, Vy. I guess you were taking care of yourself just fine when I walked in here." Begonia held her hand up in Violet's face and turned to the chubby girl standing next to her. "I asked you why in the hell were you picking on my sister."

"You need to tell your sister to stay—"

Violet punched the chubby girl right in her nose and walked out into the hall. Begonia's mouth fell open. she followed after Violet and shouted her name. Several students stopped whatever they were doing to stare at them.

"I said I can take care of myself." Violet shook out her hand. "Stay out of it, Bee." She clutched her hand to her chest and ran down the hall.

The gremlin took the chubby girl back into the bathroom to stop up her leaking nose, which left Begonia standing there facing the third girl, who looked like she would rather be anywhere else. Begonia jumped at her, and she ran into the bathroom after her friends. Laughing, Begonia started down the hall to find Violet. *She was scrapping her little ass off*, Begonia thought with a smile. She turned into the stairwell and was cut off by Charlotte and April.

Charlotte smiled brightly. "Begonia! Just the bitch I was looking for."

Begonia looked over their shoulders to see if she could see Violet. "Have you seen my sister?"

"Yeah, I thought I saw her going to class."

Begonia looked relieved. She sighed and turned to Charlotte. "So, why have you been looking for me?"

Charlotte waved Begonia back into the hall. "I have to go shopping today, and I thought you might like to go with me."

Begonia arched her eyebrow. "I don't think I need anything right now, and I usually *shop* alone."

"Shopping?" April asked accusingly. "I thought you said that we were gonna go boosting. I don't have any money for shopping, Charlotte."

Begonia shook her head. "Your girlfriend is a little reckless, don't you think?"

Charlotte turned to April. "I'm going to need you to keep your mouth shut, okay?"

"But, you said—"

Charlotte sucked her teeth. "Shut up, April, please!"

Begonia headed back to the stairwell, but Charlotte ran to catch up with her. "Come on, Bee, I've got a buyer."

Get the fuck out of here. Begonia looked Charlotte up and down with new interest. "Who in the hell has money to buy something this time of the month?"

"Big Dame's baby momma's birthday is coming up, and he said he would pay top dollar for some exclusive shit."

Begonia thought about the extra $200 that she lifted from Mr. Johnson's perverted ass. It was tucked securely in her bra. She opened up her mouth to tell Charlotte to shop on her solo, but nothing came out. *Think about Violet, you dickhead. You know that you need to get her something real nice for her sweet sixteen*. Begonia gave Charlotte another appraising look before turning and walking down the steps. *If the girl already had a buyer for the boost, Begonia, then it's worth the risk.*

She pulled a pack of cigarettes out of her back pocket. "Meet me at the corner ofTwenty-ninth and Ridge Avenue in twenty minutes."

Chapter 20

Violet called Kyle from the payphone by the nurse's office, because she left her cell phone in her book bag and she left her book bag in the girls' bathroom. *Real smart move, Violet, real smart*. She seriously doubted that it would make it to the lost and found. She put a quarter in the phone and looked up and down the hallway nervously before dialing Kyle's number.

Kyle picked up on the first ring. "Yo, who this?"

"It's me," Violet whispered.

"Who the fuck is *me*?"

"Kyle, it's me, Violet."

"What's wrong with you, girl? Whose phone are you calling me on?"

"I l-l-lost the phone you gave me." The anger in Kyle's voice was making her nervous. She swallowed a big gulp of air to steady herself. "I'm sorry," she said quietly.

Kyle's voice softened a little. "Are you crying?"

"No," Violet lied. "I just need you to come here and get me."

"I told you I'd be there about two thirty, shawty. I got some things I got to handle first."

Violet's heart sank. She curled the phone cord around her fingers, saying nothing. Her tears trailed down her face and gathered at her chin.

Kyle called her name a couple of times, but she didn't respond. "What's the matter with you, girl? Did something happen to you?"

"Yeah, something happened to me. Your sister happened to me. Your sister and her stupid friends jumped me in the fourth floor bathroom. Look, Kyle, you don't have to come and get me, but I am not staying here."

"Hold on, shawty. I'll come and get you. Just calm down, okay?"

"Okay," Violet said, relieved.

"Go across the street to the Chinese store. I'll be there to pick you up in five minutes."

"Okay," Violet said again before hanging up the phone. She wiped her eyes on her sleeve and walked straight past the office to the main exit. Violet looked around for non-teaching assistants and school security guards, but the exit was free and clear. *School security is a fucking joke*, she thought as she walked across the street to Lee's. *No wonder Begonia can come and go as she pleases.*

Violet yanked the store door open and got a glimpse of her reflection in the glass. She felt like fighting all over again. “Can I have a pack of Newports and a Pepsi, please?”

The small Asian woman behind the counter sighed and looked Violet up and down, taking in her hair and ripped up outfit. “How old you are?” the woman asked, pointing to the eighteen and over tobacco sign.

“I’m old enough,” Violet said, slapping a twenty-dollar bill down.

The woman muttered something under her breath in Chinese and slid the twenty-dollar bill off of the counter. Violet stood there, stiff and pissed, with her arms tucked tightly under her breasts.

Still muttering, the woman threw Violet’s cigarettes and change onto the countertop. She walked over to the freezer to grab the Pepsi.

Violet picked up her cigarettes and thrust the change into her pocket. “Throw my soda, bitch, and I swear that I’ll jump smooth over this counter.”

The woman took in the wild look in Violet’s eyes and gently placed her soda down. Violet smirked, grabbed the bottle, and walked out of the store.

Taking a seat on the steps of the abandoned house next door, she banged the pack of cigarettes against her free hand like she’d seen Begonia do countless times before. She took a swig of her Pepsi, opened the pack, and looked up and down the street. *Coast is clear*, she thought as she lit her cigarette and took a long drag.

Violet was choking and sputtering when Kyle pulled up. He rolled the passenger-side window down and laughed. "You look funny as hell trying to smoke a cigarette. You're not even holding it right, ma. That's the way you hold a joint."

Violet's back stiffened. She stood up and took another puff on the cigarette just to prove him wrong. Her eyes watered, but she managed not to choke. She flicked the cigarette away before getting into the car.

Kyle laughed and took the whole pack from her. "Look at you, all scraped up and shit. What the hell happened?"

"What the fuck do you think happened?" Violet rolled her eyes, crossed her arms, and eyed the pack of cigarettes under the radio. Kyle pulled out onto the street so fast the wheels screeched. Violet groped around for her seatbelt and recounted the fight to Kyle.

"Oh, you really tryna be a bad ass, huh? I was just playing when I called you that, cutie. I didn't know that you were going to try to live up to it and shit."

Violet stared out of the window. She started to think she had made a mistakc calling Kyle. "So you think this is all my fault?" she asked, reaching for her cigarettes.

"Nope," Kyle said, slapping her hands away from the Newports. He glanced at her scrunched up face and smiled. "On second thought, bad ass is definitely the right nickname for you." He brushed his hand across her chin, and she jerked away like she was dodging a punch.

"Oh, you don't want me to touch you?"

Violet stared straight ahead silently.

"That's funny," Kyle said, rubbing his chin. "You didn't mind me touching you yesterday." He reached for her breast, and she slapped his hand away. "Aww, shit, shawty, you mad for real, huh? Look, ma, you can't pay any attention to those little chicken-head girls at your school."

Violet turned her head to look out the passenger-side window because she didn't want him to see the tears in her eyes. "What about your sister, Kyle? Is she a chicken-head too?"

"Don't worry about my sister. I'll deal with her." Kyle pulled the car over on Ninth and Allegheny and ran his hand lightly up the length of Violet's arm. Chills ran up her arm, and a sigh escaped her lips before she could control herself.

She turned and faced Kyle, wide eyed. A tear spilled over her cheek. "And what about the girl with your sister, the pretty little heavy-set one. How are you gonna handle her?"

Kyle unbuckled her seatbelt and pulled her close. He wiped the tears from her eyes and kissed her softly. The heat ignited so fast between Violet's legs that she was afraid she was going to set the car seat on fire.

Kyle eased away from Violet. “Yeah,” he said softly. “I’m going to take care of her too. I told you not to worry about those little girls, and I mean it.” He opened the car door. “Come on.” He motioned for Violet to get out of the car. “Let’s get you cleaned up.”

“Is this where you live?” Violet asked, looking up at the big three-story building.

“Yup,” Kyle said. “This is one of the places I lay my head.”

Violet’s jaw dropped open when she walked into the living room. *This place looks like a department store*, she thought, eying the buttery leather sofa and big screen TV. There was a chandelier hanging over a gleaming white dining room set, and the biggest fish tank Violet ever saw separated the two rooms.

Kyle was halfway up the steps before he noticed that Violet wasn’t right behind him. “Come on, girl,” he said, walking up the last few stairs backward.

His voice snapped her out of the trance she was in. *This place is practically a palace compared to the shithole I live in*. Violet walked up the steps, letting her hands trail over the cranberry painted walls. She marveled over the gleaming white baseboards and the intricate carvings of the banister. *This place could be on TV,* she thought as she followed Kyle down the hall. *Or at least a magazine*. They walked past two closed doors before they reached the bathroom.

"Go in there and run you some bathwater, shawty. I'm gonna go and find you something to put on."

Violet looked at Kyle and nodded her head before doing what she was told. *Why do I have to take a bath?* she thought. *I know my clothes may be a little beat up, but I did take a bath this morning.*

Sitting on the edge of the tub, she turned the water on and slipped off her sneakers. Goose bumps rose up on her arms as she stopped up the tub and watched the water rise. *What are you doing here, Violet?* She looked around the bathroom nervously, not really seeing anything at all. *Are you really going to get naked in a strange house and take a bath in the middle of the day?*

Steam billowed up from the tub water, and Violet thought of Begonia. *Stop being a little baby. Begonia would take off her clothes at the drop of a dime, and you're acting like a bitch.* Violet sighed. She wiggled out of her jeans and pulled her tattered shirt over her head.

Kyle walked into the bathroom, and Violet screamed. She jumped two feet into the air and landed on her shoe and almost slipped backward into the tub. Kyle caught her by the waist and pulled her tightly to him. "Woo, shawty," he said softly in her ear. She could feel his heart pounding against her breast. Kyle whispered into the nape of her neck. "You think I'm scary, huh?" He brushed his face against her smooth skin. "What, you think I'm gonna bite you, ma?"

Violet could barely breathe. She thought that her heart was going to burst out of her ribcage. Kyle smiled. She couldn't see it, but she felt it.

He kissed her lightly on her cheek. "I'm not going to bite you. Yet." Kyle let Violet go, and she was instantly cold. She tried to cover herself with the t-shirt, and Kyle laughed. He walked around Violet, locked the door, put the lid down on the toilet, and sat down. Violet didn't know what to do. No one had ever seen her naked before, not even her sisters.

"Are you gonna watch me take a bath?"

Kyle smiled and pulled a Dutch out of his pants pocket. "Uh huh." He ran the cigar across his nose before licking it and biting the tip. He sliced the Dutch straight down the middle and dumped its contents into the trash can by the sink. "You got a problem with that, bad ass?"

Violet didn't respond. She looked straight into Kyle's eyes and let her t-shirt fall to the floor. She stepped into the tub, sat down, and turned off the water.

"That's what I'm talking about, girl. There ain't no need to be afraid of Daddy." He filled the Dutch up with weed and spread it out evenly with his fingers.

Violet didn't know what had come over her. All she knew was that she was on fire, and it had nothing to do with the hot water.

Later that evening, Violet sat wrapped around Kyle, truly happy. She kissed him on his forehead. "That was excellent."

"Look at you, smiling all big," Kyle said, picking her up off of his lap.

"Am I hurting you?"

"No, but we can't sit like this all day." Kyle rubbed his stomach and stretched.

"What's the matter?"

"Nothin's the matter, baby girl." Kyle smiled at her concern. "A brother is just hungry—that's all."

"I could make you something to eat," she said quietly.

"Okay, ma, hold up. Put some clothes on and meet me downstairs when you're done."

She slipped on the t-shirt and looked at herself in the mirror. "Kyle?"

"What up?"

"Um, do you think that I could stay here for a little while? I don't want to go home yet."

"You can stay here for as long as you want, baby girl. This is your home now."

Chapter 21

Begonia walked to the back of the bus with April and Charlotte on her heels. She flopped into a seat and put her feet up on the armrest in front of her.

April sat down in a space a couple of seats down from hers. She looked Charlotte up and down and sucked her teeth. "I thought she said for us to leave our book bags at school."

Charlotte ignored April's comment and stared out of the window, shaking her head slightly, so Begonia spoke up instead.

"I told her to bring her book bag, April, because it looks more like a pocketbook. Besides, we are going to need something to put all of our bullshit in, right?"

"Yeah, I guess," April said, sulking. "You don't have to take my head off, though."

"I'm not taking your head off, girl. Get a grip." Begonia turned to Charlotte. "So, what's up? What do we have to get?"

Charlotte dug in her bag and handed Begonia a list.

Oh, this is gonna be cake, Begonia thought. She went over the list a couple of times, mentally locating each item in the store. "Okay," she said, still looking at the list. "This isn't gonna be hard at all. We just need to take five things a piece off of here. I'll cop the perfume and the Coach bag because that's the hardest stuff to get."

Charlotte dug her fingers into Begonia's ribs.

"Ouch, bitch. What the fuck?"

Charlotte nodded her head at the girl sitting across from them. Begonia turned her head and looked straight at the high-yellow, toad-faced girl with the poppy eyes. Begonia dropped her feet off the armrest and crossed her legs. "Is there something that I could help you with, sweetheart?"

The girl quickly turned her head away,

"I mean, you're looking at me like I have the fucking antidote." Begonia leaned forward. "Are you gay?" She turned her attention to the old lady sitting beside toad-face, who was openly staring at Begonia as well. "And what about you, Grandma? You want me too?" Begonia winked at the old woman and licked her lips seductively. "I'll tell you what, Granny. Normally I'm strictly dickly, but I'll deep-sea dive for the right price."

The old woman and the young girl got up and walked to the front of the bus. April started to laugh, until Begonia's icy stare fell on her. April fixed her face and sat up in her chair.

"Okay," Begonia started, motioning for Charlotte to come closer so she could keep her voice down. "I know that you bitches boosted before, but there is a certain way that I do things." She looked them both in the eye, making sure she had their full attention. "First off, there will be no snatching and tucking. They have cameras, and I am not interested in going to jail today. Secondly, don't do anything, and I repeat *anything,* that will call attention to yourself." She ripped the list into three pieces. "The object of the game is to go unnoticed." She tucked her list into her bra and handed them theirs. "Only pick up clothes that are similar to what you have on. Make sure that you come out of the stall modeling your original clothes."

"Oh, that's hot," said Charlotte. "I never thought to do that before."

"Wait a minute, wait a minute, hold up." April frowned. "That's dumb as shit. Why do we have to model our own clothes, and how are we going to get the new clothes out?"

Begonia sat back and sighed. Charlotte just stared at her.

"What?" April asked. "If I don't get it, I don't get it. What the fuck?"

I need a cigarette, for real, Begonia thought.

Charlotte leaned toward April and spoke as if speaking to a small, slightly disabled child. "We are going to model are own clothes because we are going to wear the new ones out."

"But what happens to our clothes?"

"Our clothes go onto the hangers, and then back onto the rack."

"You can't be serious, girl." Begonia snatched April out of her seat by her collar. "Come on. This is our stop. Take those damn ponytails out of your hair. You look like an infant."

The girls got off the bus across the street from the Gallery. They entered the mall through J.C. Penney and window-shopped a bit before migrating to Strawbridge.

Everything is going according to plan, Begonia thought. She walked past the mall sensors and the security guards. She adjusted the Coach bag on her shoulder and walked over to the perfume stand.

Begonia's hand was wrapped around a red box of Gucci Rush, the last thing on her list, when she heard a scream coming from inside the department store.

"Get the fuck off of me," Charlotte screamed. "I didn't steal anything."

No, no, no, Begonia thought.

The attendant walked a few paces into the aisle to get a better look at the commotion, and Begonia dropped the perfume into the Coach bag. Begonia sucked her teeth and took the escalator up to the second level and walked calmly to the door.

"Get the fuck out of my way," April screamed.

Begonia paused and looked over the railing. She saw April running out of Strawbridge like a bat out of hell, until a security guard clipped her by the fountain.

Un-fucking-believable, Begonia thought. She walked out onto the street and mingled with the crowds on the pavement.

Chapter 22

Violet's thighs throbbed. She winced as she grabbed the pepper off the spice rack and limped over to the table. Steak and eggs sizzled on the stove, while biscuits browned in the oven. *So this is what having a man feels like,* she thought. She sniffed Kyle's t-shirt, taking in his cologne, and her stomach fluttered. She sprinkled pepper on the eggs while the memory of Kyle's hands on her hips clouded her vision. Shivers ran up her spine. Turning to grab a plate off of the dish rack, she nearly jumped out of her skin.

Keisha, Kyle's sister, was standing in the doorway.

"So this is what you left school early for, huh?" She looked Violet up and down coldly. Violet was humiliated, standing there with nothing on but a t-shirt.

Keisha barked out a laugh. "Just because he fucked you don't make you his wife!"

Violet's eyes flashed. She slammed the plate down on the counter. "So, I guess that little fat fuck you call a friend is Kyle's wifey, huh?"

"As a matter of fact, she is."

"Well, if she is his wife, then what am I doing here?"

"I don't know. Maybe you're following in your sister's slutty-ass footsteps."

Violet was confused for a second, because no one ever called Begonia a slut. Thief always, bully maybe, but never a slut. Then it came to her, and she snapped her fingers. "That's right. You go out with T-bone! That's the nigga I always see following Begonia around like a puppy dog."

Keisha stepped into Violet's face. "You got it twisted, bitch. He doesn't follow her around. She's the one always hanging around him."

Violet laughed. She knew Begonia and T-Bone were just friends, best friends at that. But if Keisha wanted to play mind games, then Violet was down for the get down. She turned toward the stove and finished fixing Kyle's plate. "It's not my fault that you and your raggedy-ass friends can't keep a man." Violet grabbed Kyle's tea off the counter and headed upstairs to give him his food.

She was almost to the stairs when she heard a knock at the door. Keisha flew past Violet into the living room. She peeked through the window and then wrenched the door open with an evil little laugh. "Oh, Violet, look at who we have here!"

Doreen stood in the doorway looking like death warmed over. Keisha smiled brightly. "It's a regular family fucking reunion! Well, don't just stand there," Keisha said brightly. "Come right on in!"

Kyle came down the steps, heated. "What the fuck are you doing, yo? I told you not to come here anymore. If I'm not on the block, then I'm just not the fuck on the block! You can't just be coming around where I lay my head! What the fuck do you think dis is?"

Kyle was shouting at the top of his lungs, but Doreen looked as if she didn't hear a word he said. Her eyes were glued to Violet's eyes, and so many things were said in silence. Keisha's bitter laughter broke the spell.

"Maybe she didn't come here for crack, Kyle. Maybe she came here for her baby girl."

"Shut the fuck up, Keisha, for real, and close the door. I don't want er'body looking in my mutha-fuckin' house." Kyle looked at Violet, unsure of what to say next.

Doreen watched as her baby's eyes hardened. She opened her mouth to say something, but Violet shook her head. "You heard what my man said, Mom. This ain't the crack house! Why don't you go wait at the bar on Thirty-first and Montgomery with the other fiends?" She put Kyle's food on the table and placed her hands on her hips. "Did I fuckin' stutter? Get the fuck out!"

Doreen put one shaking hand up to her head and pushed her hair behind her ear. She turned to Kyle, and, as always, her sickness outweighed her motherly instinct. “I got fifty dollars, K. Don’t make me leave empty handed. I promise not to come back here again.”

Kyle went into his pocket and pulled out a bundle, snatched the fifty dollars from Doreen, and passed her a couple caps of her medicine.

Doreen clutched the crack to her chest and looked at Violet. “I’m sorry, baby,” she said before turning and walking out the door.

Keisha walked over to the dining room table and took a biscuit off of Kyle’s plate. “Your mom is so sweet, Violet. I wish I had a mom just like yours!”

Chapter 23

Begonia got off the bus at 33rd and Cecil B. Moore Avenue. She was beyond pissed. *I can't believe those idiots. How fucking hard was is it? How fucking hard was is it to follow simple fucking directions? The shit was supposed to be cut and dry—fifteen motherfuckin' things that I could have stole by my motherfuckin' self with my motherfuckin' eyes closed and my hands tied behind my motherfuckin' back! I'm going straight over to Portia's house. I need a drink for real. At this rate, I'll be a motherfuckin' alcoholic by the time I turn nineteen.* Begonia sighed. *When in the hell is my luck going to turn around? Because I'm beginning to run on empty.*

Begonia walked into Portia's place like she owned it. She didn't speak to anyone. She barely even noticed anyone. Her head was beginning to pound. Portia was sitting at the dining room table, reading over some papers. Eric B and Rakim's "Paid in Full" was blaring on the radio. Portia tapped her ink pen to the beat. She reached up and turned the volume down when Begonia stormed into the room.

"What the fuck, Bee? I know Doreen taught you some manners before she started sucking on that glass dick!"

Begonia pulled out one of the chairs and sat down hard. "Pleeeeeaaaassssseee, Portia, not today! I need a shot of Bacardi and a Newport. Thank you."

"A'ight, heffa, with your disrespectful ass. What's wrong now? And why you all dressed up?" Portia leaned over and craned her neck toward the living room. "Peanut, go and get Begonia some Bacardi."

Peanut got up and stood beside Begonia. He didn't move until she pulled a five-dollar bill out of her bra and handed it to him. Portia lit a Newport, took a long pull, and then handed it to Begonia.

Begonia puffed the cigarette as if she were kissing the man of her dreams. Her eyes rolled as if she were in ecstasy. She rested her head in her hands and exhaled slowly. "Girl, you wouldn't believe the bullshit I've been through today."

Peanut handed Begonia a mayonnaise jar with a corner of rum. He set the Bacardi bottle in front of her.

Begonia knocked back the shot in one swallow. She recounted the day's events to Portia, who found it all outrageously funny. By the time Begonia was finished, she was well on her fourth shot, and Portia was doubled over in laughter.

"I'm glad that I'm fucking amusing you, bitch!"

"I'm sorry, Bee, but you gotta admit that's funny as hell. First off, I'm trying to envision your nerdy-ass sister rolling around on the floor with some—what did you say? Oh yeah, turd-faced bitch." Portia had to hold her stomach she was laughing so hard. "Let me find out that there is fire running through all y'all veins! Next thing you know, Daisy gonna be tryin' to take over kindergarten!"

Peanut sat down on a stool in the corner. "Ay, yo, but weren't you scared?"

He was so quiet Begonia almost forgot he was there. "Scared of what?"

"Scared of them girls rattin' you out at the mall."

Portia squinted at her brother. "Peanut, you're so dumb. Ain't no sista about to rat out another sister about no shoplifting. You actin' like it's a drug charge!" Portia eyed the bag on the table. "So, how much is that gonna run me?"

Begonia studied the bag "I can let it go for two fifty."

"You ain't gonna let it go for no two fifty in here." Portia leaned over and grabbed the bag. "Lemme look at this summa bitch." She opened up the flap and pulled out the box of Gucci Rush. "Aww, shit, this is that lick-me-slowly scent. This drives the old dudes wild. I'll give you two hundred even for the bag and the Rush."

Begonia rolled her eyes. "A'ight, whatever, trick. I gotta go home and make nice with Violet. She's been actin' real pissy toward me lately, and I don't like it when we fight." She got up from the table and staggered just a bit.

Portia stood and grabbed Begonia by the elbow. "I told you about drinking on an empty stomach, ho!" She slapped Begonia on the ass. "A diet of Newports and rum is the quickest way to lose all your booty meat!"

Begonia smiled as she walked to the door. "You just like to touch me."

"Whatever, heffa. If you wash the crotch out of those jeans, I'll give you forty dollars for them."

The moment Begonia stepped inside her house, she stripped out of the jeans. *I ain't trying to mess up this new shit,* she thought. She stood in the living room in her bra and panties and lit another cigarette.

Portia's words echoed in her head, so Begonia walked over to the dining room, stood up on the chair, and looked at her ass in the mirror. *Portia's crazy. Ain't nobody fittin' to lose their booty meat.* She wiggled her ass and almost fell out of the chair. *You're definitely tipsy.*

She walked into the kitchen, flicked on the light, and grabbed some lunch meat out of the refrigerator. She slapped some baloney between two pieces of bread and took a large bite out of it. She was about to grab a cup out of the cabinet when she noticed the time on the wall. *It's damn near eight o'clock. This is ridiculous. Violet's starting to take this attitude thing a little too far.*

Begonia heard the front door open and was relieved. *It's time for us to air all this shit out. I need to find out what's really going on.* She rushed into the dining room, prepared to rip her sister a new asshole; however, it wasn't Violet who came in. Shakiyya stood in the hallway, holding a sleeping Daisy.

"Where's Violet at, Bee?"

"Girl, your guess is as good as mine. I was just about to ask you that. I haven't seen her since we were in school."

"Well, my mom is worried as hell. This is the second day Violet was late. That isn't really like her, Bee. Is something going on?"

"Once again," Begonia said, taking Daisy out of Shakiyya's arms. "Your guess is as good as mine." She laid Daisy down on the couch and slipped her jeans back on. She grabbed her shirt out of the corner and buttoned it up. "Look, Shakiyya, I'ma need you to sit here for a minute while I go find my sister."

Shakiyya looked around the abandoned house that Begonia and her sisters called home, and shook her head. "How about I take Daisy back down the street? She can stay the night with us. Let us know when you find Violet, because my mom is worried sick."

Chapter 24

It was dark when Violet and Kyle pulled back up in front of the house.

"Did you have a good time, shawty?" Kyle asked.

"Are you crazy? That's the most fun I had in my life! Pop the trunk, Kyle, so I can get my bags out." Violet could have sworn that Kyle bought her the whole damn mall.

"The bags will be cool for a little bit. I need to show you something. Come on." Kyle caught Violet up into a hug as soon as she got out of the car. He kissed her on her neck and swung her around until she was dizzy.

"Stop, Kyle! You play too much!"

"Are you my baby girl?"

"Yeah." Violet blushed a deep shade of purple.

He sat down on the steps of the house and pulled her onto his lap. "You know, shawty, I been looking for a girl like you for a long time."

"You have? Really?" Violet's smile threatened to split her face in two.

"Yes, I have. All these girls out here . . ." He swept his arm out toward the street. "They don't mean nothin' to me. These dumb-ass little girls don't want nothing out of life. They're into the same old shit twenty-four-seven." Kyle hugged Violet around the waist. "I need a woman I can trust." He nuzzled her neck. "Can I trust you?"

"You don't even have to ask me something like that. I love you, Kyle."

"Is that right?"

"I wouldn't say it if it wasn't true."

Kyle rocked Violet gently on his lap. "I believe you, shawty. It's just that chicks tend to say anything to get what they want. It's hard to find women out there who will keep it real."

"Well, I'm keepin' it real, Kyle. All I want is you." She pointed to the car. "You didn't even have to buy me all those clothes, for real. I'm happy with you. I feel safe and loved for the first time in my life." She ran her hand across Kyle's cheek, and he turned his face to kiss her palm. "I'll do anything for you, Kyle. Just name it."

"That's all I want, babe. You keep it real with me, and I'll keep it real with you." He kissed Violet softly on the neck. "You have my back, baby girl, and there is nothing that I wouldn't do for you."

"I have your back, Kyle."

Kyle eased Violet off of his lap. "I'm glad to hear it, because I'm going to need your help big time, and there is just nobody I can trust in my camp, not even my sister." He stood up and brushed the wrinkles out of his pants.

"You can trust me, Kyle. Anything you need, I got you."

Kyle took Violet's face in his hands. He kissed her on the lips and looked her in the eye. "Do you mean that, Ms. Bad Ass?"

"I swear on my grandma's grave."

"Well, come on, then. It's something I need to show you." Kyle took Violet by the hand, led her into the house and down to the basement.

The basement was laid out just as nicely as the rest of the house. It looked just like another living room with the same wall-to-wall carpet and cranberry-colored wallpaper. There was a huge picture of Scarface over the black leather sofa.

Kyle took Violet straight to the back. There was a door with a padlock. He reached into his pocket, took out his keys, and opened the door. Inside the room, there was a tiny little kitchen. Kyle locked the door back.

"You said you trust me, right?"

"With my life," Violet said.

"A'ight then, shawty, this is what I need you to do. This room right here is the lab. Over there is the stove. This is where we make product. I don't know anybody that I can bring down here that wouldn't rob me blind."

"Why do you call this the lab?"

"Because, this is where we turn coke into crack."

"I thought coke and crack were two different things."

"Nah, shawty, it's like tomatoes and ketchup. You need coke to make crack."

"Oh, okay." Violet stuck her hands in her pockets. She bit her bottom lip.

Kyle looked at her closely. "Are you sure you ready for this, shawty? You look nervous."

"Oh, no, I'm not nervous. I just don't know what you want me to do."

"It's real simple." Kyle went over toward the corner and twisted off one of the pipes hanging from the ceiling. He dug into the pipe and pulled out a sandwich bag of cocaine and a box of baking soda. "Go over there and get me a pot from the cabinet. Put it on the stove." Kyle poured the cocaine and the baking soda into the pot. He stirred it up, turned the flame on, and added water.

He looked at Violet. "You have to boil cocaine to turn it into crack. The baking soda makes it hard. There are measuring cups and shit next to the sink. I can do it by sight, but you will need to use these," he said, holding up the cups and spoons. "You need one ounce of baking soda to every seven grams of cocaine. The smoke from the pot is kind of grayish." He pulled out a couple of masks from the drawer. "You have to wear these while you're cooking or you're gonna get high, and I know you don't want that.

"Once the water boils out, you have a brick. Take the brick, put it on this cutting board, and chop it up into rocks. You put a couple of rocks into each capsule. And now, you have product. Oh yeah, the smell is sort of awful. It smells like dead mice." He walked over to Violet and grabbed her by the hips. "Are you sure you can handle this? 'Cause I don't have anybody else to help me."

Violet's stomach clenched. She had never imagined her first job would be making crack. Crack was the reason her life was so fucked up now.

This is a bit much, she thought. *I can't do this.*

Kyle's hands tightened on her hips. "You just say the word, baby girl. If this is too much for you, I'ma just have to try and find somebody else. But I just wanted somebody I trusted, you know, somebody I love to have my back."

Violet's heart exploded when Kyle mentioned love. Whatever was crawling around in her stomach disappeared instantly. "I love you, Kyle," she said, throwing her hands around his neck. "If helping you means cooking crack, then I guess I'll just be cooking crack."

Chapter 25

This is the day from hell, Begonia thought as she walked down the steps from Violet's only girlfriend's house. She had been everywhere she thought Violet could possibly be. She looked around aimlessly. Her head was pounding and her stomach was churning.

"Where in the fuck are you?" Begonia rolled her shoulders and cracked her knuckles. "Can things get any worse?" As if on cue, lighting struck, thunder rumbled, and the clouds decided to piss down rain on her.

Begonia threw her hands up to the sky. "Unfuckingbeliveable!" She dug the pack of Newports that she stole from Portia out of her back pocket. However, the cigarette was instantly drenched and failed to take the spark from the lighter.

"Fuck!" Begonia screamed. She threw the whole pack, lighter and all, into the sewer drain. Her fingers itched to rub her temples, so she shoved her hands into her pockets. "Come on, Vy. How can you just disappear off of the face of the fucking earth and nobody knows where you are?" Cars whizzed by, splashing water up onto the pavement. *Where are you, Violet?* A hundred horrible images popped into her head: Violet, lying in the gutter, or being held hostage, lost, hurt, bleeding.

Get a grip, Bee, she thought as she trudged down the street. *I'm gonna need some help.*

She walked over to Tabitha and Lisa's house and banged on the door. Lisa opened up the door.

"I know somebody better be dead, you banging on the damn door like that, Begonia."

"I can't find my sister."

"What do you mean you can't find your sister? Where is she?"

Tabitha came to the door and pushed Lisa out of the way. "Move, dumb-dumb. If she knew where her sister was, she wouldn't be here. Come on in, Bee."

"Nah, I'm not trying to impose or nothing. I was just trying to see if Shanice was here because I thought maybe she could help me look for Violet."

Tabitha grabbed Begonia by the hand and pulled her inside. "Girl, it is pouring down rain. What you will do is come in here and get something dry to put on." Tabitha closed the door behind Begonia and nudged Lisa on the shoulder. "Go upstairs and get her something to put on quick."

Lisa walked toward the steps. "You want me to get her something out of your closet, right?"

Tabitha pulled Begonia toward the kitchen. "Lisa, that's not the way you get into heaven."

Lisa walked up the steps. "Tab, ain't nobody trying to rush to heaven. I swear," she said, mumbling under her breath. "Let a person go to a couple of church services and they turn into the freaking Virgin Mary."

Tabitha turned toward Begonia. "Honey, don't mind her. She hasn't taken any of her meds today." They walked into the kitchen, and Tabitha put on the tea kettle.

"I'm all right, Tab. You don't have to go through all this trouble for me. I just—I just need to find my sister."

"Girl, please, this ain't no trouble. Shanice isn't here yet. She and my mom went out the grocery store. They should be back shortly. You're crazy if you think I'ma let you stand there dripping wet till she comes back. Now," Tabitha said, taking the coffee mugs out of the cabinet. "Why don't you tell me what's going on? Did Violet run away or something?"

"No, she wouldn't run away." Begonia sucked her teeth. "Run away to where? She has nowhere to run to. I'm afraid something may have happened to her, you know? This isn't like her. I mean come on, Tab, you know Violet. She's a bookworm. All she ever does is go to school and come home with an occasional stop at the library." Begonia shrugged. "But lately she been actin' funny, you know? She was even fightin' in school today."

"You got to be kidding me! Who was she fighting?"

"Some girls I don't know. I was just tickled to see her fighting. But maybe I should have asked around or went after her when she ran off. I should have done something."

"Don't beat yourself up now, Begonia. You're not her mother, you're her sister. This was at school. You probably had stuff to do, too, ya know?"

Begonia's chest tightened with guilt. *Yeah, I had real important stuff to do, like shoplifting in the mall.*

The front door opened, and Shanice's voice blasted through the house like a bull horn. "I got movies, ladies!"

Lisa came running down the stairs with a pair of jeans and t-shirts over her arm. "Let me guess. You want the people on the moon to hear you, right?" She walked back to the kitchen, and Shanice followed.

"Am I being loud?"

"Well, you're not being quiet!"

"But I got movies! Momma Mabel took me to the West Coast Video! I got *Godzilla* for me, *Enemy of the State* for you." She walked into the kitchen, not even noticing Begonia sitting at the table. "And I got *City of Angels* for you, Mother Teresa!"

"Shanice, my name is not Mother Teresa."

"Oh, come on, Tab. You know you holy. Is that that chamomile tea? I want some."

"Well, I only made enough for me and Begonia."

Shanice whirled around. "Beeeeeee!" She dropped the videos on the table and bear-hugged Begonia. "What are you doing here?"

Lisa smiled. "Well, what she's doing right now is leaking on the floor." She handed Begonia the clothes. "You can change upstairs in the bathroom, Bee."

Shanice backed up a few spaces to let Begonia by. "What's going on? Oh my God, is Daisy sick again?"

"No, no, Daisy's fine. Have you seen Vy, Shanice? I can't find her anywhere."

"No, Bee, I haven't seen Violet all day."

Begonia clutched the clothes to her chest. "Do—" She paused. "Do y-you think you could help me look for her?" Begonia stammered as she spoke. Then she took a deep breath to steady herself. "I need help. I need to find her. I don't know what's going on."

Shanice hugged Begonia to her. "Of course I'll help you, girl. It ain't nothing but a word. Let's go. Did you check the pool hall?"

"Yeah, I checked there, and I checked just about everywhere else I could think of."

Shanice twisted her hair up in a bun. "Well, I'm sure there are some places you ain't looked, so let's go."

Tabitha put the teacups on the table. "Hold up. The girl is soaking wet. Let her go upstairs and change her clothes." Tabitha looked at Begonia. "Put those wet clothes in the hamper in my room. I'll make sure that they get dry. But changing is the first thing you need to do."

Begonia just nodded her head and turned to go upstairs. She was so relieved to have help that she didn't know what to do. Once upstairs, she ripped her clothes off. She wiggled into the jeans and t-shirt that Lisa gave her and pulled her hair back into a ponytail. She bent over to pick her wet clothes up off the floor and slipped into her sneakers.

Walking out into the hallway, she looked around. *Now how am I supposed to know which room is Tabitha's*? She shrugged her shoulders and opened the first door she came to. Miss Mabel was sitting on the bed, taking off her shoes.

"I'm so sorry, ma'am. I'm just looking–I mean–Tabitha told me to—" Begonia held up the clothes in her hand. "My clothes are wet." She took a deep breath. "Could you please tell me which room is Tabitha's so I can put these clothes in her hamper?"

"Begonia, is that you? Come in here and show me how big you got! Y'all girls are just sprouting up all over the place. How old are you now?"

"I'm seventeen, Miss Mabel."

"Seventeen! I remember when you was four years old in yo' grandmomma's backyard, pulling her azalea bushes out by the root. How time flies. Come here. Let me look atcha." Miss Mabel looked Begonia up and down. "Well, Begonia." She stared deep into Begonia's eyes. "You look much older then seventeen," she whispered. Mrs. Mabel frowned, and a thin line formed between her eyebrows. "Sit down here on this bed and catch me up on what's going on with you, baby."

"Miss Mabel, I can't. I have to go. Shanice is gonna help me find my sister. Violet didn't come home from school today."

"What do you mean Violet didn't come home from school today? Where's Doreen, and who's lookin' after the baby? Shanice told me that she has been getting sick."

Begonia's words came out in a rush. "Miss Mabel, my mom don't stay with us. She don't care nothing about us. And Daisy's all right. She's with Shakiyya and Ms. Lenora. I just gotta find Violet," Begonia said, backing up. "This ain't like her, and as much as I hate to admit it, I'm starting to get scared." Begonia was panting, and her chest was heaving. She felt as if she couldn't breathe.

"Calm down, child," Mrs. Mabel said. She took Begonia's hands and guided her toward the bed. "Look at me," Mrs. Mabel demanded, but Begonia's eyes were wild and unsteady.

What the hell is wrong with me? Begonia thought. *I can't breathe. I can't breathe.*

"Begonia, look at me!" Mrs. Mabel's voice cracked like a whip, and Begonia's eyes finally locked onto hers. "That's it. Calm down. Take deep, slow breaths just like this. Inhale one, two, three. Exhale one, two, three. That's right. Again. Inhale one, two, three, and exhale, one, two, three."

Begonia did as she was told, and the invisible bands that were wrapped tightly around her chest started to loosen. After a few more deep breaths, they disappeared altogether.

"Now, child, I know you need to find your sister, and I know that you are going to need some help, but it is foolish for you and Shanice to go out in the rain, wandering around in the streets at this time of night."

Begonia's head dropped down to her chest. Her heart sank deep inside of her stomach, and she could no longer look Mrs. Mabel in the eye. *As always, Bee*, she thought, *you're on your own.*

"You don't have to look like that, child." Mrs. Mabel cupped Begonia's chin in her feather-soft hands and brought her face back up to hers. She looked straight into Begonia's chocolate brown eyes. "Now, I didn't say I wasn't going to help you, dear. I just said that I wasn't going to have you wandering the street at all times of night." Mrs. Mabel sighed. The look of hopelessness on Begonia's face stabbed at her heart.

She took Begonia's hands firmly in her own. "I am going to drive you down to the police station so that you can put in a missing person's report."

Begonia snatched her hands away from Mrs. Mabel's and leaped off of the bed as if it had caught on fire.

"What in the hell . . ." Mrs. Mabel stood up. "Are you all right, child?"

"I am not going to no police station, ma'am. With all due respect, that's a no-no, as in no way, no how, not happening."

"But I thought you wanted to find your sister."

"I do want to find my sister, and I will find my sister, but I won't go to the police." Begonia walked to the door. "I'm not being ungrateful, ma'am. I know that you are really trying to help me, but me and cops are like oil and water. We just don't mix." Begonia opened the door, and lightning struck.

"Baby, listen to that storm out there. You don't have to go out in that mess. Just stay here tonight, and I'll go to the police station for you in the morning. Tabitha and Lisa can drive you around to look for Violet."

"I'm sorry, Mrs. Mabel, but I can't wait that long." Begonia walked out of the room and ran down the stairs.

Shanice jumped up from the couch. "I'm ready, Bee. Where do you want to go first?"

Begonia forced a smile. "Girl, the first thing I'm going to do is go to bed. I must be trippin' for real. I'll bet you any amount of money that Violet's in the house snoring her behind off. I'm going to go back home, and if she's not there, then I'll come get you so you can help me look in the morning."

"Are you sure, Bee? Because I don't mind coming with you."

"I know, Shani, but I think it would be stupid to drag you out into the rain." Begonia picked an umbrella up off the floor. "Can I borrow this?"

"Sure. You want a jacket too?"

"No, I'm good."

Begonia heard Mrs. Mabel coming out of her bedroom, so she rushed to the front door. "I'll see you tomorrow, Shani. Tell Mrs. Mabel and your sisters I said thank you, okay?" She ran out on the street before Shanice could reply.

Chapter 26

Violet was dog-tired by the time she came up from the basement. Her stomach rumbled loudly. *Dang, is it like that?* she thought, smiling. She patted her stomach and looked up at the clock on the wall. "It's damn near eleven p.m.," she said softly. *Who would have known that cooking and capping up crack would be so time-consuming?*

She was about to head upstairs to lie down and wait for Kyle when the telephone rang. She hesitated for a moment before picking it up.

"Hello."

"Hey, baby, are you finished?"

"Un huh," Violet said, smiling. *I can't believe he's calling to check up on me,* she thought as she twirled the phone cord around her finger.

"A'ight, shawty, that's what's up. Look upstairs on my dresser. I left a couple of dollars there so that you could get something from the store if you wanted to. If you don't feel like going to the store, I could pick you up something from around here, 'cause I'm about to come home soon. All this rain is making it dead out here tonight."

"Naw, Kyle, I'll just go pick something up. I am hungry as hell."

"I'm sorry, baby. I didn't mean to leave you in there starving."

"Don't be sorry. I guess I could have made something to eat. I just was busy trying to get done, that's all."

A few moments passed, and Kyle didn't say anything. Violet gripped the phone with both hands.

"Hello, Kyle. Are you still there?"

"I'm here, baby, I'm here. It's just that I told you that I was going to take care of you, and the first day of you staying with me, I got you working like a slave, all tired and hungry and shit."

Violet closed her eyes as the warmth of Kyle's concern washed over her. "Don't say things like that, baby. I'm cool, honest."

"I care about you, girl. You mean a lot to me."

"I know, Kyle. I feel the same way."

"I just don't want you to feel like I'm taking advantage of you and shit."

"I don't feel that way."

"A'ight, Ms. Bad Ass, go 'head and get you something to eat, and if you are going by the Chinese store, get me some wings with salt, pepper, ketchup, and hot sauce. A'ight?"

"Okay, baby."

"A'ight, peace."

Violet held the phone to her chest after Kyle hung up. She could hardly believe this was happening. She felt like she was dreaming.

She went upstairs to get the money and an umbrella and walked down to the Chinese store, Lee's. *After I eat, I am going to take a shower and put on one of those sexy nightgowns that Kyle bought me. Yeah, I'll bet he would love that.*

Violet was so lost in her thoughts that she didn't notice the group of girls that filed into the store behind her. She took a step closer to the counter, staring up at the menus hanging over the bulletproof glass. A girl came from behind Violet and bumped her so hard that she slid two spaces to the left.

"Excuse you. Damn."

"What do you mean, *excuse you*? You bumped into me." Violet rolled her eyes at the girl. *These bitches down here are crazy,* she thought.

Someone started cracking up laughing behind her, and Violet whirled around to see who it was. "I don't see anything funny," she said between clenched teeth.

"Well, I do," said the little fat girl in the corner.

It only took Violet a couple of seconds to recognize Kyle's ex-girlfriend, and before she could open up her mouth to say something smart in return, someone yanked her ponytail so hard she fell straight back on her ass. Pain tore down the middle of Violet's skull. She didn't have to touch her head to know that her hair was being ripped out by the root. Violet scrambled to get to her feet, but before she could get her bearings, Kyle's ex-girlfriend kicked her square in the gut.

"Not in here. You no fight in here!" screamed the Chinese man from behind the counter. "You go outside 'fore I call police." Violet couldn't make out the rest of what he was saying because she was being dragged out of the store by her hair.

The pavement was wet and cold against Violet's back. "Get off of me. Get the fuck off of me." The rain started to pour down like a waterfall. Violet was completely drenched.

"Naw, bitch, you tough, right? You want to sneak my sister in school?"

Violet grabbed the leg of whoever was talking. "I didn't sneak anybody. They tried to jump me!" Violet screamed. Punches seemed to come from everywhere. Violet's heart thudded against her chest. She could no longer see. Her eyes were swollen shut.

"Get this bitch off of me," the girl screamed, but Violet wouldn't let go. She couldn't see the girl's face, so she focused on her voice.

Violet yanked on the girl's leg as hard as she could. The girl fell straight back, slapping the pavement with a sickening thud. Violet climbed on her quickly and rained down punches, bloodying the girl's lips and blackening her eyes.

Violet thought she heard Kyle's voice in the background, but it was hard to tell. Blood rushed inside her ears, and someone kicked Violet hard in the side. Violet rolled off the girl and onto the street. She lay there stunned for a few seconds, and then she was being lifted into the air. Strong arms wrapped around her back and legs. Someone was carrying her; she did not know who.

"I got her, Kyle," a male voice said. He put something over Violet to shield her from the rain.

Violet was being placed inside of a car. She recognized the leather seats and apple incense smell. *This is Kyle's Beamer,* Violet thought. The car door closed with a thump, and Violet struggled to open her eyes. She could hear screaming, but she couldn't quite make out where it was coming from. The rain beat down on the car like a thousand tiny drums. Her stomach ached, and her side burned where she was kicked. She wrapped her hands around her mid-section and groaned.

Leaning her head against the window, she opened her eyes. She had to blink the tears away to see. The rain slowed down to a drizzle. People were running around, screaming. Four shots rang out in rapid succession. Violet turned her head around to see Kyle holding his gun to the head of his ex-girlfriend, and her heart leaped into her throat. She couldn't breathe. *No, no, no,* she thought. *Kyle, what are you doing?*

Time seemed to slow down as she watched Kyle cock his gun back. Violet sat straight up in the car, ignoring the pain. She banged on the windshield with all of her might, trying to get Kyle's attention.

She screamed. "No! Stop! Kyle, please! What are you doing?"

Kyle had his fingers wrapped tightly around the girl's neck. She was sputtering and clawing at his hands. Kyle turned and faced Violet. His eyes were cold, hard, and flat. He looked demon possessed. He sneered and turned his back on Violet.

Violet brought her shaking hands up to her mouth and shook her head. *No, no, noooooooo.*

Kyle let his hands fall down to his sides. The poor girl doubled over as if in pain and puked all over her shoes. He took a step back, and with out warning, he lifted his right hand and struck her in the temple with the hilt of the gun.

He ran around the car and hopped into the driver seat. Violet thought she heard sirens in the distance but couldn't be sure because her eardrums had popped from her frantic screaming. The car pulled away from the curb with the wheels screeching.

Violet sat back in the seat and closed her eyes. Her fairytale had ended almost as quickly as it had begun, and she had never wanted her big sister more than she did right at that moment.

Chapter 27

Violet wasn't home when Begonia returned. She looked in every nook and cranny of the house as if they were little again and Violet was just playing a game of hide-and-go-seek. However, they weren't little, and this wasn't a game.

Begonia sat in the middle of the living room floor, chain smoking and listening to the old house creak. She stared at the front door for what seemed like an eternity, waiting for Violet to walk through with a stupid-ass lie about where she'd been.

Violet never came.

So, Begonia got up off the floor rolled her shoulders and trudged back out into the rain. She walked fourteen blocks down to the police station with Mrs. Mabel's words echoing in her head. Stopping short at the entrance, Begonia looked at the crumpled box of cigarettes in her hand and decided that she needed one more smoke before walking into the pig pen.

Begonia stood on the steps of the corner store down the block from the police station. The storm had passed, leaving the streets shining like black ice. *This is crazy*, she thought, tearing into a fresh pack of Newports. Her hand shook slightly as she put a cigarette to her lips. *Your little sister is just coming into her own, that's all. She's not the little bookworm that you've come to know and love, and it's past time that you accept it, plain and simple.*

Begonia sighed. *Grow some hair on your nuts, Bee*, she thought while flicking her second cigarette butt into a puddle. *They don't arrest people for asking for help, and if they do, they can't possibly hold you for that shit for long*. She laughed at herself for being a pussy and walked into the precinct.

The place made Begonia's skin crawl. She stared at the broad oak door that led to the courtroom before walking up to the counter. Three cops sat behind the bulletproof glass, shooting the shit. Begonia waited for a few minutes before banging on the glass like she wanted to knock it out the window. The cops looked up, surprise and irritation sweeping across their faces.

"May I help you?" asked the lady cop, coming up to the glass. She must have had a million donuts too many because her gut hung down her lap like a fanny pack, and the little white buttons of her baby blue uniform shirt screamed bloody murder.

That's your fucking job, ain't it? Begonia thought. She cleared her throat. "I need help finding my sister. She didn't come home tonight."

Begonia dropped her head in her hands, raking her fingers through her hair. "I need to fill out a missing person report."

"Well, honey, it ain't that simple. Are you your sister's legal guardian?"

"Yes."

The lady cop looked at Begonia like she had bumped her head. "How old are you?"

"Twenty."

"Honey, if you're twenty, then I'm sixteen and skinny."

The two cops behind porky started laughing as if the fat fucking bitch was performing on Def Comedy Jam. Begonia's head started to pound. She punched the glass so hard that the lady cop jumped back. Her two friends were on their feet in an instant.

Begonia's eyes darted wildly from one officer to another. "Look, my sister's only fifteen years old. Okay, she's fifteen, and she's been missing since early this morning. I've been looking everywhere for her in the rain. Everywhere! And I can't find her. I was told that you would help me. Her name is Violet Brown. She's fifteen. She's my sister, and I can't fucking find her, okay?" Begonia dropped her voice. She smoothed back her hair and stood up straight. "I am sorry for hollering. I'm sorry. I just want to fill out a missing person report because I need help. I can't find my sister, and I need your help."

The big, bald-headed white cop walked over to the counter. “Well, first off, you’re not going to get any help banging on the glass like a lunatic. What you will get is the inside view of a cozy little cell.”

“I’m sorry for banging on your glass. I am, but I was told that if I came here, you were gonna help me.” Begonia pointed at the lady cop. “She said that’s not the way it works.”

“Well, it’s not the way it works.” Officer Cue-ball leaned on the counter. “Where do you live?”

“Why? I already checked there. If she was there, I wouldn’t be here.”

“Do you want help or not?”

“I live on 3062 Clifford Street.”

“All right,” Cue-ball said. “Now we’re getting somewhere.”

Officer Fat-ass walked back to her seat and flopped into her chair, smiling. Begonia would have given everything to go back there and punch her teeth down her throat.

Cue-ball snapped his fingers in front of Begonia’s face, bringing her deadly stare back onto him. “I’m fully willing to help you find your sister.”

The ice that stole through Begonia’s blood just before she was about to do something dangerous started to melt. “Thank you so much,” she breathed. “I was just—”

He held his hand up to cut her off. “There is this little thing called procedure that we must abide by, young lady. I am going to need you to go home and have you and your sister's legal guardian call 911. A squad car will come by and investigate the property to insure that there wasn't any foul play . . ."

Are you kidding me? Begonia thought. She stood there rigidly taking in everything that the officer said. *Are you fucking kidding me? My legal guardian is a fucking crack whore, and calling the police is the last thing she would do.*

"Do you understand what I'm saying to you?"

Begonia nodded.

"All right, then." He slipped a business card onto the silver tray under the dip in the window. "My name is O'Neal. If you have any problems, call that number, and you'll get me directly."

Begonia didn't trust herself to speak. She took the card, nodded her head again, and left the precinct. She couldn't think. The pain in her head was slicing. She took shallow little breaths through her mouth and forced one foot in front of the other.

It didn't take her long to get home, though. She walked into the house and straight up the stairs. It was too late for her to get Daisy, and as hard as she was supposed to be, it felt strange to be alone. She stood in the hallway, staring at the room that she shared with her sisters. It hurt too much to sleep in that room staring at Daisy's crib and thinking about Violet, and the thought of going in her mother's room made her ill. She cracked her neck and walked into the bathroom. Stepping into the tub, she curled into a little ball.

"Please, God," Begonia said softly, "let my sister be okay." She squeezed her eyes tight, trying to shut out the pain. "Let her know that it's okay, and I'm not mad. Just bring her back to me." She repeated that last part until she drifted off to sleep. "Just bring her back to me."

Officer Marlene Anderson sat back in the seat until the chair squeaked. "You know damn well that girl wasn't listening to a word you said just then. Why don't we send a squad car by her house just to make sure everything is on the up and up?"

O'Neal looked at her as if she were crazy. "A squad car will drive by when she calls 911. Look, Marlene, we don't have time to be dicking around with this little girl because she wants some attention. For all we know, her sister is out at a party or making out with some kid."

"Or for all we know her sister is hurt somewhere and needs help. Hell, the little girl probably needs help herself."

"Marlene."

"James."

They stared at each other silently until James O'Neal looked away. "Okay, Marlene, damn. Stop staring at me like I have horns or something. I'm not sending a squad car over there."

Marlene opened her mouth up to protest, but O'Neal put his hands up. "If she wants a squad car, then she's going to have to call 911 like everyone else in the city, but I'll ride over there personally after I get off if we don't hear from her by the morning."

Marlene smiled and turned back to her desk. "You're a saint, honey."

"Yeah, I know. I'm the patron saint of idiots."

Chapter 28

Violet didn't like being carried around like a doll baby, but she was too weak to protest. Her mind was stuck on Begonia, and she cried out silently for her sisters, her mother, and even the broke-down abandoned building that they called home. Every last part of her ached right down to her toes, so she stayed as still as she possibly could in Kyle's arms.

She opened her eyes and looked around. *Oh my God,* she thought. *If Kyle's house is a palace than this must be a, uh . . . whatever the fuck is better than a palace.*

Violet winced as Kyle laid her down on the plush leather sofa in what looked to be a huge-ass bathroom. "Where are we, Kyle?"

"We're at a friend's crib. Cops will be crawling all over my block tonight, so we're gonna chill here for a day or two until the shit dies down." He pushed the hair out of her face and kissed her on the forehead. He got up from the couch and ran water in the Jacuzzi tub. Violet tried to sit up so she could get a good look at it, and the room started spinning. She fell back against the sofa with a groan.

"Slow down, shawty. I'm gonna hook you up." He poured bubble bath in the water and leaned over to flick a switch on the wall, which turned on the jets.

Although Kyle was being gentle with her, he clenched and unclenched his fist like he was ready to beat somebody down. His jaw was clamped together tight, and the crazy-devil look was still in his eyes. Violet was terrified.

"What's the matter?" Kyle asked, standing up and turning off the water.

"Nothing."

"Nothing, my ass. You look scared as hell, but don't worry. Kisha is going to pay for the bullshit she shot off tonight. Please believe me."

Violet sat up despite the pain. "What do you mean, Kisha? I didn't see her out there."

"Oh, she was out there. Ben said that she was one of the girls kicking the shit out of you when he pulled up, and that she ran into the store when she spotted his Jeep hop the curb."

Violet couldn't believe it. She knew the bitch didn't like her, but she never thought it was that deep. *That psycho could have killed me.*

"Don't worry about her, Violet. I told her not to be bringing that project shit out to my house. She can take her ass right back to the pj's with her drunken daddy after I fuck her up. You don't shit where you eat, baby girl. That's rule number one. You hear me? That fucking girl knows better."

Violet sat up even though it hurt like hell to do so. "I hear you," Violet said as he walked to the door. *I hear that you're more concerned with your operation being compromised than me getting my ass whooped.*

He took off Violet's clothes with a gentleness that surprised her. His face was murderous, but his hands were soft and light. "I'll be right back to wash you up. I'm going to go get you something that will make you feel better."

Kyle returned with a bottle of Hennessy and two fat-ass blunts. He gave her two shots before she got into the tub."This is to knock the edge off."

He washed her up as if she were a newborn infant, and despite her pain, she couldn't help but be turned on by the way the soapy sponge slipped over her skin. Hennessy warmed her body from the inside out.

Kyle lifted her out of the tub and carried her into the bedroom. He laid her on the bed soaking wet, and then went back into the bathroom to get the weed and the Hennessy. Kyle swigged it straight from the bottle and handed it to her to do the same.

The Hennessy slid down Violet's throat and rushed through her system. Her body buzzed and tingled from the liquid fire.

Kyle lit the blunt and kneeled down in front of her. "Open your mouth."

Violet did as she was told. Kyle put the blunt in his mouth backward and blew the smoke straight into her mouth. Violet coughed and turned her face away.

Kyle took the blunt out of his face and laughed. "Hold still, girl. This is called a shotgun, and you got to catch the smoke, not choke it up."

Violet let the shotgun fill her lungs. She held the smoke in for a minute before blowing it out through her nose just like Kyle. The weed seemed to rush straight to her head, making her feel light and airy.

Kyle put the blunt out on his shoe. He pulled his shirt off over his head and clicked the radio on. Biggie Smalls' "Big Poppa" blared out of the speakers.

Violet raised her hands above her head and fell back against the bed. She felt good, like she was floating. Absolutely nothing was hurting her now. Her heart beat in time with the drums of Biggie's track. "I love you," she whispered in his ear.

"I know, baby. I love you too."

Tears spilled out over Violet's swollen cheeks. That was all she wanted to hear. *Fuck everybody and everything else!*

Chapter 29

Officer O'Neal turned too sharply on the crooked little block of North Clifford Street. He banked the corner doing about forty-five miles per hour, slammed on his brakes to avoid crushing a cat, and spilled piping hot coffee right onto his crotch. "Jesus, Mary, and Joseph!" he screamed while knocking his cup onto the floor and frantically mopping up the mess on his lap. "Great, James, just great. You're on a roll now, big boy. Damn fine way to start the day." He adjusted himself on the seat, ignored the burning sensation between his legs, and continued up the street at a crawl, peering at every address until he found 3062 Clifford Street. He couldn't believe his eyes. He peered down at his pad to make sure he had the address right. He sighed. It was the right address all right. Right as rain. He parked the car and went to knock on the door.

An elderly woman from across the street got up from her lawn chair and came to the end of her porch. "Is there a problem, officer? Is everything okay?"

"There's no problem, ma'am. I'm just looking for the legal guardians of two young girls that live here." He glanced quickly at his pad. "Uh . . . little girls named Begonia and Violet."

"Well, I don't think she stays there with them anymore. I saw her drag some stuff out the other day, and she ain't never came back."

"Who's that, ma'am?"

"I'm talking about Doreen, them girls' momma."

"Did she take the girls with her?"

"No sir, I don't believe she did."

O'Neal looked back at the house and frowned. "You wouldn't by any chance chance know where the girls are now, would you?"

"Of course I do. Those some good girls. I s'pose they're in school."

"School, right." He slapped his pad in his left hand, took one last look at the house, and nodded to the old woman before returning to his squad car.

He called Marlene from his cell. "Those girls are living in a damn slum. And a neighbor said that the mother left a couple of days ago."

"I knew something was wrong, Jim. Something about that little girl just didn't sit well with me."

"I know. Shit, I should have come here sooner. See if you can get one of your friends from Child Protective Services over here."

"All right. I'm on it."

***

Begonia walked home from school completely wiped out. She knew that her blood pressure was dangerously high because she had a punching headache that just wouldn't quit. Her body was stiff from sleeping in the tub, and she was mentally drained from all the questions about Violet at school. She told every last person who asked about Violet a different story.

Fuck those people, she thought, irritated. *Nobody is really concerned about my sister. They're all just nosey as hell.*

Mr. Johnson was standing on the corner by an empty lot when Begonia turned onto her block. He'd been hanging around a lot more since she ganked him. Begonia rolled her eyes and sped up her pace.

"Rob anybody today, you little cunt?"

Begonia ignored him because she had to. Every time she saw the fat fucking pervert, she fantasized about slitting his pudgy throat and ridding the world of one more child molester.

Daisy flew into Begonia's arms as soon as she stepped into the door. Her cheeks were wet with fresh tears.

"You left me."

"I know, baby girl. I'm sorry."

"Don't leave me no more," she said, burying her face into Begonia's neck. "Don't let nobody take me."

"I won't, baby, I promise." Begonia shouldered Daisy's bag and mumbled some garbage to Mrs. Lenora about Violet before rushing out the door. She was beginning to lose track of the stories she told, but she really didn't care.

Cradling Daisy as if she were an infant she walked into their house and closed the door with her foot. She dropped the bag by the door and walked into the dining room. She stood Daisy up on the table. She smoothed her hair back and wiped her big eyes. "Are you hungry, baby girl?"

"No, Bee. Where's Vywet?"

Begonia's chest tightened. "Violet's not here, honey. She's at a friend's house."

Daisy held her hands out to be picked back up. "When is she coming home?"

Begonia swept Daisy off of the table and pretended to eat her belly. Daisy squealed with laughter. "I don't know when she's coming home, baby. Let's watch some TV, okay? I bet you cartoons are on." Begonia flopped down on the couch and sat Daisy in her lap. She switched on the TV and reached in the corner for the bottle of Bacardi she left there the other day. She opened up the bottle then looked down at her sister and rolled her eyes.

Yeah, Bee, she thought, *why don't you just get smashed right here in front of the baby*? She closed the bottle and put it back where it came from. She kicked off her shoes and turned the channel to PBS.

Daisy yelled her approval. "Sesame Stweet, Bee!" She clapped her hands and giggled.

Begonia wondered what they were going to eat for dinner. She had no idea what was left in the freezer, and she only had ten bucks to her name. She picked Daisy up off her lap. "You sit right here, baby girl. I'm gonna put dinner on." Begonia smiled. Daisy was staring at Big Bird and didn't hear a word that was said.

Begonia walked into the kitchen and opened the freezer. "There is a God," she said softly. The freezer was stuffed. She had almost forgotten that Shanice went to the supermarket for them. She pulled out a big bag of wing-dings and was looking in the cabinet for cooking oil when she heard the front door bang open and Daisy screamed.

Begonia dropped the chicken wings on the floor and ran out of the kitchen. "Get the fuck off of my sister!"

A women in a cheap pin-striped pants suit picked Daisy up off the couch. She whirled around when she heard Begonia.

A cop grabbed Begonia by the waist, pinning her arms to her side. Red spots danced across her eyes. She hollered and bucked but could not break his hold.

"Beeeeeeeeeeeeeeeee, nooooooooooo!" Daisy twisted her tiny body around in the lady's arms. Her eyes were wide and frightened. She stretched her arms out for Begonia. "Beeeeeeeeeeee, pleeeease."

Begonia froze. Her hands curled into fists, and she took slow, deep breaths to steady herself. Another cop came down the stairs to stand beside the woman who held Daisy.

"There's no one upstairs. I'm going down to check the basement." The woman nodded at him absently while trying to calm Daisy down.

"Who are you?" Begonia asked through clenched teeth. "And why the fuck are you in my house?"

The cop came up from the basement, and the woman handed Daisy to him. Daisy bit his hand, and Begonia smiled coldly as the officer tried to shake off the pain. *That's my baby girl,* Begonia thought with approval.

The women walked into the dining room. "My name is Regina Dean. I am a Social Worker with DHS."

"DH who?"

"DHS stands for the Department of Human Services. We received notice that you and your sisters were living in an abandoned building without a legal guardian." She looked around the house and frowned. "I'm afraid that you and your sisters can not stay here any longer."

Begonia snapped. "What the fuck do you mean we can't stay here? I am my sisters' legal guardian, and I say that we stay wherever the hell we want to stay."

Regina took a step closer. "Begonia, isn't it?"

Begonia just stared at her. Daisy's screams died down to soft sobs, and it was tearing her heart apart.

"Well, Begonia, I know that you are only seventeen years old. I know that your mother has a severe drug problem, and I also know that you have no idea where your sister Violet is. I'm afraid you don't have any say at all." She motioned for the cop to take Daisy outside, and Begonia snapped.

"Put my sister down, you fucking pig, or I swear to God I'll fucking kill you."

Daisy screamed again, fat tears streaming down her face. "Beeeeeeeee, don't let them take me."

Begonia knocked her head back into the face of the officer who held her as hard as she could. Blood spurted from his mouth and nose.

"My nose!" he screamed. "She broke my damn nose." He loosened his hold, and Begonia broke out in a run as soon as her feet hit the floor.

"Daaaaaaaaaaaaaaiiiiiiiiiisssssssssssy. I'm coming!"

"You're not going anywhere!" hollered the cop as he wiped the blood from his nose on the back of his hand. He dove after Begonia and managed to catch the edge of her shirt before she reached the front door. He yanked her backward, and she tripped on one of Daisy's doll babies and fell. There was a loud crack as her head bounced on the hardwood floor. Begonia was out cold.

"Was that necessary, Jim?" Regina asked coldly.

"What? I was trying to stop her from bolting."

"You didn't have to hurt her."

"I wasn't trying to hurt her, Regina. And you don't have to look at me like I'm the devil. Did you not just see her break my nose?"

Chapter 30

Kyle sexed Violet all night long. They didn't fall asleep until four o'clock in the morning, and they didn't wake up until about one o'clock in the afternoon.

Violet was in heaven. She managed to forget almost every bad thing that happened to her the day before. Thoughts of Begonia and Daisy were the only thing that stuck in her mind. She rubbed the soft hair on Kyle's chest and sighed staring out of the window.

"What's the matter, baby?"

Violet jumped at the sound of his voice, and Kyle's arm tightened around her back slightly. Violet laughed.

"I'm sorry, baby, but damn, you are a jumpy little thing, aren't you? What's the matter? You hungry? I could go whip us up something real fast."

"I am hungry, baby, but that's not what's the matter with me. I just miss my sisters, that's all. I've never spent the night away from them, and it feels kind of funny, you know?"

"Yeah, I know, shawty, but I'm sure they're fine. I know Begonia can take care of herself. She's a straight little hustler."

Violet was kind of jealous of the pride in his voice when he mentioned her sister. "I guess you're right," she said, sulking a bit. "I just didn't want them to worry about me," she said, rising up to straddle Kyle. "But I think you're right. I'm a big girl, and I can take care of myself just as good as Begonia can." She worked her hips slowly on Kyle's lap, trying to get him hard again.

Kyle laughed. He grabbed Violet's hips to stop her from grinding on him. "Slow down, Ms. Bad Ass. You have to give a brother a chance to recharge, you know?" He sat up quickly, causing Violet to fall off of his lap and roll onto the bed.

She pouted, and he slapped her on her bottom playfully. "I'm going to get us some grub." He stood up and pulled on his boxers and jeans.

He was about to grab his t-shirt when somebody knocked on the door. "Sit tight, sweetheart. I'll be right back." He walked out of the room and closed the door behind him.

Violet got out of bed and crept over to the door.

"I'm not trying to hear that, Kyle. You know how I feel about having hoes I don't know at my crib—especially an underage ho."

"Yo, Trip, I'm sorry, dawg. I wasn't trying to disrespect you, for real. It was a split second decision. I let off a round on the block, and I knew it wouldn't be long before Jake was crawling all up and down my spot. I heard sirens in the distance as soon as I pulled off."

"Don't none of that shit sound like my problem, Kyle. You get dressed and take that little-ass girl up out of my house. I love you like a son, man, but I'm telling you straight up. You let another dumb-ass split-second decision bring you to where I lay my head, and you're going to find your ass full of hot lead."

"I'm sorry, Trip. I meant no disrespect."

"I know you didn't, K, and that's why I'm going to let your ass slide this time with a warning. Is that the little girl that's gonna be making our runs?"

"Yeah, I'm trying to groom her."

"Look here. Take half of last night's profit and get you a hotel or something. Keep me up on your progress. We gonna squash all this drama, all right? Ancient history."

"I really am sorry, Trip."

Violet could hear them shake hands.

"I said it's ancient history. Just get that little girl out of my house."

Violet ran to the bathroom and started putting her clothes on. She thought she heard fear in Kyle's voice, and she was scared of anybody that scared Kyle.

Violet was completely dressed when Kyle called out to her, "I've decided that I'm going to take you out to eat, okay?" He sat down on the edge of the bed and pulled her on his lap.

Violet had a million questions in her head, but she knew better than to ask about a conversation that she wasn't even supposed to hear. She looked into Kyle's eyes and melted. She knew that he would tell her. All she had to do was be patient.

"I'm going to take and buy you something to put on, baby girl, 'cause you look kind of busted. We can grab something to eat at the diner in South Philly. What do you think about spending a couple of days in AC?"

Violet threw her arms around Kyle, excited. "When are we going?"

Kyle laughed. "Right after we eat. We can't stay here, and I'm not ready to go home just yet, so how about we take us a little vaca?"

"Are you kidding me? I have never even stepped out of the city before. As far as I'm concerned, we can skip eating and go straight to the beach."

Kyle picked them up something from the McDonald's drive through and drove straight for the shore. He was quiet for the majority of the ride, and Violet was too afraid to break the silence. She pushed down all the questions that were building up inside of her ever since she'd overheard Kyle's conversation. Being dirt poor for most of her life had taught her patience, and she knew that Kyle would tell her what was up on his own time. Besides, Violet started buzzing with excitement the moment they crossed the Walt Whitman Bridge into New Jersey, and her eyes were glued to the trees that lined the Atlantic City Expressway.

"Do you have dreams, Violet?" Kyle's tone was so soft Violet wasn't sure if he had spoken at all.

"Did you say something, Kyle?"

"Yeah, I asked you about your dreams, you know. Like, what do you want to be when you grow up and shit?"

"Oh, I don't know." She shrugged. "I never really made any plans like that, but I guess if I had a choice, a different life or something, I would want to be a history teacher. I love everything about history."

Violet was embarrassed the moment after that shit came out of her mouth. She slumped down in her seat and stared out the window.

"I think that's hot." Kyle smiled over at Violet. "I think that's hot as hell."

"You do?" Violet said brightly. She beamed at Kyle.

"Hell yeah. We all got to have dreams. I don't see shit wrong with being a teacher. A history teacher at that. Naw, ma, that shit is hot as hell." He looked over at her and returned her smile. "You know what? I always wanted to be a veterinarian."

"You're shitting me."

Kyle laughed. "No, I'm not. I love animals, all kinds of animals. I wanted to be a vet ever since I was knee-high to a chicken." He looked at Violet, who was laughing so hard her shoulders were shaking. Kyle smiled. "What? You can't picture a nigga like me being a vet?"

"I don't know, it's just, you know . . . funny. It's hard to picture Nino Brown being an animal doctor."

Kyle laughed. "Okay, you got jokes. I'm serious, though, girl. I can't do this kinda stuff forever. I want to live my dreams, and with you by my side, I'm starting to think I can." He ran his hand down her arm and laced his fingers through hers.

Violet looked down at their fingers and then up into Kyle's eyes. She was touched. "Are you serious, Kyle?"

"Girl, I wouldn't play about no shit like that. I'm hella serious. From the first time I laid eyes on you, I knew that I wanted you to be my wifey, and now that I have you by my side, I can't help but to think about our future. I want to get out the game, and I got a plan to do it, too."

"You do?"

"You damn straight I do, and as soon as I put my plan in action, we are going to have enough money to go to school, live our dreams, and put this drug shit far behind us." He lifted Violet's hand to his lips and kissed her fingers softly. Violet was speechless.

Chapter 31

Begonia woke up in the ER of Women's Medical Hospital a bit disorientated. She cracked her neck and looked around the room. Her eyes fell on the irritated and rather frumpy-looking social worker.

"Well, hello there, star-shine. You've had a nice nap now, didn't ya?"

"What in the hell did you guys do to me?" Begonia asked, bringing her hand up to lightly examine her head.

Regina walked over to Begonia's bed. "A better question is what didn't we do to you? We didn't lock your butt up for attacking a police officer, so I think a little gratitude would go a long way, don't you?"

Begonia rolled her eyes and clasped her hands together on top of her chest. "Why, gee golly, ma'am, thank you ever so fucking much."

Regina's eyes flashed. "Now listen here, little girl. I had to do a lot of begging to get the officer with the broken nose standing outside not to press charges against you. Please don't make me think that I made a mistake, because I could easily correct it."

Begonia sat up on the side of the bed. She looked at the cop's silhouette outside of the curtain and the anger in the social worker's eyes and sighed. "I'm sorry," Begonia said softly, and she meant it. "I won't be no help to my sisters behind bars."

My sisters. Begonia hopped off of the hospital bed. "Where's Daisy?"

"Calm down, Begonia. Your sister is fine. She is in a foster home in Northeast Philadelphia."

Foster home. Begonia's head spun. Daisy's round little smiling face popped into her head. "She told me not to leave her." Begonia's voice was barely a whisper. "She told me not to let anybody taker her." Begonia's chest tightened.

She slid off the hospital bed and put her sneakers back on. "Take me to her."

"That's not possible."

Begonia felt the ice sliding through her veins. "Oh, you don't know just how possible it is. All you have to do is take me to your car and then take me to my sister." She reached into her back pocket for her switch-blade, but it was gone.

Regina's lips curved into a thin, cold smile. "Did you misplace something, Begonia? Back pockets empty?" Regina barked out a cold laugh. "I threw your tiny knife into the trash before the ambulance came." The smile fell off her face when she saw the dangerous glint in Begonia's eyes.

Begonia looked around the room for something heavy enough to bash Regina's skull in with.

Regina stepped into Begonia's face. "You're looking for something to hit me with? You bad, right? You think because I have on a suit I'd be shook by a petty small-time thief from around the way?" She dropped her voice. "I'm here to help you, Begonia. Help you. I'm not here to fight you."

Begonia smirked.

"Oh, I'm not scared of you, if that's what you're thinking. I'm North Side born and bred, honey, and it ain't a drop of bitch in my blood." She stepped out of Begonia's face and took a deep breath to calm herself. "The reality of it, Begonia, is that you're going to have to play nice with me if you want to see your sister again. Breaking bad ain't going to do nothing but get your feelings hurt. As of right now, I'm the only person on your side, and I'm on your side because I know how much you care about your sisters and how hard you tried to take care of them. I'm not going to fight you to help you, Begonia. You must have bumped your head harder than I thought if you think I can be bullied by a seventeen-year-old thug wannabe."

The nurse walked in with Begonia's discharge instructions, and they both fell silent. Begonia half listened as the nurse ticked off all of her do's and don'ts. She snatched the offered plastic cup filled with two horse-sized ibuprofen pills and knocked them back without water. *Could this day suck anymore*?

She followed Regina out of the ER and down to her car. Her head pounded and her stomach rolled. She couldn't stop thinking about Daisy being in some strange place with some strange-ass people.

Regina tried her hands at small talk, but it wasn't working. Begonia rode in the back seat with her head glued to the window. She felt helpless and worthless. She closed her eyes, put her head back in the seat, and counted down from one hundred as slow as humanly possible. *Truth is, I need help*, she thought. She needed help to find Violet. She needed help to get Daisy. She needed help period, and it was starting to piss her off.

Regina made a left onto Lehigh Avenue and pulled over in front of a three-story house a couple of doors down from the corner. Begonia got out of the car and stared at the house for a few seconds. She sighed and closed the car door gently, despite the fact that she wanted to slam the son-of-a-bitch so hard that the windows cracked.

They stood outside for what seemed like an eternity. Then the door swung open, revealing a tall white woman with flaming red hair, Coke bottle glasses, and a wide smile. She waved them inside with a fluid flick of her wrist.

I don't believe that they are gonna make me stay here with Mary friggin' Poppins. She walked into the cluttered living room and immediately began to case the joint. She had her eyes on the VCR and the antique clock on the mantel when Regina cleared her throat.

Begonia looked over at Regina, who was standing stiffly by the door. "Begonia, this is Diana Richardson, and she's going to be looking after you while we try to straighten everything out."

Begonia slid a pair of earrings in her pocket, flopped down on the couch, and put her feet up on the coffee table. "When am I going to get to see Daisy?"

Regina's shoulders sagged. "I will schedule a meeting as soon as I can. But I want you to know that there is no such thing as instant gratification in the foster care system."

Begonia just looked at her as if she had two horns sticking out of her forehead.

Diana walked back to the door. "It'll be all right, Gina. Don't worry. Me and this little gal are gonna be fast friends." She gently ushered Regina out of the door. "You go on ahead and do what you need to do. I'll take care of Begonia."

"Taking care of me ain't easy."

Diana sighed. She closed the door on Regina and walked over to the couch. "Take your feet off my table and take my earrings out of your pocket."

Begonia dropped her feet down and sat up. "You saw me snag the earrings? Sheesh, lady, those are some powerful friggin' glasses."

Diana sat down on the coffee table in front of Begonia. She took her glasses off, rubbed the bridge of her nose, and put them back on. She held out her hand, palm up, and waited.

Begonia stared at Diana's hand for a minute before reaching in her pocket and handing her the earrings.

"See now, that was easy." She put the earrings back on the end-table and made a little face. "Now, look here, girlie. It's late, I'm tired, but I would like to make a deal with you. You need a little help, a little care, and a place to stay. I am going to provide you with all three on two conditions. First, I'm going to need you to trust that I'm not giving you any bullshit. You can have my help, my care, and a place to stay free of charge." She looked into Begonia's eyes and waited a beat to make sure that what she said sunk in. "Now, for the second thing." She stood up and stretched. "I am real partial to my things, so I am going to need you to keep them out of your pockets. Do you think it's a deal you can handle?"

Begonia nodded her head.

"Good. I'm going to take a shower. There's food in the fridge, and I laid a pair of pajamas out for you in the back room." Diana walked upstairs and left Begonia staring at the steps.

You gotta be fucking kidding me.

***

For the next couple of days, Begonia went to school faithfully, hoping that Violet would show up. She didn't know what else to do. She couldn't eat, couldn't sleep, she could barely function. Shanice and T-Bone took turns following her around while she went through the motions—every day after school she'd hit the police station, the Department of Human Services, and every library, playground, and hang-out that she could think of.

No Violet.

After a few weeks and no breaks, she started to feel like she was losing her mind. She sat in her last period class, staring out of the window trying to wrap her mind around everything that had happened. She just couldn't.

"Begonia? Begonia? Ms. Brown?" Mr. Wharton dropped a textbook on the desk in front of her.

Begonia pulled her eyes away from the window. She stared at the geometry book and then looked up into Mr. Wharton's wintergreen eyes. "What?"

"Here's a pass. Go up to the art room. Mrs. Blake would like to speak with you."

Begonia snatched the pass and left. *I don't even know why I'm here,* she thought. She took the stairs two at a time. She knew what Mrs. Blake wanted to talk about. She cut her last few art classes so she could hang around Violet's first period. She told herself that she would eventually run into her, but it was bullshit and she knew it. She cut art because she no longer had the stomach for it. She didn't want to paint anymore. *Maybe if I would have spent less time painting and more time paying attention to my sisters, we wouldn't be in this mess.*

Mrs. Blake beamed at Begonia when she walked through the door. She shot around her desk and wrapped Begonia up in a warm hug. "Oh, sweetheart, you've won. You've won."

"What are you talking about?" she asked, stunned by Mrs. Blake's affection. She looked around at the other students in the classroom, embarrassed, and quickly freed herself from Mrs. Blake's embrace.

"The competition, of course. I know that you said you didn't want to enter, but I couldn't resist. Your piece was too special. You have a definite future in the arts, Begonia. The little old lady that you have painted has taken you to the Nationals." Mrs. Blake picked up a manila envelope and proudly thrust it toward Begonia. "Take it. Everything is in it: your award letter, your plane tickets—everything. All you have to do is get you mother to accompany you and you're in!"

"Thank you," Begonia said, stunned. She didn't know what else to say. She sure as shit wasn't going to tell her that she lived in foster care and her mother was free-basing in some broke-down crack house at this very moment.

A brief feeling of happiness floated across Begonia's chest at the news. *My painting won. It fucking won.* The joy was quickly replaced by a crushing feeling of guilt.

Begonia turned on her heels and ran out of Mrs. Blake's class as fast as she could. She needed air, and she needed it bad. Bursting through the exit doors, Begonia kept on running until her chest burned and her side ached. She was ten blocks away from the school when she finally stopped. She bent over and rested her hands on her knees to catch her breath. It was too much. It was just too fucking much. She sat down hard on the pavement. She hugged her legs to her chest and rested her face lightly on her knees.

Begonia's chest was tightening up. *God, girl, calm down before you kill yourself.* Raising her head up, she took deep breaths to open up her chest. She lifted her arms over her head, but stopped dead in the middle of her stretch.

"Momma," she whispered.

A dingy little homeless woman was being thrown out of an abandoned house directly across the street from where Begonia sat. The woman's long black hair fell out of the dirty ball cap she wore when she hit the pavement, and Begonia's heart sank into her stomach.

She scrambled up off the ground and darted out into the street screaming, "Momma, oh my God! Momma."

Rodney appeared in the doorway, laughing with one of his flunkies by his side. "I told you we don't take wrinkled-up, dried-up, and rotted-out pussy in here. Don't come 'round here again with no money."

Doreen rolled onto her stomach and started crawling up the steps. "Don't be like that, Rodney. Come on, baby. You know I can make you feel good."

Begonia's stomach rolled, and she had to swallow hard to keep from throwing up. She slid her hands under her mother's arms and hauled her up onto her feet. "Momma, is you okay?"

"Get off of me." Doreen flailed her arms, wildly shaking and screaming until Begonia let her go. Rodney was laughing his ass off at the top of the steps. Doreen spun around and stumbled back over the steps when she recognized her daughter.

"Momma." Begonia reached out to her, but Doreen pulled away.

"Stay away from me, girl. Don't you touch me." She turned toward Rodney, but he went back inside the house. Doreen ran up the steps and banged on the door. "Come on now, Rodney. Don't act like that. I can make you feel real good, just like I used to."

Begonia took a few paces back, shaking her head. She didn't know what to say. This wasn't her mom. Her mom was gone, dead. Her mom died the same day her grandma did. This crackhead was just using her body.

Doreen stopped banging on the door and just stood there with her head hung low.

"Violet's missing, Momma. I can't find her."

"So, what do you want me to do about it? You kicked me out, remember?" Doreen turned around and sat on the steps. She scratched her neck and her arm. There was a wild, hungry look in Doreen's her eyes that Begonia had never seen before.

"Don't you care, Momma?"

"Honey, what I care about is behind this door. Now, go on and leave me alone."

The door opened, and Doreen shot up like a rocket. Nate and Bunky walked down the steps. "Hi, boys. How y'all doin?"

Nate looked at Begonia sadly and then turned to her mother. "Hi, Ms. Brown."

She giggled and licked her lips seductively. "It's just Doreen, baby. Call me Doreen." She made a move to pull him into a hug, but he side-stepped her neatly and walked toward the curb. His brother Bunky stepped into her embrace. She ran her hands up and down his arms and pressed her hips into his pelvis.

"Momma," Begonia yelled. "What about Violet? Are you going to help me find her?"

"Honey, yo' sista ain't lost. She is somewhere mindin' her business, like you should be doin'."

Bunky pulled a twenty-dollar bill out of his pocket and waved it in front of Doreen's face. "I heard you used to have some of the sickest head skills in the hood."

"Have, baby. I *have* the sickest head skills, and for twenty bucks, I'll suck the skin off your dick."

Bunky took Doreen's hand and led her back up the steps.

"Momma, wait. What do you mean she ain't lost? Do you know where she is? Momma!"

Doreen ignored her and went inside the crack house. Begonia could see Bunky starting to unfasten his pants. She charged up the steps after them, but Nate grabbed her arm.

"Hold up, shawty, you don't want to go in there."

"The hell if I don't. Let me go, Nate," Begonia said, pointing to the now closed door. "She knows where my sister is."

"So do I," he said as he released Begonia's arm.

Begonia just stared.

Chapter 32

Violet was tired, and her head was knocking from the fumes in the lab. She wore the little mask, but the putrid smell of crack cocaine seemed to slide right through it. Kyle wasn't home yet, she noted, as she entered their bedroom. The king-size bed was covered with black satin sheets and a mess of pillows in all different shapes and sizes. *If Kyle was here, those damn things would be all over the floor*. Violet pulled her tank top over her head and shimmied out of her shorts. It was hot as hell in the lab, so she tried to wear as little as possible.

All I need is a bath and a book, she thought while wiping the sweat off her brow. She pulled the silk kimono that Kyle bought her last week out of the closet. It was a pretty thing—black with red Japanese characters scrawled all over it—a pretty thing, indeed. That was Kyle's style. She pulled a beer out of the little refrigerator by their bed and walked down the hall toward the bathroom.

"Why, if it isn't Kyle's little slave girl," Kisha said with a smirk. She was sitting cross-legged on her bedroom floor.

Violet laughed and leaned against the banister. "At least this little slave girl is getting fucked royally, you lonely, dusty-crotch bitch."

Kisha jumped up off the floor and rushed into the hallway. "I can't stand your bony ass, and as soon as my brother gets tired of helping the homeless, I'm going to drag you out of here by that long, pretty hair."

Violet took a swig of her beer and smiled at Kisha. "Until that day, sweetie, you are going to just have to put up with the fact that I'm here, in your brother's house, in his bed, and in his heart."

Kisha's eyes blazed.

"Oh, what's the matter, honey? You want to hit me don't you, Ki-Ki? But you're scared of what your brother might do to you," Violet said, tapping the beer bottle on her chin thoughtfully. "Oh, I know. Maybe I could get T-Bone to come over and give you a charity fuck. Tricks need love too!"

Kisha's lips curled into a snarl. She stepped into Violet's face. However, both ladies froze when they heard the front door slam and Kyle run up the stairs.

"Hey, babe, are you hungry? 'Cause I got you some soul food from Wanda's." He walked down the hallway and got a whiff of the tension between Violet and his sister. "What the fuck is going on here?" he asked, putting his arm around Violet. "I know you're not starting your shit again, Kisha."

"No, baby," Violet said before Kisha could open her mouth. She turned into his embrace and kissed him on the cheek. "There's no problem. Kisha was just offering to get me something to eat, but there's no need now. You took care of me like you always do."

Kisha swallowed anything she was about to say and headed downstairs.

Kyle released Violet and leaned over the banister. "Good lookin' out, sis. There is some food downstairs for you, too. You keep behaving yourself, and I may just let you out of the house every now and again." He walked into their room, put the food on the dresser, and knocked the pillows off the bed before flopping down.

Violet opened her tray and pulled out a chicken wing. Breaking off the tip of the wing, she sucked the juice off her finger and stared at Kyle. "What are you smiling at?"

"I'm smiling at your pretty ass, girl." He grabbed the remote off the table and flicked the TV on. "Hook up my Nintendo, shawty."

Violet put her chicken down and did what she was told.

"You know I'm proud of you, right? Don't think I don't appreciate how much time you put in the lab. My shit has been running super smooth since you came here. That's why I got mad love for you. You ain't like these lame-ass little chicken heads. You about business."

Violet glowed under his praise. "Really, Kyle?" she asked while loading his NBA Live game into the Nintendo.

"Fuck, yeah. You my little boss bitch, and we got just enough cash to take this shit to the next level." Kyle lit a cigarette and started the game. "Why don't you go and take a shower. Make yourself all pretty for Daddy. When you come back, I'll tell you about how you're gonna help me change the game."

Violet skipped into the bathroom, buzzing with excitement.

It took a few hours and all the strength that Nate had to keep Begonia from rushing over to Kyle's house. When she finally calmed down, he told her everything he knew about the situation. Begonia stood there with her mouth hanging open.

"Look, ma, I went over to Kyle's crib the other day to drop off product and shit, and ya sister Violet was in the kitchen, cooking dinner. She's playing house for real."

"What do you mean *playing house*?"

"I mean she's cookin' and cleanin' and servin' that nigger hand and foot, and she's doing it all with a smile."

Begonia shook her head in disbelief. Kyle continued talking, but Begonia couldn't hear him because she was too wrapped up in her own thoughts.

But it doesn't make any sense. Violet is a good girl. She loves to go to school and read books. She's a regular homebody. Then the scenes from her last couple of weeks with Violet started replaying in her mind. All of a sudden, her sister's attitude and fucked-up behavior made sense. Then she thought of Kyle's house and recounted how many times she passed it looking for Violet—how many people she talked to on his block. Her stomach rolled again. She blinked hard so she could refocus on Nate's face.

"You all right, shawty?" Nate asked, grabbing Begonia's hand.

"Why didn't nobody say anything?"

"Because Kyle's a crazy-ass, trigger-happy nigga. Ain't nobody gonna answer any questions connected to him."

"Well, why did you tell me?" she asked a bit too sharply.

Nate ignored her tone. "I told you because I think you should know. I told you because your sister is too young to be mixed up in Kyle's shit. She's living in a fairytale, and I think maybe you're the only one who could convince her that there ain't no happily ever after with a dude like Kyle."

Begonia just walked away. Nate called her, but she ignored him. Her mind was going a mile a minute, and she could feel her blood pressure rising. Emotions flashed through her system with enough force to make her throw up: happiness over finding Violet, anger over Violet's betrayal, guilt over the way she'd ignored her, and fear, mind-numbing fear, that she wouldn't be able to convince Violet to get away from Kyle. If they were truly living like Nate said they were living, how could she compete with the lifestyle that Kyle was providing?

"Money, that's how," she said softly.

Well, if its money you want, Violet, I can get money like nobody's business.

Chapter 33

Begonia's heart thumped like crazy in stark contrast to the cold calm she felt sliding over her body. She sped up her pace, cutting across the street. She cracked her knuckles, looked over her shoulder for traffic, and bumped into the man standing at the light post. "Sorry," she mumbled. She turned the corner and stuffed the man's wallet in her back pocket and slid into the alleyway.

Dogs barked as Begonia picked her way through the narrow trail of overgrown weeds, broken fences, and trash. She pulled the wallet back out of her pocket, took the cash out of the billfold, and tossed it into an abandoned yard. Tucking the money into her bra, she was cold as ice when she came through on the other side. She looked up and down the block quickly and spotted another target. She'd picked five more pockets and even scored a tennis bracelet by the time she reached her foster home.

"Diana, I'm home." Begonia said, closing the door with her foot. She walked to the foot of the stairs. "Aye, yo, Diana?"

Nothing.

Begonia flew up the steps. She flung her drawers open, scooped out her clothes, and flung them on her bed. She kicked off the stupid penny loafers that Diana bought her and tugged on her beat-up Nikes. She pushed the mattress and box spring off the frame and tore off the money she had taped to the bed slat.

She looked around for her book bag. "Fuck. Where in the hell did I put the damn thing?" She saw the handle peeking out from behind the door and rolled her eyes.

She was stuffing her clothes in the bag when Diana's soft voice penetrated the silence. "You planning a trip, honey?"

Begonia kept packing. "No, I'm leaving."

"You're leaving," Diana said, leaning against the wall. She massaged her neck and rolled her right shoulder. "Where are you going?"

"I've found my sister," Begonia said while scooping the jewelry in her bag. Then she zipped it and flung it over her shoulder. She kept her head down, not able to look Diana in the eyes.

"So, you go get Violet and then what?"

"Then we're gonna get Daisy."

"And then what?"

Her head came up, and her eyes locked onto Diana's. "What do you mean *and then what*? We'll be together, that's what. We'll be together, and that's all that matters." Begonia tried to push past her, but Diana stood her ground.

"Just hear me out, okay? I'm not going to stop you because I'm sure you're just going to find a more creative way to slip out of here. I just want you to think about what I'm going to say to you. Think on it real hard." When Begonia stopped pushing against her, she lowered her hands and sank against the wall. "I'm not saying that finding your sister isn't a great thing, because it is. However, sometimes people are lost by choice."

Begonia rolled her eyes, but Diana pressed on.

"You'll be eighteen in a few short months, Bee. You'll time out of the foster care system and truly be on your own. If you stay here, you will be able to finish school and really give yourself a chance. You are a bright and gifted girl who has had far more pain than the law should allow."

"What the hell are you trying to say?"

"I'm trying to say that Violet may not want to be rescued. I don't want to see you get hurt."

"Diana, look. I like you, okay, and I'm real thankful for all that you have done for me. But you don't know my sister. Hell, you don't know me, not for real. I'm going to get my sister, and it's a wrap. So chill, 'cause it's a wrap."

Begonia tried to push past her again, but Diana's hand shot right back up.

"What?" Begonia asked through clenched teeth.

"I just want you to know that it's okay to let go. Sometimes it's all that we can do . . . let go and let God. You are not Jesus, baby girl. It's not your job to save the day, even though you took care of your sisters from the cradle. It's not your job." She stroked Begonia's cheek. "It's really okay to let someone take care of you for a change. There's nothing wrong with being loved, safe, and cared for. You don't have to feel guilty for that."

Begonia's face contorted in pain. Then she shook herself roughly and tore Diana's hand from the wall. "I don't let go of family. Shit maybe easy for you. You sittin' up in here, playing Barbie with a couple of niglets from the hood, but my sisters are my family. They are my blood, and I will never let them go."

Begonia's stomach clenched at the hurt look on Diana's face, but she ignored it and flew down the stairs.

"Begonia," Diana called. Her red hair tumbled over her shoulder when she leaned over the railing.

Begonia paused at the door.

"You are always welcome here, okay? Eighteen and older, no matter what, my door is always open."

Begonia didn't respond. She didn't know how to. She just left and closed the door quietly behind her.

***

Violet barely let the water hit her skin before she jumped out of the shower and dried off. *Oh my God! I can't believe he's finally gonna spill about his plans,* she thought while slathering herself with Victoria's Secret body lotion. *I don't even care what it is, as long as it gets my ass out of the lab!* She quickly got dressed and waited for Kyle to join her.

He walked into the bedroom and kissed her on her forehead. "A'ight shawty, let's talk business. I just got off the phone with a real close friend of mine from North Carolina. We about to make some real big moves, and you are going to be at the heart of it."

"Me?"

"Yes, you." Kyle laughed and looked around the room. "I don't see anybody else up in here, do you?"

Violet sat up straght. She didn't really understand what was up but was proud of the trust that Kyle had in her. "Well, what do you need me to do? 'Cause you know I'm down for whateva."

"Okay, Ms. Bad Ass, now that's what I like to hear." He stood Violet up and smacked her ass lightly. "Get some clothes on, 'cause Rodney and Carmen are coming over tonight to school you on everything you need to know. You are about to move major weight across state lines."

"State lines?"

"Yeah, shawty, all that lab shit is over. I told you I was going to take you places. Well, this is just the beginning. After you make a few runs, we'll be set. Anything you want is yours. We gonna start living our dreams, baby girl." He stared into Violet's eyes. "If you can make this happen for Daddy, we gonna straight make this official."

Violet's heart did a summersault. "For real, Kyle?"

He pulled a ring out of his pocket and slipped it onto her finger. "For real."

Chapter 34

Begonia walked down to Kyle's house, waiting for the cold comfort that usually slid through her system when shit was about to go down, but it didn't come. She felt normal, warm, and a little afraid. Diana's words had cut to the heart of it.

Where are we going to go and what the fuck are we going to do? Begonia cracked her knuckles. *Shit, I'll burn that bridge when we come to it.*

She dipped into the alley across from Kyle's house and noted that the ammonia was strong in that particular piss-pit. Her nostrils flared.

She lit a cigarette, stared at Violet's hiding place, and took a long pull. She watched as Kyle's sister, Kisha, switched her stank ass up to the door and went inside. *You have got to be kiddin' me. Violet would rather live with a motherfuckin' gutter whore than her own family.*

"I don't think so." She flicked her cigarette away, cracked her neck, and walked across the street.

I may not be numb, she thought as she knocked on the door, *but I'm starting to get pissed.*

"Who is it?"

"Begonia."

"The welfare office is right off Broad and Lehigh."

"Open the door, Kisha. I know my sister is in there."

"Bitch, you trippin' if you think I'm letting your crazy ass up in here."

Begonia eyed the lock on the door. *You trippin' if you think I can't get in if I want to*, she thought. She pulled a bobby pin out of her back pocket and jammed it into the door knob. Then she wracked the lock as hard as she could. The door sprang open with a flick of her wrist.

"Bitch, I know your ass is crazy now." Kisha looked toward the stairs and opened her mouth to holler out, but Begonia's fist smashed into her face. The force of the blow knocked her against the wall. She slid to the floor, momentarily dazed.

Begonia took the stairs two at a time. "Violet!" she screamed. She was getting more frantic with every passing second. "Violet, are you okay?" Images of Violet gagged and bound flashed through her head. She headed straight to the front room because the door was closed. Her heart raced, and cold sweat beaded on her forehead. Begonia banged through the bedroom door, shrieking Violet's name, and found herself staring straight down the barrel of Kyle's gun.

The next few minutes were total chaos. Begonia couldn't breathe, her body was locked in place, and she couldn't hear anything besides her own heartbeat. She began to shake as she inched backward. Kisha raced up the stairs, screaming, with blood trailing from her nose to her chin. Kyle cocked the gun, and Begonia froze.

Violet was in front of Kyle in a flash. She was saying something, but Begonia couldn't hear her. She watched helplessly as Violet gently placed her hand on Kyle's arm. He lowered the gun, and all at once, her hearing came back, air filled her lungs, and her heart stopped trying to break through her rib cage.

Kyle walked into the hallway, and Begonia's eyes dropped down to the gun at his side.

"If I didn't have so much love for your sister, you would be a memory." He tapped the gun on Begonia's chin. "If you ever come in my house again, you won't be walking out." He turned back to Violet. "Make this shit quick."

"Oh, hell no!" Kisha screamed. She took a swipe at Begonia, but Kyle grabbed her hand. "Get the hell off of me, Kyle. You should have smoked her ass. Coming up in here like she crazy."

"Shut the fuck up, Kisha, and go wash the blood off your face. Don't break bad now. You should have never let her in here."

"I didn't let her in, Kyle. She broke in." Kisha tried to push past Kyle, but he yanked her back by her hair and tossed her toward the bathroom.

"Like I said, you weren't bad a few moments ago, so don't test me. Go clean your fucking face up. Don't come out of your room until I tell you to." He turned back toward Violet, pointed to his watch, and stuck his gun into his waistband. Without another word, he walked down the stairs.

Begonia was freed from her invisible prison. She walked over to Violet and pulled her into a tight hug. "Are you okay?" she breathed. "Did he hurt you? I was so scared. My God, Vy, I was so scared for you."

Violet pulled away from her. "Scared of what, Bee? Scared I may be comfortable, safe, and well fed?"

"What? No." Begonia shook her head earnestly. "I thought you were hurt—that he was holding you hostage or some shit. I came here to—"

"To what, save me? Are you serious? You were never scared when you left me in that fucking shack." Violet plucked a cigarette off of the dresser and lit it. She had finally got a handle on smoking, and she wanted to emphasize the fact that she wasn't a little girl anymore.

She walked away from the dresser slowly, swaying her hips gracefully. Begonia struggled to connect the chick she saw in front of her with the sister she knew.

Violet sneered. “No, Bee, I think you came here to see what the fuck you could get.” She sat down on the edge of the bed, crossed her legs, and let the smoke slide through her nose. “I’m sorry to say that we ain’t got nothing for ya.”

Begonia’s back stiffened. “I don’t want anything from you, and I damn sure don’t want anything from Kyle. That nigga is just as foul as Rodney, maybe worse. I came here to get you.”

“And take me where, Bee? Have you found another slum for us to live in? Bitch, please. As you can see, I’m fine. I won’t go back to living like a dog. I’ve got bigger and better things to do.”

“So you’d rather be a slave, Kyle’s little live-in trick.”

Violet’s jaw clenched, and her eyes bugged out of her head. “More like his queen. We’ve got major shit planned, and I’m going to be at the heart of it, moving major weight right by his side.”

Begonia laughed. “Is that what he told you? You’re going to be a queen.” Her eyes squinted. “Or are you gonna be his little mule?” She looked at the suitcase by the bed with the plane tickets on it. “Is that the next level shit you planning? A trip, huh?”

Violet looked up at the door, and Begonia whipped her head around to see Kyle walking back into the room. He bumped Begonia when he walked past, knocking her into the dresser. She steadied herself, keeping her eyes glued to the gun in Kyle’s waistband.

He sat down on the chair beside the bed and motioned for Violet to sit on his lap. His hands roamed up and down her thighs possessively.

Begonia's stomach rolled. "You can't stay here, Vy. You can't." Her voice shook. It was thick and heavy with the tears she fought to keep inside.

Kyle laughed. "I know that you're not going to cry, shawty. Let me find the fuck out."

Begonia looked at Violet longingly. She felt helpless and frustrated as she watched Violet's eyes shine and twinkle when she looked at Kyle. Her breath hissed out of her chest, and big fat tear spilled over her cheek.

"Oh, shit. She's crying for real. Say it ain't so, girl. I thought you was a little gangsta bitch, a junior hustler. I know you aint cryin' like a little punk. Y-you w-want y-your s-sister?"

Begonia didn't answer she looked at Violet, and the slow smile that spread across her sister's face broke her heart. She ran from the room, weeping.

A small part of Violet wanted to run after her. She'd never seen Begonia cry before, but she stayed on Kyle's lap

Diana was standing in the hallway talking to Regina when Begonia ran through the door. Her eyes registered shock, but she shook it off smoothly. Diana walked over to Begonia as if she'd been expecting her.

She wrapped her arms around Begonia and whispered in her ear. "You just play along, honey, and everything will be okay."

Begonia nodded weakly. Her heart was bruised and aching. Her stomach was hollowed, and her head pounded. Rejection from her sister was almost too much for her to bear, and all she wanted to do was lie down and close out the entire world.

"Hello, Begonia," Regina said softly. She checked her watch and gave Diana a strained smile. "I'm not trying to be rude, but I have a meeting to go to in twenty minutes. What is the urgent matter that you wanted to discuss?"

Diana grabbed the manila envelope off the table and handed it to Regina. "Our young lady has won a regional art competition and is going to the nationals."

Regina pulled the award letter out of the folder and read the results. A hint of a smile tugged at her lips. Regina's breath caught when she saw the photo of the painting included with the letter.

"Oh my God, Begonia, it's beautiful." She looked from the painting to Begonia and back again. "Truly remarkable." She snatched Begonia up in a hug. "I am so proud of you. This is just, well, it's just wonderful." She let go of Begonia and stared at the picture again. "Stunning. Do you have another picture? I would like to show it to my supervisor and hang it on the wall of my office."

"Take that one," Begonia croaked. Her throat was still raw from her sobs. She shoved her hands in her pockets.

"Are you sure?"

Begonia gave a quick nod, not trusting herself to speak.

Regina looked down at her watch, gave Begonia another quick hug, and headed to the door. "I'm really sorry, guys, but I do have to go. Thank you for including me. Maybe we could go out on Friday to celebrate." Regina tucked the picture carefully into her pocketbook and paused at the door. "I want you to know that Daisy is doing really well in her foster home. The Claytons are real good people, and they expressed an interest in adopting her. I am going to try to arrange a visit for you this weekend. Would you like that?"

Adoption, Begonia thought. The room started to spin.

Diana took one look at Begonia's face and rushed Regina out of the door. "That would be wonderful, Regina. You go ahead to your meeting now. I don't want you to be late." She gave her a gentle push and locked the door behind her.

Begonia collapsed onto the floor, and Diana was barely able to stop her head from hitting the stairs. "Oh, sweetheart, come on now." She sat down on the floor and rocked her like a baby. "Come on now, let it out."

Begonia took one deep breath, and her whole body rocked with her sobs. "I tried so hard," she wailed.

"I know, sweetie, I know."

"But—" Begonia began.

"Shhh, hush now. It's not your fault, honey. It was never your fault, and it should never have been your responsibility." Diana smoothed her hair and held her close as if she were a small child.

Begonia had never felt that amount of pain in her life. She thought she would die it hurt so badly. However, death did not come. The pain eased a tiny bit as she lay there clinging to her foster mother. Seconds slid into minutes, and minutes rolled into hours.

It was dark before her tears stopped falling and she loosened her hold. Begonia wiped her eyes and sat up, feeling weak and small. Begonia looked at the wet stains on Diana's shirt and put her head down, embarrassed.

"There now," Diana said, lifting her chin up. "There's no shame in crying when it hurts."

Begonia drew her knees into her chest and wrapped her arms around them. "My sisters are my life. I don't know what to do without them." She sniffed and wiped her nose on her jeans. "I don't know who I am without them."

Diana took off her glasses and wiped her own tears away. "I know who you are. You are Begonia

Brown, a wonderfully gifted artist, a fierce and loyal sister, and a cunning and beautiful young lady who has a shot at a bright future."

Begonia's shoulders shook with fresh tears.

"It is okay, honey. The pain will pass. It truly is time for you to be a child now, and in time, you will see the truth of what I'm saying."

Begonia wasn't so sure. . . .

Part Two

Violet

Chapter 35

It's time for this nightmare to end, Violet thought as she pushed 85 miles per hour down Allegheny Avenue. Her wheels screeched and her tires blackened the street as she banked a right onto Broad. "I'm tired of all this shit," she said while mashing the gas pedal. The shiny black Lexus revved up to 100. Violet flew through a red light like a black blur. A kilo of cocaine sat open on the passenger seat, and Biggie's "Ready to Die" blasted on the radio. "I'm so fucking tired." Tears streamed down her cheeks, turning gray as they mixed with the coke on her nose and upper lip.

She looked down at the pregnancy test on her lap, and a moan bordering on madness rumbled deep in her belly and exploded out of her mouth in a wail. She couldn't get the look in Kyle's eyes out of her head. Those beautiful chocolate brown eyes that she adored turned cold and flat as he sneered down at her.

"No, God, no" she cried. She hopped the curb, trying to avoid a young lady crossing the street, carrying a sleeping toddler. She honked her horn as she slid into the intersection.

She saw the truth in Kyle's eyes. He didn't give one flying fuck about her, and the pain of that truth was more than she could bear. Begonia's words rang in her head. She turned the volume up on the radio, but she couldn't block her sister's voice out of her head.

"So you'd rather be a slave, Kyle's little live-in trick." Begonia's voice was filled with so much pain. It was all she could do not to drop the tough girl act and go to her big sister.

"I am worse, Begonia," Violet said softly, "so much worse."

The traffic on Broad Street was becoming too thick for Violet to weave through, so she made a quick right on Cecil B Moore Avenue and a left on 15th Street. She dug her hand into the kilo of coke and snorted deeply. She could feel her pulse increase with the speed of the car. Her heart thudded against her chest in time with the bass line of Biggie's track. Sweat beaded on her forehead. Her skin was blazing, and she rolled the windows down so she could feel the wind.

She just wanted it to be over. She wanted it all to be over. She had betrayed her family for a man who didn't matter. Kyle didn't matter. Nothing mattered anymore. She'd left the people who loved her, left the only home she knew, dropped out of school, and transported major weight across state lines all for Kyle. Everything for Kyle and the love she thought they shared. Now she had nothing and no one. She was pregnant, and she didn't even know who the father was.

She could still feel their hands on her. It had been six weeks since they raped her, and she still felt everything like it was yesterday.

She snorted the rest of the coke on her hands and licked her fingers. She didn't want to feel anything. Her body shook with sobs, and tears blurred her vision. Thoughts of Begonia and Daisy flitted across her mind: Daisy's laughter and the half smile Begonia wore when she was painting.

Violet heard the sirens, before she saw the cop cars in her rearview. She smiled through her tears. *It's all going to be over soon. . . .*

The kitchen smelled like heaven. Violet had all four burners going. Chicken was frying, greens were simmering, stuffing was steaming, and spaghetti was on boil. She had homemade biscuits in the oven with her mac and cheese. Dinner was going to be slammin'.

Kyle was in the living room with his boys. They were talking major shit waiting for the game to start. "Aye, yo, Violet, bring me another beer, and bring some more chips and shit out here 'cause the game is about to start."

"Okay, babe," Violet hollered. She put her cigarette out and poured more vodka into her Kool-aid cup. Being around Kyle's friends made her nervous. Kyle always made her wear these skimpy little outfits that left nothing to the imagination.

She pulled her ponytail out and let her hair swing down past her shoulders. She bent over to buckle the strap of her red stilettos, and pulled the cuffs of her red checked booty shorts out of her crotch. She dumped chips and pretzels into a large mixing bowl, grabbed a beer from the fridge, and took a deep breath before walking out of the kitchen.

She switched into the living room, carefully avoiding all of the mirrors that hung on the wall. I don't need to see my reflection to know that I look like a five-dollar ho, *she thought.*

Bunky licked his lips and sighed as Violet walked by. He was dressed in a baby blue North Carolina jersey and matching hat. His dark skin glowed like patent leather in stark contrast with his outfit.

She raised one delicately arched eyebrow. Make that a two-dollar ho. *She set the pretzels and chips on the coffee table and handed Kyle the beer. "Everything will be done soon, baby, but we're getting low on ice." She looked down at him dressed in an oversized white T and baggy jeans and frowned slightly.* Everybody gets to wear clothes but me.

"A'ight," Kyle said. He looked her up and down, eyeing the outfit that he bought her. She could tell that he approved because his eyes glazed over and his hand unconsciously went to his dick. "I'll send one of those little niggas out to get you some, a'ight?"

She nodded her head, and he smacked her lightly on the ass, dismissing her to the kitchen.

"Damn," Bunky said to the way her butt bounced after Kyle tapped it. All eyes were on her.

She wanted to run into the kitchen, but she forced herself to walk. She hated game night, and she hated to have to serve Kyle's friends dressed like she was about to swing around a pole. Hating it didn't matter. She did it because it was what Kyle wanted. Her whole life had become what Kyle wanted. She downed her glass of spiked Kool-aid and tried not to focus on what they were saying about her in the other room.

"Damn, Kyle, I never thought you would go out like that."

Kyle took a swig of his beer. "What the fuck are you talking about, Bunky?"

“You know. Li’l shawty.” Bunky nodded his head toward the kitchen. “She got your nose wide open.”

“Fuck outta here.”

“I don’t know,” Amir said while brushing imaginary lint off of his black jeans. “If I had a bad-ass little girl like that living with me, I’d be playing house too.”

Kyle smiled, but his eyes hardened and his grip tightened on his beer. “I’m playing house, Amir. You think so?” Kyle wanted to punch Amir straight in his fat mouth. “I don’t play house, nigga. I don’t play period, and my nose ain’t open. Y’all trippin for real.”

Bunky smiled. He knew that Kyle was getting heated. This nigga ain’t nothing but a little sucka, and I’m gonna prove it. I don’t know why Rodney put so much faith in his nut ass anyway.

He walked around the couch and sat directly in front of Kyle, blocking the TV. “Nigga, that little girl got your nose so wide open that you could drive a truck through it. I ain’t mad at you, though, ’cause that little trick is bangin’. Chocolate shawty with all that long hair, tight little waist, and fat ass. Shit, I’d be trippin too.” Bunky leaned into Kyle’s face and smirked. “If I was a punk.”

“Who in the fuck are you calling a punk?” Kyle asked, clutching the chrome at his hip.

Bunky sat up slowly, careful to keep the smile off of his face. Kyle can be played like Sega. *"Calm down, nigga. We just fuckin' with you."*

"Yeah, nigga," Amir said. We know you wouldn't trip over no ho, no matter how fat her ass is." Amir winked at Bunky, and Bunky pulled a bag of wet out of his pocket.

Kyle relaxed his grip on his gun. He sat back and laughed, but it was forced, and it showed. "Nigga, get the fuck up from in front of the TV, 'cause yo' ass ain't see through!"

"My bad." Bunky got up, stretched, and started off toward the kitchen.

Kyle watched him out of the corner of his eye. He took a swig of his beer and tried to remain cool. That wasn't easy because Bunky made him nervous.

Bunky turned his hat to the back and pulled a Dutch out of his shirt pocket. "Hi, Vy," he said in a low, sing-song voice. He pinned her to the sink. "Pass me the knife, will you?"

She pushed away from him and backed up to the refrigerator. "Hey, Bunky, what's up?"

Bunky grabbed his balls. "Something big. You want to help me get it down?"

Violet swallowed hard. "You b-better st-stop playing, Bunky, before I call Kyle back here. That shit ain't cute."

The corner of Bunky's mouth turned up slightly. "Call him, shawty." He pulled a knife out of the butcher block on the counter and stared at Violet menacingly. "Go ahead and call him."

Violet's heart skipped a beat. She gripped the counter and forced a laugh. "Yo, Bunky, for real, stop playing around."

Bunky slid the knife down the Dutch. He walked over to the trash can and dumped out the guts. He poured the wet into the open Dutch, winked at her, and walked out of the kitchen without saying another word.

Violet sagged against the refrigerator. "Kyle is not going to let that crazy motherfucker hurt you." She repeated that sentence over and over while she did the dishes and washed down the stove, but no matter how much she said it, she couldn't bring herself to believe it.

Blunt smoke and laughter floated into the kitchen. Her bottom lip trembled as she listened to them talk about widening the gap between her legs.

Bunky lit the blunt, took a long pull, and passed it off to Kyle, who hit it, lazily letting the smoke curl out of his mouth in slow circles. After two more quick pulls, Kyle passed off to Amir and sat back enjoying the daze that settled over him.

"That's some good shit," he said, closing his eyes. "I ain't never felt this good over a few puffs."

"Oh, yeah?" Bunky asked, sitting back onto the coffee table.

"Yeah, man," Kyle said, not opening his eyes. "Where the fuck did you get this shit from?"

Bunky took the blunt from Amir and inhaled deeply. "Aww, man, this is that homegrown. You know how I do."

"Yeah, I know how your crazy ass do." Kyle's head rolled back on the couch, and he tapped his feet to the rhythm of his heartbeat—boom bop, boom bop.

"This weed is the shit," he said softly.

Amir leaned closer to Kyle. "Naw, man, your little bitch is the shit."

"Yeah," Bunky said, puffing the blunt and plucking the ashes on the floor. "You should let us hit that."

"Man, get the fuck out of here," Kyle said, putting his hand up for the blunt; however, Bunky held it out of his reach. Kyle's eyes turned hard and flat, so Bunky took one quick pull and passed it to him.

"It ain't no fun if ya homies can't have none."

"Y'all on some other shit," Kyle said, taking a long hit off the blunt.

"No, you on some other shit," Amir said while holding his hand out for the blunt. "I know you not in love with that little trick."

"Hell yeah, this nigga in love. His jaw gets tight every time we say something about her."

"Oh, it's like that, huh?"

Kyle leaned back on the couch and looked up at the ceiling. "Naw, it ain't like that. Y'all trippin'!"

"You mean to tell me you ain't hooked on that little round ass?"

"I mean her ass is tight, but I ain't hooked on shit, nigga. A ho can't be no housewife, ya mean? She serves a purpose, point blank."

"Aww, man, she serves more than one purpose. I bet you that pussy is hella tight."

"Damn straight it's tight. I am the first and only one in it!" The rush of weed through his system was electrifying his senses.

Amir was talking about all the things he would do to Violet, and to Kyle's surprise, his dick was getting brick hard.

"Shut the fuck up, yo, before I knock that ass out," Kyle said, but his threat held no sting.

Bunky plopped on the couch beside him. "You know we did the same thing to Rodney's girl last week."

"Get the fuck outta here, man. I know Rodney ain't let y'all greasy asses touch Carmen."

"Shiiiit," Amir laughed. "I was donkey fuckin' that bitch all night."

Bunky leaned over Kyle. "Hey, Amir, come on now. You know Rodney is a real-ass nigga."

"What you trying to say? I'm not?"

"I'm just saying, we know you got feelings for your shawty."

Amir laughed. "Everybody can't be hard, Kyle. The world needs soft niggas too. You know, balance. You love your bitch, and that's cool."

Kyle jumped up off the couch. His heart was thumping in his chest. "Aint shit soft about me. Anything Rodney do, I can do, and I don't have love for nothing but white rock and green paper. I don't have love for no hoes. You hear me?" Kyle was screaming at the top his lungs. He pulled his shirt up to reveal a rock-hard six pack and the chrome handle on his gun. "I'm king around here, as hard as they come." He grabbed his dick and motioned to the kitchen. "Bring that bitch in here!"

Bunky smiled as he rose from the couch. A little bit of angel dust mixed with chronic gets them every time!

Violet stood in the kitchen, shivering despite the heat from the oven. It was becoming hard for her to ignore the conversation in the front room. Amir and Bunky had always creeped her out. Bunky was cool when he was with his brother Nate, but when he was with Amir, things got real. It was like their special brand of crazy fed off of each other.

Violet turned away from the door and stared at her reflection in the window. She wanted to go upstairs but was too afraid to walk back past them. She swigged her vodka straight from the bottle and looked at the back door longingly.

Run, Violet. Just open the door and run.

Violet sighed. You're acting like an idiot, *she thought.* They are just fucking around. *She turned the oven off, slipped on her mitts, and pulled the mac and cheese out. She set it on the stovetop to cool by the biscuits, pulled off her mitts, and gave a little shout when Bunky appeared in the doorway.*

A slow smile slid across his face, and Violet's heart jumped into her throat. His smile made fear wash over her like a flood. With a scream, she raced to the back door. Bunky caught her by the hair and yanked her into his chest. He pulled her into the living room and threw her on the table like a rag doll.

Violet gagged at the memory of Bunky and Amir ripping inside of her while Kyle watched. She forced her mind back to the present. Her inner thighs burned as if it were yesterday. Tears blurred her vision. She blinked hard to clear her eyes. There were at least three cop cars tailing her. She ignored them. She heard the sirens, so she turned the music up. Violet jack-knifed the turn on Broad and Vine and entered the expressway doing 120 miles per hour. She sideswiped a blue Cavalier and lost control of the car briefly. Her back end slid into the passing lane, sending a Jeep onto the shoulder.

"I'm so sorry, Begonia," she said softly. "I miss you so much, and I am so sorry." She eyed the cops in her rearview. "Come on," she whispered.

A vision of Kyle's smiling face flashed before her. She could still taste the dirty sock he stuffed in her mouth to stop her screams. She shook her head as if she could shake away the memory.

"Come on!" she screamed.

I-95 became a blur as Violet accelerated to 140. *I just need this to be over*, she thought as she approached the WELCOME TO DELAWARE sign.

"I'm tired."

A helicopter bathed her Lexus in white light.

"I'm so tired."

She closed her eyes and let her arms drift from the steering wheel. The car smacked into the median and flipped over the divide. Violet's airbag deployed, knocking her out cold.

Chapter 36

Shanice stepped on a squeaky floorboard outside of Tabitha's room and froze. She thought that they had heard her for sure, but Tabitha and Darren kept talking and giggling in their own little world. Shanice breathed a sigh of relief and almost choked to death on the thick cloud of perfume floating in the hallway. *God, Tab, use the whole bottle, why don't ya*? she thought as she pulled her t-shirt over her nose.

Shanice was nervous as hell but determined to get her sister's car keys. Begonia was going to walk all the way to Southwest Philly to see her baby sister Daisy, and Shanice wasn't having that. She tried to get Begonia to wait on the steps for her, but only God and all of his angels could stop Begonia from doing what she wanted do. Shanice sure as shit wasn't going to see her girl walk across the city when there were two cars parked out front.

She eased the rest of the way to Tabitha's door. Her sister's voice floated through the crack.

"Come on, Darren. You know that we can't do that in here. You said you wanted to see me in it, not screw me in it."

"I just want a little bit," Darren said.

Tabitha giggled. "Okay, but we have to be quick."

"Okay, baby, whatever you say. Now, come on and climb on top of Daddy."

"Yes," Tabitha whispered, responding to the deep timbre in Darren's voice.

The room light clicked off, and Shanice thought she would be sick. She waited until she heard the first moan escape her sister's lips before switching the hall light off and opening Tab's bedroom door.

"Yeah," Darren growled. "That pussy fits Daddy like a glove."

Oh my God, Shanice thought. She got down on all fours and began to crawl into the bedroom.

"You like Mommy's pussy, don't you?"

"Yeahhhh, baby." Darren was grunting like a dog in heat.

Oh, I know I'm going to throw up now, Shanice thought as she crawled toward the dresser. *I am going to get sick and die.* She reached her hand up on the dresser and patted around blindly for the keys. When her hand brushed up against them, she sighed heavily. Their keys were side by side, so she grabbed them both.

Tabitha and Darren were deep into it now, and the room was filled with the sounds of their love-making. Shanice shivered. *I am never going to sit on her bed again.* She slipped one set of keys into her bra and crawled backward outside of the room.

Tabitha screamed like someone slid a knife in her back.

Okay, brother-in-law!

The lamp on the nightstand flicked on, and Tabitha scrambled to cover herself with the sheet. "What are you doing in here, girl?"

Oh, shit! "Ummm, my uhhh earrings . . ." Shanice patted around on the floor. "You know the ones Momma Mabel bought me? I think I lost them in here."

"Yeah, un huh, sure, the little diamond studs that Momma gave you?" Tabitha growled.

Shanice stood up and nodded. "Yeah, that's right. The studs." She looked at Darren and nodded again.

Darren laughed. "Those wouldn't be the studs that are in your ears right now, would they?"

"What?" Shanice asked. She slid the second set of keys in her pocket and felt her ears. "Uhhhh, duh! They were in my ears the whole time." She walked toward the door. "You know, I really should lay off the weed."

Tabitha sat straight up in the bed and gave Shanice a stare hot enough to melt butter. "Yup, Shanice, I think laying off the weed would be a real good thing, real good. Now, get out of my room!"

Shanice opened her mouth to say something, but Tabitha cut her off. "I don't know what you are up to, and I don't care. Just get out of my room."

Darren sat back against the headboard and tried his very best not to laugh at the look on Shanice's face.

"I'm going, I'm going. Sheesh! I know when I'm not wanted. Carry on with the fucking, 'cause I'm gone." Shanice glanced at Darren's bare chest. "Looking good there, brother-in-law. What, you working out?"

"Get out!" Tabitha screamed. She chucked a pillow at Shanice, who dodged it and slipped out of the room.

She ran to the end of the hall.

"Not so fast, you little fucking thief. Stay right there."

Shanice looked at the stairs longingly then turned around to face her sister. Her jaw dropped when she saw what Tabitha was wearing: a baby doll lace teddy with sheer, thigh-high stockings and black pumps. "You are such a freak!"

"Shut up, Shanice, and give me whatever it is you slipped in your pocket."

Shanice rolled her eyes and pulled the car keys out of her pocket and tossed them into Tab's outstretched hand.

"Oh, yeah, you're trippin' hard now. You *are* smoking too much weed if you think I'm going to let you drive my car. It's almost midnight. Where in the world are you trying to go?"

"I gotta make a run."

"You got to make a run, my ass. You better run along to bed before I call your mom."

"You gonna call my mom and Momma Mabel all the way in Atlantic City because I want to use your car? You trippin'! I'm not a little girl anymore, Tabitha."

"Well, stop acting like one, Shanice!"

Tabitha rolled her eyes and walked back into her bedroom. Shanice sighed heavily and continued on down the stairs. She was on the third step when Tabitha ran back into the hallway.

"Give me Darren's car keys too."

Shanice didn't say a word, nor did she look at Tabitha. She just pulled the second set of keys out of her bra and threw them on the hallway floor before running downstairs.

"You keep playing with me, girl, and I'm going to have Lisa kick your ass."

Shanice sat down hard on the last stair step. "Lisa ain't gonna kick shit," she mumbled under her breath.

"Is that right?" Lisa asked, walking out of the kitchen. She wore her trademark braids and a McDonalds' uniform.

"Lisa, when did you get here?"

"I've been here long enough to know that you need your ass beat. Why are you stealing car keys?"

Shanice sighed. "Begonia doesn't have carfare to go and see her baby sister, so she's walking. She's walking all the way across the whole damn city. I just wanted to give her a ride, that's all."

Lisa was quiet for a long time. She dug in her purse and handed Shanice her car keys. "All you had to do was ask, retard. I owe Begonia for helping to free me from my crazy-ass mom. The least I can do is give her a ride."

Shanice hopped off of the steps and hugged Lisa with all of her might. "Thank you, sissy."

"Yeah, yeah, right, right. Just be careful, and tell Bee that I'll be expecting to see her at work on time tomorrow."

Shanice caught up with Begonia on Fortieth and Girard, a good twenty blocks from where they lived. "Damn, girl, what where you, running? I asked you to wait."

Begonia shrugged. "I may have jogged a little bit. I couldn't wait for you, Shani. I know Daisy won't go to sleep until I get there."

"Well, hop in then. I had to go through hell to get this ride."

Begonia got in the car and buckled her seatbelt. "Sweetheart, you really don't have a clue as to what hell is."

They pulled up in front of a large two-story house off of Limburg Avenue. “Damn, this is nice,” Shanice said, taking in the front lawn sprinkled with flowers.

“It’s okay,” Begonia said. “Pull over around the corner, will you?”

Shanice parked the car. “I can come back in the morning to get you.”

“Naw, Shani. I don’t think that would be necessary.” Begonia hopped out of the car. She ducked her head in before closing the door. “Thanks for the ride, for real.”

Begonia closed the door and walked to the back of the house where her sister was being held hostage. She looked around to make sure no one was out before scaling the wall using the gutter bolts as a stepladder. After bracing herself on the ledge, she tapped twice on the window and waited for her sister’s smiling face to appear.

“Why’d you take so long?” Daisy asked. Her face was crumpled into a frown, and her little hands gripped her tiny hips.

“Unlock the window, little girl.” Begonia was trying her best not to laugh at the expression on her sister’s face. She waited somberly as Daisy pushed a chair from the corner over to the window. After she unlocked it, Begonia slid the window up and entered the room soundlessly. She scooped Daisy up and swung her around and around until they were both too dizzy to stand. They fell onto the bed, giggling softly.

Daisy climbed up on Begonia's stomach. "Well?"

Begonia chuckled and bucked slightly, sending Daisy tumbling onto the side of the bed. "Well, what?"

Daisy's face crumpled again. "What took you so long?"

"I had some things that I needed to take care of."

"What kind of things?" Daisy sat up on the bed and grabbed her teddy bear from the corner. "You mean like stealing and stuff?"

"No, not stealing. I told you that I don't do that kinda stuff no more. No bad stuff. I want us to be together as a family again, so I won't be doing any bad stuff. No stealing or robbing or boosting. Things are gonna change for us. You'll see, munchkin. Everything is going to work out fine." Begonia scooted up in the bed to get under the covers, and Daisy scrambled up after her.

"Have you seen Violet?"

Begonia's chest tightened, and a lump rose in her throat. "No, baby, I haven't seen her."

"What about Momma?"

"No, I haven't seen her either," Begonia lied. She made it her business to see Doreen at least every other day. She would pull her out of one crack house or another and make sure she got something to eat.

Begonia hugged her sister close and stroked her hair until she fell asleep. She alternated between watching the clock and gazing out the window at the stars. Daisy began to snore, and Begonia smiled. It had taken a full year for Begonia to find her. It wasn't easy breaking into the state building that held her records, but she did it. She would do anything for her family—any and everything.

The feel of Daisy's heartbeat, the rise and fall of her chest, and the sound of her soft snores acted like a sweet lullaby that threatened to ease Begonia gently into sleep. Begonia fought the feeling, however. She couldn't afford to stay the night because there was so much she had to do in the morning, on top of walking all the way back to North Philly.

Begonia scooted out of bed, careful not to disturb Daisy. She said a little prayer while tucking her in tight. When she stood up to go, her heart almost leaped out of her chest at the sight of Daisy's foster mother standing in the doorway.

Mrs. Briggs put a finger up to her lips and motioned Begonia into the hallway. Begonia instantly went cold. She curled her hands into fists and walked out into the hall without saying a word.

Mrs. Briggs closed the door and leaned against it. "I need to talk to you," she said in a hushed tone. "My name is—"

"I know who you are, Mrs. Briggs. What do you want?"

Mrs. Briggs looked at Begonia like she'd been slapped. "I want you to stop coming here. I know that you break into my house every night to be with Daisy. I don't know how long it's been going on or when it started, but I need it to stop. My daughter is never going to adjust to her new life if you keep this up."

Begonia went from cold to frozen instantly. She trembled with the need to punch Mrs. Briggs in her face; however, she steeled herself against that need. She spoke slowly through clenched teeth. "Daisy Brown's mother is in a crack house somewhere beaming up to Scottie as we speak. You are not Daisy Brown's mother. You are not Daisy Brown's anything. That is my sister, my blood, and the only family I have left to hold onto. You may want to burn those facts into your memory."

Mrs. Briggs backed away from the crazy look in Begonia's eyes. She took a deep breath and stood up to her full height. "That may be true, but we have filed for adoption. Daisy *is* going to be a member of this family now, and you are going to have to accept and respect that."

Begonia raised her hand as if to hit Mrs. Briggs, but she pushed Daisy's door open instead. She started to go in and then changed her mind. She gave Mrs. Briggs a frosty smile. "No need for me to go out the window, since you know I'm here." She walked toward the steps. "I think you are a nice lady, Mrs. Briggs. You take good care of my sister, and I appreciate that. As a matter of fact, that is the only thing stopping me from beating the shit out of you right now. I need you to accept and respect *that*. I'm going to leave. Do me a favor and tell my sister that I will be back tonight."

"You don't scare me, Begonia."

"Well then, you're dumber than you look."

"Maybe I'll put bars on the windows."

Begonia looked up at Mrs. Briggs from the middle of the stairwell. "You really are an idiot if you think bars will keep me out of here. That's funny." Begonia laughed as she walked out of the house. "You are funny as hell!"

Chapter 37

Violet woke up handcuffed to a hospital bed. For a few brief and beautiful seconds, she thought she was dead. However, the pain killed that dream. She was alive but not well at all. Violet was covered with a million and one bumps and bruises. The beeps of her hospital monitor echoed like a sledgehammer in her head, and the smell of hospital disinfectant was nauseating to say the least.

Violet opened her eyes slowly. *You can't even manage to kill yourself right,* she thought. She turned her head slightly so that she could look out the window to the hall. *It's like I am caught in some cheap-ass movie.* She watched the cop flirt with one of the nurses bustling around outside of her room. *That explains the handcuffs.* She brought her free hand up to her face and ripped the oxygen tube out of her nose. Her monitor started dinging and buzzing like a car alarm. The pretty blond nurse stopped gazing into the police officer's eyes and ran into the room.

"Are you okay?" the nurse asked. She hit a few buttons on the monitor. She leaned over Violet's head and looked into her eyes. "Are you having any pain?"

Violet tried to speak, but nothing came out. *I'm in a whole lot of pain, lady*. Violet thought. *Morphine, Vicodin, or Percocet won't dull the pain that I'm in. I can't even seem to die right.*

The nurse leaned over and brushed Violet's hair behind her ear. "Don't worry, sweetheart. I'm going to see what the doctor can give you that will be safe for the baby."

Baby. Violet gripped the side rails as pure anguish flooded her system. *Baby. I'm having a baby.* Kyle, Bunky, and Amir's faces flashed before her.

"I don't want a baby," Violet said softly.

The nurse frowned slightly and left to get the doctor.

A bald man with glasses and a white lab coat walked into the room with the police officer in tow. He walked over to the sink and washed his hands.

"Hello, Ms. Brown, my name is Dr. Hertz. I'm here to tell you that you are a very lucky young lady, and you are carrying one very strong and special baby." He pulled out a little flashlight and stared at both of Violet's eyes. "On a scale of one to ten, how bad is your pain, with ten being the worst pain you ever experienced?"

Violet laughed. "The worst pain I've ever experienced happened six weeks ago. I don't want anything for pain." She nodded to the officer. "Am I going with him?"

"I'm afraid so," the doctor said sadly.

"Well, what's the hold up?"

I just need to examine you once more, and then the nurse will be in to go over your discharge instructions. You've been here for three days, Violet. I had to administer Narcan to combat the high levels of cocaine in your system."

The doctor kept on talking, but Violet stopped listening. She went through the motions and said whatever they wanted her to say. She was going to jail, and Kyle was going to walk free. *Free as a fucking bird.*

Violet stuffed her hospital shirt in her jeans. They had explained to her that her shirt and bra had to be cut off in the ambulance. She put the call light on and waited for the nurse and the police officer to come back into the room.

"You all right, honey?" the nurse asked. Her voice was laced with compassion, and it made Violet's stomach roll. "All you have to do is sign here, and you are free to go."

Violet looked at the handcuffs in the officer's hand and shook her head. *Not exactly,* she thought. She signed her discharge papers and held her hands out to the cop, He read her Miranda rights and escorted her out into the hall. People stopped, stared, and whispered as they walked by, but Violet gave less than a fuck about what they thought. She put her head down and counted the floor tiles until they left the hospital.

There were four other girls inside the paddy wagon already. Violet avoided their eyes but could not avoid their smell. The whole damn wagon reeked of sweat, liquor, and pussy. The officer cuffed her left wrist to a little light-skinned girl who smelled like sushi and Absolut. They strapped them in with one long seatbelt and then proceeded to hit every damn pothole in the city.

"Get the fuck off of me," screamed the heavy-set girl in the back of the wagon.

The rat-faced crackhead she was cuffed to looked at her like she was crazy. "Bitch, please. You think I want to be on you? You fat fuck. Nobody wants to be on you. These damn cops are driving like assholes."

Violet squeezed her eyes shut and took small, shallow breaths out of her mouth because she was afraid the smell was going to make her toss her breakfast. The wagon came to a complete stop. The cops got out and stood around, shooting the shit.

"They gossip like women," one of the girls said. Violet couldn't tell who because she kept her eyes closed tight. She was scared, she realized—scared out of her mind— and all she wanted to do was close in on herself and disappear.

After about five minutes, the back of the wagon opened to the gray and smoky light of a parking garage. The officers helped them out of the wagon but did not free them from their handcuffs.

They walked into the precinct linked like ducks in a row. The heavy-set girl and rat-face began to argue about something, but Violet blocked them out. Her stomach was fluttering, and her hands were trembling.

"Shut the fuck up," the black cop with the 1975 Shaft sideburns hollered. "You are going to walk in here like you got some damn sense. You will stand against the wall and wait until it is your turn to be processed. You chose the right to remain silent, so keep it zipped. If I hear one more word, just one, I'm gonna get real ugly, and as you can see, I don't have that far to go!"

Just breathe, Violet, breathe, she thought as they filed against the wall. Their forced silence was forgotten as soon as Shaft walked away. Sushi girl nudged Violet's arm.

"Hey, what did you get knocked for? You don't even look like you belong in here."

Violet looked at the girl, who wore a dirty purple mini dress, and sighed. They looked to be around the same age. The girl was kind of cute, with pudgy cheeks and round eyes. Violet eyed the needle tracks on her arms. "I tried to kill myself."

"Damn, I didn't know they locked people up for that. I mean they should put you in the looney bin or something, but not lock you up with people like us." Sushi girl smiled like she just bestowed the greatest compliment.

Violet wanted to smile back at her, but she couldn't. She had no smiles left in her to give.

Officer Shaft came back over, yanked Violet off the wall, and un-cuffed her.

"All that ain't even necessary," sushi girl said.

"I thought I told y'all to shut up."

She mouthed *fuck you* to his back as he carted Violet off to a smaller room to be fingerprinted. A female officer pushed a plaque with her name and a series of numbers in front of her.

"I'm going to need you to take that wig off and step in front of the camera."

"I'm not wearing a wig," Violet said quietly.

The lady cop reached over the camera and tugged at Violet's hair. "No, you're not." She shrugged. "Step in front of the counter and hold that plaque up. That's right. Now turn to the side."

Violet blinked her tears away. "Don't I get to call somebody?"

The lady cop took her arm and walked her to a holding cell. "After you're arraigned."

***

Kyle screamed into the base of his cell phone so loud that they could hear him around the corner. "I swear to God, you little bitch, if you don't show up at Rita's with my shit, I'm gonna cancel you and every muthafucker you know!" He hung up the phone and threw it across the room. "Kisha, come the fuck on."

"Damn, Kyle, I'm getting my stuff."

"We don't have time for that, girl. Bring your ass."

"Fuck that. You leave your shit. I'm taking mines." Kisha pulled the bottom drawer out of her jewelry box and dumped the contents into her Fendi bag. She went over to her closet and grabbed her shoe box off of the top shelf. Five rubber-banded knots of money lay under the tissue paper.

Kyle smacked the box out of her hand. "Bitch, I said to come on."

"What the hell is wrong with you, Kyle?" Kisha asked, dropping to her knees. "That's my money."

Kyle yanked Kisha off the floor by her hair. "It's going to be your ass as soon as Rodney finds out about the load Violet copped." He dragged Kisha out of the room.

"Get off me," she screamed. "Let me get my money."

He wrapped her hair around his fist and pressed her against the wall. "A couple of thousand ain't gonna cut it, Kisha. I need to get the hell out of here and think. We are going to Rita's, and that bitch better be there with my Lexus and my work."

"Let me go, Kyle," Kisha said between clenched teeth.

He flung her against the banister. She had to grip the rail to keep from flipping over.

Kyle ran down the stairs. "I'm going to Rita's. You better come on, or stay the fuck here, but I'm out."

"Wait, Kyle. Damn, I'm sorry." She ran back into her room, rubbing the tears out of her eyes. She caught a glimpse of her mascara smeared over her cheeks in the mirror. "Oh, great. Just great." She grabbed her wipes off of her vanity, wiped her face, and kicked off her stilettos. She didn't have time to change out of her dress, but she managed to wiggle her feet into her Nikes by her bed.

"Don't fucking leave me, Kyle. I'm coming. Don't you fucking leave me." Kisha bent down and picked her money up off the floor. "Asshole," she mumbled under her breath.

Once she gathered everything she thought she could possibly use, she ran down the stairs two at a time and froze. She was staring down the barrel of a semi-automatic 9 mm handgun. "Jesus Christ," Kisha whispered.

"Ah, ah, ah," Bunky said, shaking his head. "His name is Smith and Wesson."

Chapter 38

Begonia was in disguise. She was dressed to the nines: Gucci jeans, milky white Prada blouse, and 4-inch black Prada heels. She was tired from arguing with Diana, her foster mother, all night. Daisy's foster mother had contacted their social worker and told her about Begonia's nightly visits. Diana was angry as hell, and Begonia felt a little bad about that. *However, nobody, and I mean nobody, is gonna keep me away from my sister.* She leaned against the light pole, lit a cigarette, and peeked over the rim of her dark shades.

"Fucking disgusting!" She puffed the cigarette and let the smoke curl out of her nose. "You can have the fucking National Guard set up a perimeter around this damn house, lady, but you are not going to keep me away from my sister. Believe that."

A security company was installing a high-tech surveillance system at Daisy's foster parents' house. Bars covered every window, and the doors looked to be reinforced steel. "You have got to be kidding me." Begonia dug inside of the Coach bag she stole from some woman on the bus. She pulled out the cell phone and called T-Bird.

He answered on the first ring. “You love me and you want me inside of you.”

“Still smoking that shit, I see.” Begonia smiled despite herself. “How did you know it was me?”

“Nobody in their right mind would call me at this hour but you.”

“T, it’s eleven o’clock.”

“A nigga don’t wake up until two p.m. Eastern Standard. Where’d you get the phone?”

“From your momma. Look, I need access codes to a shelter’s surveillance system, and I need something to cut through bars.”

“Aw, Bee, come on. I thought you were going to take a different route. If you’re not making enough at your gig, you know I got you.”

“I’m not going to rob anyone, T. I just need to get inside of a place, that’s all.”

“Why do you need to get inside of a place that is so well protected?”

“Are you going to help me or what? I mean, what’s up with all these fucking questions? You practicing to turn state’s evidence or something?”

“That’s fucked up, Bee.”

“Yeah, tell me about it.”

“I’ll call you around five with the codes. Should I use this number?”

“Seeing as how I’m about to throw the phone and the pocketbook it came from in the trash, I’d say you’d need another way to reach me, homes.”

"A'ight, bet. Take your ass to work, and I'll call ya there."

"T-bird, I aint goin' to work to—"

T-bird hung up the phone.

Fucking prick, Begonia thought. She tossed the phone and the purse on the ground and kicked it into the sewer.

Violet didn't wait inside the holding cell long before they called her name. Nothing seemed to last long. Her mind was racing, and she couldn't hold onto a thought. Fear, hurt, shame, and anger crowded down on her all at once. And, on top of all of that, she was freezing. *It's cold as balls in here.* She wished for death. *Anything to stop the pain,* she thought as she arrived in what looked like a small conference room.

Someone who Violet didn't know read off all of Violet's charges. They asked her if she'd understood what they were saying, and she nodded weakly. *I don't understand anything.* Tears slipped down her cheeks.

"Your bail is set at one million dollars."

The air rushed out of Violet as if she were punched in the chest. "I don't have a million dollars." The guard, or cop—Violet wasn't sure who he was. She just knew he was stronger than a motherfucker—yanked her to her feet, but her knees gave way, and she fell back into the chair.

Violet was screaming inside of her head, but nothing was coming out of her mouth. *I don't have a million dollars*. She was yanked out of the chair again and pushed down the hall. It was a female cop this time. She was saying something, but Violet couldn't make out the words.

The cop pushed her down on a cot inside the cell. "Look at me," she said, squatting down and leaning into Violet's face. "Understand something, sweetheart. The crazy routine won't get you far in here. You're just going to manage to piss a whole lot of people off." The officer gripped her face. "Do you understand me?"

"Yes," Violet whispered.

"Good." The officer backed out of the cell and closed the door. The bars clicked into place with a loud pop.

Violet lay down on the bench and rolled into a ball.

"I'll be back in twenty minutes so that you can make a phone call." She looked at Violet with pure hatred in her eyes. "Maybe you could have your kingpin boyfriend throw up a hundred K to get your narrow ass back out on the street." She walked away from the cell. "Oh, that's right. He left your dumb ass for dead on I-95. You may just be shit out of luck, princess."

Violet yanked her hospital gown out of her jeans and tried to wrap up in it the best way she could. *Oh my God*, she thought as she stuck her thumb in her mouth. *Oh my God*.

***

"What's going on?" Kisha whispered. She wanted to run, but she couldn't make her legs move. Her eyes darted around wildly until they landed on her brother. Kyle was on his knees in the dining room. His mouth was duct-taped, and his hands were tied behind his back. He was actually crying. *I think I'm going to throw up*, Kisha thought.

"Don't just stare at him, sweetheart." Bunky grabbed Kisha by the hair and pushed her on the floor next to her brother. "Get over there with him." Bunky looked at Amir and smirked. "Tie this bitch up too. She's coming along for the ride."

Amir grabbed Kisha's arm, but she yanked it away. Bunky walked over to her and shoved his Glock in her face. "Ah, ah ah, be nice, sweetheart."

Kisha gave Bunky a murderous stare and slowly placed her hands behind her back.

"Aww, shit, man. Ya little sista gots some heart. Well, would ya look at that." He walked over to Kyle and squatted in front of him. "You over here crying like a little bitch, and ya sista's ready to go to war." He grabbed Kyle's face and kissed him on the forehead. "It's going to be okay, man. Don't cry."

Kyle yanked his head away, and Bunky laughed. "Why don't you give ya brother some of your heart, Kisha?"

"Fuck you," Kisha said as she lunged at Bunky. Amir gripped her arms and held her still.

"You want to fuck me, do you?" Bunky stood up. "I'm sorry, baby. We don't have time for that." Bunky grabbed the crotch of his pants. "Although," he said, sticking his gun on her temple, "you can suck my dick."

Kyle screamed against his gag and tried to lunge toward his sister.

"Oh, now you got some balls."

Amir pushed Kyle on the floor and pulled his gun from his waist. He cocked it against Kyle's forehead. "I don't need much of a reason to cancel you, youngin'. Move again."

Bunky unzipped his pants and fumbled with his boxers.

Nate walked out of the shadows in the corner of the room. Kisha didn't even notice he was there. He and Bunky were identical in every way but their eyes. Nate's eyes were a quiet brown that held a deadly glint.

"Zip up your fucking pants, Bunky. We don't have time for this shit."

Bunky pulled his dick free and started jerking it in Kisha's face. "Not until this bitch gets a chance to taste this nut."

Nate pulled his gun out and pointed it at his brother. "I won't tell you again."

Bunky paused in mid stroke. He knew his brother meant what he said. Nate would erase a nigga without a second thought and zero remorse. Bunky put himself back in his pants, zipped up, and knocked Kisha out cold with the hilt of his gun.

"Was that necessary?"

"It was either knock her off or knock her out. I'd figured you would prefer her sleep."

"Whatever, man." Nate walked over to the window but didn't put his gun away. "Let's get out of here before Kyle's little crew decides to check in." He peeked out of the curtain. "Bunky, take them to the car." He pulled his glare out of the window. "I don't want to come out there and see any perverted shit, either. This is supposed to be simple. Don't make it hard. Amir, you give this place a thorough sweep. Any and all work and cash you find belongs to Rodney."

"All right. Come on, princess. Rise and shine." The cell door slid open and hit against the opposite wall with a loud pop. "It's time for you to make a phone call. Let's see if you can reach out and touch someone with deep pockets."

Violet rose from the cot slowly. She was stiff from the cold and a little queasy. She stretched and started to stuff her gown into her jeans.

"Come on, princess. We don't have all day. You look like shit."

"At least I have an excuse."

"What you say?"

"Nothing."

"I fuckin' thought so. I don't need an excuse to bring the pain right to your ass."

Jesus, give me a break. These cops act like they take their lines straight from the movies, she thought. She stepped outside of the cell and waited.

"Straight ahead, sweetness. You've got ten minutes."

Violet didn't say anything. Her stomach started to rumble and growl. *Maybe I shouldn't have refused the damn cheese sandwich and juice box,* she thought.

The women in the surrounding cells started hollering as soon as they spotted Violet. "Why the hell does she get to use the phone first?"

"Because she actually has someone to call, Angie. Now shut up and sit down." The officer slapped her baton against the bars. "Everybody shut up and sit down, or I'll make sure this is the first and last phone call of the day."

The cat calls didn't stop, but Violet wasn't paying attention anyway. *Who the fuck am I going to call*? she thought frantically. Calling Kyle wasn't an option, and Begonia didn't have a phone. Her stomach turned violently. When she picked up the receiver, she called the only other number she knew.

Chapter 39

The phone rang, but Tabitha ignored it. She stared at her little girl, who was sitting on her lap, tracing her letters, and smiled. Erica was wearing a purple princess dress, and she had a pair of her grandma's stockings on her head to mimic long, flowing locks. She wasn't exactly in a good mood. *We'll be moving in a few weeks, baby girl, and I'm still not sure if that's a good thing*, she thought as she rubbed Erica's back.

"Mom, can you get the phone?" Tabitha didn't feel like talking to anyone but Erica at the moment.

"That's right. You have to trace the words. *A* is for apple. Let me hear you say it."

"*A* is fo' apple."

"Good girl."

The phone kept ringing, and Tabitha rolled her eyes and pushed away from the table. "You keep working, baby. I'll be right back."

She walked into the living room, shouting upstairs, "How come you didn't get the phone, Mom?"

"Baby, I'm in the tub. I ain't about to leap out of it and prance around naked for a call I know is not for me."

Tabitha smiled and answered the phone. "Yellow."

"Hi, umm, is Shanice available?"

"No, she's not. Can I take a message?"

Violet couldn't help it. Her voice broke, and tears spilled from her eyes, blurring her vision. "Can you tell her that I'm, I'm in trouble? Tell her I'm in jail and that I'm, I'm pregnant."

"Wait, wait, slow down. Shhh, it's okay."

Violet's cry was full blown now. She could barely make out what Tabitha was saying.

Erica ran into the living room with her notebook. "Momma, Momma, look it. I did it."

Tabitha put her hand over the receiver. "That's great, sweetie. Go show Grandma."

Erica's smile split her face in two. "Grandma, Grandma!" She ran up the stairs. "I did my letters. *A* is fo' apple."

Tabitha watched her daughter disappear up the steps.

"Okay, I'm going to need you to take a deep breath, calm down, and tell me everything."

Tabitha could barely think straight. "Mom, I need you to watch Erica for a while. I have to make a run," she shouted up the steps, then grabbed her purse off of the table and hit the door. The image of Violet she had in her head did not match the girl on the phone. Violet was a quiet little bookworm, so the things she had told Tabitha just did not and would not compute.

She opened the door to the black Jeep that Darren bought her for her birthday, sat down, and stared off into space. "Jesus Christ. I don't know how to help this little girl, Lord. Send me some guidance because I just don't know." Tabitha shook her head, took a deep breath, and started up the car. "Dear Lord, please grant me traveling mercy," she said softly as she peeled away from the curb and mashed on the gas.

Tabitha made it to McDonald's in five minutes. She didn't want to think about all of the traffic laws she violated. She rushed into the store and headed straight to the back.

Lisa and Begonia were arguing. She heard them before she saw them.

"What the hell is wrong with what I got on?"

"What do you mean what's wrong with it? It's not a uniform. That's what the fuck is wrong with it."

"Lighten up, Lisa. The burgers aren't going to taste any different just because I ain't wearing a blue shirt with golden arches on it."

"You just think you can walk in here and do whatever you want to. Your shift started an hour ago. You spent the first twenty minutes on the phone with some dude, and now you won't even change into your uniform."

Tabitha asked Dave to let her into the back office.

"You sure you wanna go in there? It's going to get ugly."

Tabitha smiled at the young guy. "I'm sure. They don't scare me."

He opened the door. "Then you must be the only one they don't scare."

Tabitha walked through the door and stepped in between Lisa and Begonia.

Lisa rolled her eyes. "Tabitha, what the hell are you doing here, and who let you in the back? You guys just can't come back here whenever you want."

Tabitha threw her hand in Lisa's face. "You can flex your brand new boss muscles some other time because we have to go."

"Go where? I can't go anywhere."

"Fine. You stay here. Begonia, we have to go." Tabitha didn't wait for a response. She turned her back on both of them and walked out the door.

Begonia took one look at Lisa and followed Tabitha out.

"Oh, no you don't. You come back here. Your shift starts in ten minutes."

"Um, sorry, boss, but I have to go with Tabitha."

"You've got to go my ass."

Begonia waved bye to Lisa and walked out of the office and out of the building.

Lisa rolled her eyes, took off her visor, and threw it across the room before running after them.

Tabitha walked around the front of her Jeep. “Get in.”

Begonia raised her eyebrows but did not object. Tabitha was about to put the key in the ignition when Lisa tapped on the back window.

“Open the damn door, Tabitha, and tell me what’s going on.”

Tabitha let Lisa in, started the car, and pulled off.

“Where are we going?” Lisa demanded.

“To get Shanice.”

“Well, what the fuck is going on?”

Tabitha looked over at Begonia and then back at the road. “Violet’s in trouble.”

Shanice swept her long chocolate curls up into a ponytail and sighed. She didn’t feel like being in school today, but Momma Mabel threatened to paint her behind red if she ditched again. Shanice had never been beat with a belt a day in her life.

She walked to the back of the class, thinking about the conversation they’d had at her mother’s apartment.

"Child, you don't even know the pain I'm gonna bring to you if your mother tells me that your little butt skipped school again." She was waiving a belt around like it was a lasso and she was Indiana Jones.

Shanice looked at her like she was crazy. "I don't get whoopin's. I'm too old for that."

"And that's your whole damn problem, but don't worry, sweetheart. I'm not going to whoop you. You skip school again and I'm going to beat your ass like someone was paying me to do it."

Shanice shivered. *I think that old woman would really try to beat me. Oh, well. It looks like I'll be exploring the wonderful world of high school all damn day.*

She plopped down in her seat and stared at the overgrown cuticles on her fingernails. *That is so gross.*

Mrs. Thompson walked around her desk to the blackboard. "All right, class, I would like everyone to turn to page one forty-five in their textbooks. We are going to examine the politics behind the Spanish American War."

Oh, hell no, Shanice thought. *I can't sit through this shit. I'd rather have my ass whooped.* She stood up, took her jacket off, and wrapped it around her waist. She walked to the front of the class and cleared her throat.

Mrs. Thompson rolled her eyes. "What is it, Shanice?"

Shanice put her head down. "I need to be excused because I messed up my pants," she whispered.

"You did what?"

Shanice looked up and faked a pained expression. "My monthly came on. I need to go home and change."

"Well, can't you just clean yourself up in the bathroom?"

That is fucking gross! Shanice thought. She looked at Mrs. Thompson like she was crazy. "Uh, no, I need to go home, wash up, and change my clothes. May I please be excused?"

Mrs. Thompson turned back to the blackboard. "Go ahead, Shanice. Stop by the main office and sign yourself out."

Shanice walked out of the classroom barely concealing a smile. *Fuck if I'll do that*. She walked right past the nurse's office and out the door.

Tabitha took a deep breath and cut her eyes at Begonia before telling her about the phone call she had received. She was trying to get to Strawberry Mansion as fast as she could to pick up Shanice. *I should have gone there first* she thought as she turned onto 31st Street. *How the heck do you tell someone that their little sister is locked up?* she thought as she sped up the street.

Tabitha kept opening her mouth, but nothing would come out.

Lisa rolled her eyes and sucked her teeth. "Damn it, Tab, you just can't say Violet's in trouble and leave it at that. What the fuck is wrong with her?"

Tabitha was about to respond when a horn blared. She barely had enough time to slam on the brakes at the red light. Lisa was flung out of her seat onto the floor of the car. Her thick braids were strewn all over the console.

Tabitha twisted in the driver's seat, picking braids out of the cup holder. "You okay?"

"Do I look okay?" Lisa picked herself up. "Just hurry up and tell us what's going on so we can get back to work."

Tabitha sighed as she crossed the light and pulled over by the school just as Shanice was walking out the door. "Unbelievable."

Shanice walked over to the car. "You bitches must have ESP."

Lisa scooted over on the back seat so Shanice could get in. However, Shanice was staring at Begonia.

"What the hell is wrong now?" Shanice asked.

Begonia looked up at Shanice. Her face was like a stone mask. "Your sister says Violet's in trouble."

Chapter 40

Begonia held her breath as she listened to Tabitha. She hung on to every word that came out of her mouth as if it were the gospel. *Violet is in jail, and she's pregnant,* she thought as images of her sister sitting in the living room with her face buried in a book floated in her head. *Breathe, Begonia. Breathe and focus.* She closed her eyes and inhaled deeply. She counted to ten and then to twenty. Her head started to pound, and it took a moment to hear the silence. Tabitha stopped talking, and she could feel everyone's eyes on her.

Shanice rubbed her shoulder from the back seat of the car. "Bee, are you okay?"

Begonia twisted around in her seat to look Shanice in the eyes because that was the stupidest question she had ever heard. Her brows were knitted with honest concern that Begonia mistook for pity. "Stop the car."

Tabitha pulled over without a word. Begonia hopped out of the car. She had a full-blown migraine now and was finding it harder and harder to catch her breath. She squinted up into the sunlight to peek at the street sign and get her bearings. They were on 22nd and Lehigh Avenue, not too far from her mother's favorite crack house. She began to walk toward it.

"Begonia!" Lisa shouted. "Where in the hell are you going?"

"I'm going to find my mother."

"I thought Diana worked in the daytime."

"Not Diana. My real mother."

"Well, what the fuck is that going to accomplish?" Shanice grabbed Lisa's arm to quiet her, but Lisa jerked away.

"Get off of me, Shani." She walked toward Begonia. "Look, Begonia, I can only imagine what you're going through, but I know that Doreen ain't got nothing for you. Let's go back to Momma Mabel's house and see what we can come up with. If we put our heads together, I'm sure—"

"You're sure of what? This ain't no shit that could be cured over tea and cookies at your mom's house. This is some street shit, and if my sister's in jail, I'll bet you all the fries at McDonald's that my mother knows what went down. Go back to work, Lisa. Everyone needs to go back to what they were doing. Violet is my responsibility, and you best believe that I got this." Begonia turned on her heels and ran away. Lisa started to run after her, but Shanice grabbed her arm.

"Get off of me. What's wrong with you? We have to help her."

"How, Lisa? How the fuck do we help her?"

Lisa just stared at Shanice, her eyes brimming with tears.

"Exactly," Shanice said. She spit on the pavement and walked to the Jeep. "Take me back to school, Tab. It ain't shit we can do for Begonia right now."

"God, please let those girls be all right." Tabitha breathed while starting the car.

Lisa knocked on the window. "Ya'll go 'head. I'm gonna walk.

"You sure?" Tab asked.

"I'm positive."

Begonia stopped running when she noticed that Lisa wasn't following her. She leaned up against thc wall, gulping mouthfuls of air like water. A slow ache started to pulse deep inside of her chest when Tabitha spoke of Violet. Guilt filled her, twisting her stomach. *I'm going to throw up,* she thought as she leaned over and rested her hands on her knees. *Why the fuck did you leave her there, Bee? She's pregnant and locked up. Oh my God.*

Tears fell from her eyes and stained her jeans before she even realized that she was crying. She watched the cars roll by through the haze of her tears. The scenes of her family ripping apart at the seams raced through her head: her mother stealing and selling everything that wasn't nailed down, Daisy's illness, and the look in Violet's eyes as she gazed at Kyle like he was her fucking lord and savior. Her stomach twisted violently at the last image. She'd walked away from her sister and left her in the hands of a stupid-ass thug wannabe.

I just walked away from her.

"I'm so sorry, Violet," she whispered as she wiped her tears and stood up straight. "I'm so sorry I left you with him, but I'm going to get you out of this shit. I swear to God I will." She shook herself and walked toward the closest crack house.

Doreen was yelling at the top of her lungs. Begonia could hear her from halfway up the block. She couldn't hear what she was saying, but there was no mistaking her mother's high, squeaky voice. Begonia stopped at the bottom of the steps, waiting for the familiar cold feeling to wash over her, but nothing happened. A lot of different emotions were raging inside of her. She was hurt, sad, angry, and scared out of her mind for her sister, but she wasn't cold. She couldn't stop feeling anything, no matter how much she wanted to.

She gazed up at the abandoned building. It was decorated with trash, dirty needles, and discarded condom wrappers. She shook her head and rolled her eyes. She didn't really want to go inside, but the yelling became worse as more people joined in on the argument. Begonia cracked her neck and went in.

"I didn't steal nothing from you and this big-Bertha bitch," Doreen screamed at the top of her lungs. Spit flew out of the corners of her mouth like a rabid dog.

"Nobody said you stole it. I was just asking if you seen it." A tall, lanky crackhead stepped into Doreen's face. "You're the one who got all suspicious actin'. You actin all guilty and shit."

"Get the fuck out my face, Gary, 'cause I ain't scared of you like the rest of these bitches in here."

"I'm not going to be too many more bitches, you dogged-out, raggedy ho. I don't think you know who you are talking to," said the short, dark-skinned woman who stood at Gary's side. She looked like a miniature sumo wrestler.

Doreen stepped into the woman's face just as Begonia walked into the room. "I call them like I see 'em, you fat, ugly—"

Gary grabbed Doreen by the hair and flung her to the ground before she could get the last word out.

"Get off of me, you piece of shit," Doreen screamed. She clawed at his face and shirt, but he did not loosen his grip on her hair. His little sumo friend looked scared and backed up a few paces.

"Get off of her, Gary. Let's get out of here. She's not even worth it."

Begonia stood in the archway, frozen. She hardly recognized her mom, but she was familiar with this scene. *What the hell are you doing here, Bee? What do you expect this woman to help you with? She can't even help herself.*

"Get the hell off of me."

"Not until you tell me where the hell my radio is. You were the only person here all day."

"Fuck you and your fucking radio."

Gary raised his fist like he was about to slap Doreen, but Begonia leaped forward. She grabbed his free hand, pulled it behind his back, and punched him in his throat. He dropped Doreen's head on the floor and grabbed his neck, gagging. His little sumo friend screamed, but Begonia ignored her. She grabbed a fistful of Gary's hair and kneed him in the face. He slumped forward, unconscious. Begonia stepped over him and picked her mother up off the floor.

"Get the hell off of me, Begonia. Jesus," Doreen said while pulling away and straightening out her dingy shirt. "What the hell are you doing here anyway?"

"What do you mean what am I doing here? I'm saving your ass as usual. That's what I'm doing here."

Doreen stormed out of the house, and Begonia followed. "Where are you going?"

"I'm getting out of here. I'm getting away from you and the rest of the crazy motherfuckers in that house." Doreen crossed the street and headed up the block.

"Mom, hold up. Damn. I need to—"

Doreen turned the corner. "I really don't give a damn about what you need."

"Can you please tell me what happened to Violet? I need to know what happened to her."

"Why don't you go ask her?"

"She's locked up, Mom."

"Yeah, I know. But I'm sure that they have visiting hours up there." Doreen darted between two cars riding down the street. A horn sounded, and she flipped the driver the bird. Begonia waited for a third car to pass before following her mother.

"Look, Mom, just tell me what you know and I won't bother you anymore."

"Why should I tell you anything, huh? Don't you already know everything? You kicked me out, right? Yeah, that's right. You kicked me out because you wanted to play at being Mommy. Not as easy as you thought it would be, huh? Not quite working out for you, is it?" Doreen tossed her nappy hair over her shoulder and folded her arms beneath her small breasts. "What do you want me to say? Your little sister got herself locked the fuck up. She made a bunch of really bad people angry along the way."

Begonia walked over to her mother. "What do you mean? How did she get locked up, and who did she piss off?"

"That's all I know, sweetie." A slow smile spread across Doreen's face. "Your sister played a dangerous game with dangerous people, and now she's paying a seriously heavy price."

The look Doreen was giving her made Begonia's skin crawl. "That's it? That's all you know?"

"It depends."

"It depends on what?"

"Can I borrow a few dollars?"

"Are you shitting me?"

Doreen looked Begonia up and down. "I know you got some money in those tight jeans of yours. Why don't you give me a few bucks so I can get something to eat?"

Doreen's words slapped at Begonia. Her bottom lip quivered, and her eyes moistened. She looked away from her mother in shame.

"Oh my, God, Begonia, are you crying? I know you're not crying. Not Mrs. Big and Bad. Nope can't be." Doreen started laughing. "I've seen it all now." Her laughter tapered off, and her hands dropped down to her hips. "If you're not going to give me any money, then you can fuck off, because I stopped caring about what happened to you and your sisters a long time ago. I think it was just about the same time you kicked me out."

"Okay," Begonia said quietly. She wiped her eyes and walked away. "Okay."

Doreen began to laugh again. "That's right, baby girl. Run along and go play at being Momma. Or better yet, why don't you play at being Superman? That way you can fly in and save the day! You hear me, Mommy dearest? Fly in and save the fucking day!"

The walk to Kyle's house was short. Begonia's chest ached, her head hurt, and her high heels were beginning to pinch her toes. She walked up Kyle's steps and started to bang on the door, but it swung open on the first knock. Begonia arched her eyebrow and looked up and down the street before walking in.

The place was trashed—chairs were overturned, pictures lay shattered on the floor, and all the pillows were ripped and gutted. She walked from room to room, and they all looked the same. For the first time that day, Begonia's heart started to beat cold, and ice slid through her veins. There were no signs of Kyle or his ditzy sister. There was also nothing of value left in the place. The only emotion that penetrated the cold was anger, and Begonia was pissed.

She leaned up against the wall in the upstairs hallway and looked around. "No one with good sense trashes one of Rodney's houses no matter who lives there." She frowned. "At least not without Rodney's permission." She walked into the bathroom and opened the medicine cabinet. She dumped pills, cologne, and toothpaste into the sink. She pulled out a box of razor blades and put one in her bra, one in her hair bun, and one in her mouth. She closed the cabinet and stared at her reflection in the mirror. *It's time to dance with the devil.*

She kicked her heels off and walked into the middle bedroom, which she assumed was Kisha's. Her eyes swept across the floor until they rested on an old pair of beat-up Jordans in the corner.

She sat down on the box spring to slip the sneaks on, because someone had sliced the mattress and leaned it up against the wall. *This wasn't no crackhead job,* she thought as she laced up the shoes. *Whoever did this ran through this place with a purpose*. Begonia got up, ran down the steps and through the back door to the alleyway. *I'm going to find out what happened to my sister, and then I'm going to relieve Kyle of his balls.*

It didn't take her long to find a target. She ran up to the corner of 29th and Allegheny Avenue, tripped on a crack in the pavement, and fell into a man leaning on a fire hydrant. Begonia smilled up at him and then played shy. She put her head down so he wouldn't see the razor in her mouth.

Dusting off her clothes, she spoke softly. "I'm so sorry."

"It's a'ight, shawty. Don't sweat it."

Begonia didn't intend to. She walked swiftly across the street, going through his wallet. She found three crisp twenties and a bus pass, so she tucked the wallet in her back pocket and hopped on the bus heading to 29th Street.

Begonia picked the lock and walked right into Rodney's crib like she belonged there. One of Rodney's goons, an ex-con named Big Mike, jumped up off of the couch and stepped into Begonia's face.

"Yo, what the fuck is wrong with you, shawty? You got a death wish or something?"

Begonia kicked him in the nuts, and he fell to his knees in front of her. She pulled a razor blade from her bra and backhanded him with it, slicing his face open. Big Mike screamed and grabbed his face as blood spurted out across Begonia's blouse. She dropped the razor and put her hands in the air when three guys came out of the dining room with their guns drawn and pointed at Begonia's head.

Begonia recognized Bunky's twin brother, Nate, but the other two dudes weren't from Strawberry Mansion, so she didn't have a clue who they were.

"Talk or die, Bee. You have five seconds before I empty this clip in your ass."

"I want to talk to Rodney."

"Well, this isn't the best way to go about it, sweetie."

Begonia looked up at the camera mounted in the corner of the room. "I wanted him to know that I am serious."

The basement door opened up, and a young white boy named Tweet motioned for Begonia to follow him. Nate put his gun away, and his two friends followed suit.

"I hope you know what you're doing, Bee."

"I always do, Nate. I always do."

The basement was cold dark and damp. The floor was covered with plastic. *Not a good sign, Bee. Not a good sign at all.* She stopped when she got to the foot of the steps. She wanted to be as close to the exit as possible, even though she knew if Rodney wanted her dead, there wasn't too much she could do to avoid it.

Security monitors lined the back wall of the basement. Tweet walked over to them and took a seat. Rodney sat behind a large oak desk. He was smiling. He motioned for Begonia to take a seat in front of him.

Begonia swallowed hard and walked over to the chair. She was surprised to see Kyle on his knees, bound, gagged, and bleeding all over his t-shirt. *What the fuck is going on*? She sat down in the chair slowly. *Be cool, Bee. You wanted to know, so now you are about to find out.*

Amir walked over to Kisha and ripped the gag from her mouth. She let out a hollow moan while Amir pulled a wicked-looking knife out of a holster strapped to his ankle and sliced the duct tape off her wrist.

She tore her gaze away from Kyle and Kisha and locked eyes with Rodney.

Rodney's smile fell away as he leaned back in his chair. "What make you so serious, Begonia?"

"I want to know what happened to my sister."

"Well, your sister took two hundred fifty K worth of work from my boy Kyle here and got caught with it." He gestured to Kyle. "My boys found twenty-five K on Kyle and are willing to pay me twenty-five K for Kisha."

As if on cue, Kisha started to scream. "No, please, anything but with them." She tried to run to Rodney, but Bunky punched her in the back of her head, and she fell to her knees, sobbing, with snot pouring from her nose.

Begonia rolled her eyes. "I don't give a fuck about Ren and Stimpy over there. All I care about is my sister. I'm sorry about your work, and I give you my word that I'll pay off what I owed to you, but I need help to get my sister home."

Rodney started to laugh uncontrollably, and a sliver of fear worked its way up Begonia's spine. *He's not going to help you, Bee.*

Kisha crawled up to Rodney's desk. "Please, Rodney, I'll do anything. I'll do anything. Just don't let them have me, please. I'll do anything."

"Get the fuck up, bitch." Bunky hauled Kisha to her feet and started dragging her back over to her brother. Kyle broke out of his restraints and grabbed Bunky's leg.

"Get the fuck off of me, yo. Are you insane?"

Kisha elbowed Bunky in the gut. She punched him in the face and grabbed his gun. She swung the gun around the room, trembling and backing up against the wall.

Amir placed his gun at Kyle's temple. "You're about to be a memory, nigga. Make a move."

Bunky touched his broken nose and spit out blood. "You little fucking bitch."

"You stay back or I swear I'll shoot your fucking head off."

Rodney stood up and leaned over his desk. "Don't hurt yourself with that big gun, little girl."

Kisha looked at Begonia. "I was there when, wh-when they raped Violet. I heard her scream all n-night. I saw the look in her eyes afterwards. They were dead. They stayed dead. I'm not going through that shit. You hear me." She swung the gun back and forth around the room. She was shaking violently now. She wiped her eyes and stood up straight. "I'd rather die first." She put the gun in her mouth and pulled the trigger.

Kyle lunged for his sister, and Rodney walked around his desk, grabbed the gun from Amir. He put two bullets in Kyle's back and one in his dome. Blood splattered against Begonia's sneakers, and her cold shield slid off of her like water. She didn't know she was screaming until Rodney slapped the shit out of her.

"Shut the fuck up, Begonia, and listen to me carefully." He hauled her up out of the chair. "I'm going to give you one month to get me my money, or you and your little sisters are dead. Do you understand me? Can you tell that I'm serious?"

Begonia nodded.

"Good. Now get the fuck out of my house and don't come back unless you have my money."

Chapter 41

Violet kept her eyes on the woman in front of her as they walked to the bus that would ship them off to the county jail. She had to resist the urge to look over her shoulder for Begonia. She'd dreamed of her last night, and a false kernel of hope remained that Begonia was going to show up and make everything all right.

They stood off to the side as the men were loaded on first. After they were seated, Violet was cuffed again. She looked down at her wrist and cried. Her stomach fluttered, and she clamped her mouth shut so she wouldn't throw up all over herself. Thoughts flew through her mind too fast for her to hold onto. *Dear God, I don't really know how to pray, and I don't know if you're listening, but I don't want to be here anymore. Please just let it come to an end.*

Violet looked at the building as they pulled up, and every bad prison movie she'd ever seen sprang into her head. *Oh my God*, she thought.

They were separated from the men and led into a hallway with large windows and empty holding cells. A male guard entered the room. He was about five feet ten inches, brown skinned, with a small mustache and dark brown eyes. He paced up and down the room like a drill sergeant, looking everyone in the eyes before speaking.

"Listen up, ladies. My name is Officer Mike Davis. You will now be processed into this facility. It will take up to three days. The process can run as smooth or as rough as you want it. The choice is yours. You will stand here until your name is called, and then you will be escorted into the med office. After you're examined, you will be assigned rooms in D-block for quarantine."

Whatever, Violet thought. *Let's just hurry up and get this over with so I can lay down*. Violet watched as the women were led into the room one by one. *Oh, this really fucking blows*. She leaned against the wall and stared straight ahead. A few people tried to talk to her, but she ignored them.

Officer Mike stuck his head out the door. "Violet Brown."

About fucking time. She pushed off the wall and made her way to the door. She entered a small office and was greeted by a light-skinned black woman wearing a white lab coat. She picked a manila folder up off the desk and offered Violet a seat.

"Hello, Violet, my name is Wanda Mintz. I am the intake nurse here."

Violet nodded her head and rolled her eyes. *Let's get this the fuck over with, lady,* she thought as she sat down and fidgeted with the strings of her gown.

Wanda smiled. "This file says that you're approximately seven weeks pregnant." She looked over the file again. "I will not be able to administer a tetanus shot." She looked up at Violet. "That wouldn't be safe for the baby. I will still have to test you for tuberculosis. It's a very simple test that I will explain to you later. First, I need to ask you a few questions."

Violet suppressed the urge to be sick. She crossed her arms tightly underneath her breasts. Locking her knees, she took a deep breath and forced herself to look the nurse in the eye. "Well," Violet said, "shoot."

Wand pulled a pen out of her lab coat. "Do you have any police-related injuries?"

"Nope."

"Are you having any suicidal thoughts?"

Violet cracked up laughing. *Bitch, I flipped a Lexus over three times on the expressway, on purpose*, she thought. *What do you think*? She was laughing so hard that tears came to her eyes. It took Violet a moment to regain her composure.

"No, ma'am, I do not have suicidal thoughts."

Wanda looked at Violet like she was a nut case. She wrote furiously on her notepad. "Do you think you will be a danger to people around you?"

Violet smiled and wiped her eyes. "No, ma'am."

Wanda frowned at her tone but continued to ask questions. Violet sat up straight in the chair. The moment of humor had passed, and the weight of her situation fell back on her like a ton of bricks. She stopped talking and just nodded her head yes or no, refusing to elaborate.

Wanda grew tired of her attitude, and the syrupy sweet tone of her voice fell away. She put her little pad down and walked over to the sink to wash her hands. She pulled out a little kit from the med cart in the corner. "Please extend your arm. I am going to give you a small shot that will let us know if you've been exposed to Tuberculosis."

Violet stuck her arm out. "Are we done after this?"

"Yes, we're done for now." She swabbed her arm with alcohol. "I will see you in three days to check your arm for a reaction."

A female officer knocked on the door and stepped inside the room.

"This is CO Brandi Lyons. She will conduct your search, and then you can shower and get changed."

"Just call me Brandi," the officer said. She handed Violet papers. "This is a receipt for your personal items, and this is a call sheet. I will put all of your belongings in this bag, and this is a jumpsuit you will wear until you get your blues."

Violet stood up and rolled her shoulders. Her stomach fluttere,d and she brought her hand up to her belly to fight off a wave of nausea.

"Are you all right?" Brandi asked, handing her soap, a washrag, and a towel.

Violet ignored her. She took the carrot suit off the nurse's desk and stepped into the hallway.

Brandi led her to a large shower room. "Okay, Ms. Brown, I need you to strip." Brandi closed the door and put on plastic gloves.

"Are you going to stand there and watch me?"

"I sure am, darling. I have to make sure you're not smuggling any contraband into our fine facility."

Violet shrugged. *What the fuck does it matter*? she thought as she pulled off her gown. She started to toss it on the floor, but Brandi stepped forward to grab it. Violet backed up against the wall, holding her breasts. "Don't touch me."

Brandi stuffed her gown in the bag and sighed. "I told you I wasn't going to touch you."

The cold tiles sent shockwaves through Violet's system, but she didn't move.

"You need to calm down."

"I am calm. I just don't want to be touched."

Brandi cocked her head to the side and gave Violet a look that said *you are making this harder than it has to be.* Violet gave Brandi a look of her own and stepped away from the wall. She took deep breaths to calm herself as she unfastened her jeans. She kicked off her sneakers and pushed her jeans down her hips. When she stepped out of them, Brandi picked them up and put them in the bag along with her hospital gown. Violet took off her socks and then did a very poor job of covering herself with her hands.

"What now?"

"Now I need you to place your hands straight out from your side and spin around slowly."

Tears came to her eyes as she spun around. Visions of Kyle jerking off while Bunky held her down and Amir stuck a broomstick up her ass floated through her mind.

"I need you to stand with your legs apart, squat, and cough."

Violet squatted down slowly. The room tilted, and she became dizzy and started tipping backward.

"Oh my God," Brandi said. She leaped forward and grabbed Violet's shoulders before she fell over.

"Get off of me," Violet screamed. She didn't see Brandi; all she saw were Bunky's evil eyes as he pressed her to the table and forced himself inside of her. "Get off of me!"

"Look, girl, I'm trying to help you." Brandi tightened her grip, and Violet went wild, screaming and kicking. She fell on her butt with a thump.

"Help me!" Brandi screamed

Three female guards rushed inside the room. They had to fight hard to restrain Violet as she punched, kicked, and scratched to free herself.

"Please get off of me. Kyle, get him off of me, please. Don't let them hurt me." Violet brought her knees up and kicked out as hard as she could, but the guards maintained their hold. "I love you, Kyle. I swear I love you. Why are you doing this? Why?"

Officer Brandi held Violet's head up so she couldn't knock it on the floor again. Wanda ran into the bathroom with two other nurses in tow. Violet wrenched one leg free and kicked one of the nurses in the face. The nurse hollered out as she fell backward.

"Get the fuck off of me," Violet screamed at the guards who now had her pinned securely to the shower room floor. Her sobs rocked her body violently. "I love you, Kyle. Don't hurt me. Please, don't let them hurt me."

"No one's going to hurt you," Wanda said while she stuck a needle in Violet's arm.

Violet's eyes drooped instantly. "I'm sorry, Begonia. They hurt me so bad," Violet mumbled as she drifted off to sleep.

Wanda motioned for the guards to back away then turned to Brandi. "Go get me something to cover her up with." She looked Violet over for injuries. There were jagged scars between her legs and various bite marks on her breasts, and cigarette burns covered her stomach. *Jesus, Mary, and Joseph*, Wanda thought. *What happened to this little girl*?

Chapter 42

Begonia sat on the park bench with a fifth of vodka. She took a swig and held her hand up in front of her. She couldn't seem to stop shaking. She had a hard time coming up with 200 bucks, so the thought of squeezing out two hundred thousand was unbelievable. *I'm gonna get it though. I'm gonna get it, or I'm gonna die trying*, she thought as she looked down at her clothes. Although it had been days since she saw Kyle and Kisha die, she still expected to see their blood on her jeans and sneakers. *I think you're going to have to change first, Bee.*

Getting up from the bench, she stretched and threw the empty bottle into the street. She walked down three blocks to the house that Child Protective Services took her from two years ago. She stood there watching it for a long time while the vodka simmered in her system.

"It's all on you, Begonia. Now what the fuck are you gonna do?" No answer came from the boarded-up house she was staring at or the heavens up above, so Begonia kept it moving. She walked down to the payphone at the corner store. A young woman was walking down the street pushing a stroller, and Begonia's eyes were immediately drawn to her pocketbook, which exposed a fresh box of Newports. Begonia picked up the receiver and fished a quarter out of her pocket.

"Can I buy a cigarette off of you, miss?"

She smiled at Begonia. "You don't have to buy it, honey, 'cause I shares the cancer sticks." She handed Begonia two out of the pack and lit the first one for her.

"Thank you."

"Oh, no problem," the lady said as she walked away.

Begonia called T-bird, and he picked up on the first ring.

"Hello."

"Hey, T, did you get that stuff we talked about?"

"Bee, where the fuck have you been? I went by your job and your foster mom's house. Ain't nobody seen you in days."

"Yeah, well, I've been kind of busy."

"Busy my ass. You in trouble? Why you ain't call me?"

"I'm calling you now."

T-Bird was silent for a while. Begonia did her best to calm down. She took one long pull on her Newport and exhaled. "Look, T, I'm really sorry.

I know I should have called you, but I'm in some real deep shit, and I needed some time to get my head on right."

"Damn, Bee, how far we go back? You know I got your back no matter what."

"Yeah, I know."

"Well, then tell me what's wrong."

"Ain't shit wrong now. It's all handled."

"Are you sure? Because the streets are buzzing."

"Don't listen to gossip, T-Bird. You're better than that."

"I'm just sayin' . . ."

"Look, T, I need to see my sister. Do you have what I asked you for or not?"

"I'll meet you at Portia's in fifteen minutes." He hung up the phone, and Begonia stared at the receiver.

"He is tripping for real!" Begonia walked around to Portia's and ordered a drink.

Honey was on the steps rubbing her feet. "Bitch, you smell like pure vodka. I ain't giving you a drink."

Begonia smiled. She liked Honey almost as much as she liked Portia. "Where the fuck is your boss?"

"Out minding her damn business and leaving yours alone."

Begonia sat on the steps. "Stop playing, Honey. I want a drink."

Honey put her feet down and squeezed it back into a black pump. “I ain’t playing, Begonia. You are a little fucking girl, and I’m not giving you shit to drink. Now, give me those sneakers ’cause these heels are really killing me.”

“Go put on your own sneakers.”

“Portia threw them all the hell away. She says I have to learn how to dress like a lady.”

Begonia laughed, and Honey stood up and gave her a dirty look. A white Grand Cherokee pulled up in front of the house.

“Looks like that’s my ride, young buck.” She turned toward the house. “Aye you, Peanut, I’m leaving. Tell Portia I’ll be back tomorrow and don’t give this little-ass girl nothing to drink.” Honey tip-toed down the steps and wobbled to the Jeep.

Begonia smiled. “Where are you and your date going, Honey?”

“Foot Locker, of course. Didn’t I just tell you that a bitch don’t got no sneakers?”

T-Bird walked up the street just as Honey was pulling off. He handed Begonia a bag. “You gonna tell me what’s going on?”

Begonia riffled through the bag and smiled at the hunter’s knife. “Hell no.” She pulled 200 bucks out of her bra and handed it to him. “But you already knew that, didn’t you?”

T-Bird opened his mouth to speak, but Begonia cut him off. She grabbed his shirt and pulled him into a passionate kiss. “No matter what, T, you gots to know that I’ve got mad love for you. I’m gonna call you as soon as I can.” Begonia started walking down the street.

“Why won’t you let me help you?”

Begonia held the bag up in the air. “You already have.”

T-Bird had become brick hard as soon as she started kissing him. She had stroked that meat log in his pants hard and fast so he didn’t notice his piece or his money being lifted from his jeans.

“I’m going to have a serious talk with that boy one day.” She slipped the two hundred she stole back in her bra, and then checked his gun. It was loaded.

Begonia rode the El train to the end of the line twice, trying to think of what to say to Daisy. She tried so hard to protect her from everything that was going on, but she couldn’t help thinking that if she’d told Violet the truth every once in a while, they wouldn’t be in this predicament. She got off the El at 30th Street and crossed over to the trolley stop. She would have walked the rest of the way, but her gear was heavy, and T-Bird’s gun felt awkward in her waistband.

Begonia had made an additional $400 from boosting on the train, but it wasn’t enough. *I ain’t gonna get nowhere by pickpocketing people,* she thought as she got on the trolley.

She stared at her reflection in the window. It was too dark outside to see out of them. The woman sitting in the seat in front of her had an infant on her lap and forty dollars visible in an open diaper bag. Begonia shook her head. *I'm going to let you and the baby have that,* she thought as she got up to exit the trolley on 63rd Street. Begonia pulled the cord and moved toward the door.

She turned to the woman. "Your bag is open, and your money is showing."

Begonia didn't wait for the woman's response. When the doors opened, she flew out of them like she'd actually taken the cash. *I'm tired,* she thought as she hefted T-Bird's bag on her shoulder. *I am so damn tired.*

When she got to Daisy's block, she sat across the street from her house and looked longingly at the bar on the corner. "Come on now, Begonia. Focus. You can't do what needs to be done if you are all drunk and high."

She walked across the street into Daisy's back yard and dropped her bag in the dirt. Bending down, she unzipped the bag and riffled through it. *Aw, shit, T-Bird, you really know how to come through for a sister.* The bag was loaded with enough stuff to break into a bank.

Begonia pulled out the envelope with the codes to override their security system and a container of acid for the bars on Daisy's window. She pulled her ski-mask from her back pocket and placed it on her head.

A car door slammed, and Begonia jumped. She had the mask halfway over her face when the image of Kisha blowing her brains out all over Rodney's wall hit her like a hammer. Begonia's breaths came hard and fast. *Kisha died not to go through what they did to Violet.* Tears ran down Begonia's cheeks. She wiped her nose on her sleeve and looked up at the sky.

"What's worst then death, God? What did they do to my baby sister?" She snatched off her ski mask, then dropped the acid and the envelope back into the bag. Hefting it back onto her shoulder, she walked out of the yard and up to the front door.

Begonia rang the bell and banged on the door. A light flicked on, and Mr. Briggs snatched open the door. "Why are you here in the middle of the night, banging on the door like you're crazy?"

Begonia walked by Mr. Briggs without waiting on an invitation. "I need to talk to your wife."

Mr. Briggs rolled his eyes and closed the door. "That's obvious, Begonia." He wrapped his robe tightly around his towering frame. "Do you have to talk to her in the middle of the night?"

Mrs. Briggs came down the steps in a matching robe. "Who is it, Jim?"

Begonia walked into the living room and grabbed the TV remote off of the coffee table. Mrs. Briggs gave her a look hot enough to melt butter.

"What the hell are you doing here?"

"Nice to see you too, sweetheart." Begonia turned the TV on and turned the volume up to max.

"God damn it. This is crazy." He tried to snatch the remote from Begonia, but she dodged his advance and walked around the sofa.

"Don't tell me you came all this way to watch cable?"

"No, I came all this way to talk to you, and I don't want my little sister to hear what I have to say."

"Daisy is asleep," Mr. Briggs said, leaning against the door jamb. "Turn the tv the hell off, say whatever you came to say, and then get out of here before I call the cops."

"Look, just hear me out." Begonia felt like kicking Jim in his temple. She turned to his wife. "You know that Daisy isn't sleep. She's upstairs, standing by her window, waiting for me." Begonia closed her eyes. *She'll always be waiting for me.* Begonia's heart broke in a thousand places. She gasped at the feeling and grabbed at her chest. Tears sprang to her eyes, and Mrs. Briggs came around the couch to console her.

"Are you all right?"

"No, I'm not." Begonia placed her hand up, halting Mrs. Briggs in her tracks. "You said you wanted to keep Daisy. You said you want her. Did you mean that?"

"Begonia, what's going on? What's the matter with you?"

"Did you mean it?"

"Yes, I meant it."

God, help me, Begonia thought. Tears fell in a steady stream. She pointed the remote at Mr. Briggs. "Do you mean it?"

Mr. Briggs nodded, looking concerned. "Begonia, what is the matter? Are you in some sort of trouble?"

"Mr. Briggs, I'm in more trouble than you could imagine." Begonia walked around the couch and handed the remote to him. "I'm not going to come back here. You tell my sister that I love her very much." Begonia gulped in a mouthful of air and wiped her eyes. She stepped into Mrs. Briggs' face. "You protect my sister, you hear? Don't let anyone hurt her."

She looked over Begonia's shoulder to her husband, who just shrugged. "I love her. I would never let anyone hurt her."

Begonia searched her eyes, looking for any hint of deception.

Mrs. Briggs laid her hand gently on Begonia's arm. "I love Daisy, and I will protect her with my life."

"Okay." Begonia sighed, "Okay." She looked around at their house, with its bright colors and nice furniture. "You have a nice house, Mrs. Briggs. I can't give her this. I can't protect her." She wiped her eyes again and walked out the front door.

I can't protect anyone, but I can try.

Begonia walked away from that house as fast as she could. Her stomach heaved, but she refused to get sick. *God, please watch over my sisters.*

She was a good six blocks away before she slowed down. Scanning the cars on the block, she looked for a good solid hoopty that she could jack quickly. Her eyes landed on a gray beat-up Chevy Celebrity. *That'll work*, she thought as she walked over to the car. She looked up and down the block for movement before squatting down and opening up her bag of tricks. She put her gloves on, pulled out a slim jim, stood up, and stuck it into the driver-side window, popping the lock. It took her two minutes to hotwire the car.

She pulled off the street and headed to South Philly. *Time to go to work*, she thought.

Begonia pulled over on the corner of 17th and Reed. She watched the corner boys make a couple of transactions, waited for their traffic to die down, and then got out of the car. The corner was jumpin'. They had to have made three hundred dollars in the last 45 minutes.

She switched up to the dude she thought was calling the shots. "Aye you, can I talk to you for a moment?"

The young boy looked her up and down and licked his lips. His eyes lingered on her thighs before returning to her eyes. "What can I do for you, sweetheart?"

Begonia returned his smile and eyed the two guys that were with him. They were all babies playing at being hard. *You would think that whoever really ran this corner would put at least one merc on the job,* she thought. *Oh well.* She pulled the gun out of her pants and stuck it in his crotch.

"I'm gonna need ya money, homes."

"Oh, shit, this bitch is strapped."

"You're a fuckin' genious, youngin'. Do you know that? Now, hand over your money and your work, or I'm gonna put three holes in your dick." Begonia patted his pockets with her free hand. She pulled his gun out of his jeans and put it in her bag. "Come on, baby," Begonia said sweetly. "I'm sort of pressed for time."

"Bitch, you must be crazy."

"You're right."

He looked over at his boys. "Aye, y'all just gonna stand there and let this trick jack me?"

Begonia eyed his friends. She pulled dude's gun back out. "Unless you fuckers are faster than a bullet, I'd suggest you lay the fuck down before I lay you down."

His friends hit the deck, no questions asked.

"Aww, y'all some pussies for real." He pulled his money and his bundle out of his pockets and put it Begonia's bag.

"That's a good boy. Now lay down. Gooood." She backed up with both guns trained on them. When her butt hit the car, she licked two shots in the air, hopped in the car, and sped off. She hit two more corners before ditching the car in Frankford and hopping on the shuttle to go home.

Begonia spent the next three nights the same way. That's how long it took for the word to get out that a young girl was sticking up the corners. Word spread like lightning, and real killers were put out on the street with the young boys. *All good things must come to an end*, she thought as she drove by a heavily armed set.

She boosted some couture clothes from Lord and Taylor and sported a short cut wig to change her image. She had only made fifteen grand off of the young boys that she robbed, so she figured it was time to step her game up to robbing ballers, because she was 185 grand away from lifting the bounty off of her and Violet's head.

Shanice walked into McDonald's and headed straight to the counter. Denise leaned over the register and patted her arm.

"Hey, Shani, what's good?"

"Ain't nothing good, girl. Where's my sister? Oh, never mind. I see her." Shanice leaned over the counter and screamed at the top of her lungs. "Hey, Lisa, come here."

Lisa took off her headset and sucked her teeth. "Stop hollering like you're crazy. I'm in enough trouble as is."

"I need to talk to you."

"Okay, we will talk when I get home."

Shanice walked around the counter and swiped at Lisa's headset.

"What are you doing? We talked about this. They are threatening to fire me, girl. Get from back here."

"Lisa, I need to talk to you, and I honestly don't give a flying fuck about this job when it comes to family."

"Family." Lisa pulled her headset off. "What's wrong with our family?" She looked through thc crowd in the front of the restaurant. "Where's Tab? What's going on?"

Shanice frowned. "Tabitha and Erica are fine. I'm talking about Begonia and Violet." Shanice dropped her head down to a whisper. "They have a contract out on them, Lisa. No one has seen Begonia in days, and there is some serious stuff going on. If we don't help them, who will?"

"How in the hell are we supposed to help them, Shanice?"

"Tabitha is outside waiting in the car. We are heading over to Portia's to get to the bottom of what's going on and see if we can help." Shanice turned and walked out.

"Hey, wait," Lisa said. She took her headset off and put it on the counter. "I'm going with you."

Denise picked up Lisa's headset. "I know you're not walking out again. What am I going to tell the manager when she gets back?"

Lisa pulled her purse from under the counter and took her name tag off. "Tell her I quit!"

Chapter 43

Violet put her pillow over her head, but it didn't drown out her cellmates snoring. *This bitch sounds like she's operating a buzz saw,* she thought. Violet almost wished she was back in the infirmary they stuck her in when she flipped the fuck out during her intake. They had her drugged up for two days until one of the staff doctors intervened for the baby's safety. Violet could give a fuck about the damn baby. She longed for the sweet oblivion that the drugs provided. She couldn't feel a thing and spent 40 hours of those two days knocked the fuck out. Her third day, she was examined by every nigga with a lab coat on, they pronounced her well and transferred her over to A-block with all the other pregnant prisoners.

She kicked the top bunk. "Barbara!"

"Huh, what's the matter, Mommy?"

"Shut the hell up. I can't sleep with all that noise."

"What you mean? I'm sleepin', baby. I'm not talkin'."

"No, but you're snoring loud as shit."

"How the fuck can I stop snoring when I'm sleeping, Mommy? That shit don't make no sense." The top bunk creaked loudly as Barbara repositioned herself. "Let me sleep, mamacita. I'm tired as hell."

You're tired, Violet thought. *I know she didn't just say she was tired. I should climb up there and smother this bitch with her own pillow*. Violet counted to ten because she could feel herself about to snap, and she liked Barbara's psychotic ass.

She looked around the cell at all of Barbara's posters and pictures taped to the wall. The entire place was plastered with pink butterflies and Hello Kitty bullshit. Good old Barb was determined to give herself the childhood she never had on the outside. Violet couldn't understand that, but she didn't knock her for it. *Hell, if I can overlook the fact that this bitch stabbed her ex-boyfriend's fiancée to death, than I can overlook her obsession with Rainbow Bright.*

Violet turned on her side and pulled the covers over her head in an attempt to get some kind of rest before the night was over; however, nothing worked. Barbara's snoring became louder, and memories of Kyle floated through her mind; his soft kisses and the way he felt inside of her. He would smile at her in a way that made her feel like she was the only girl in the world.

"Leave it alone, Violet. None of that shit was real," she said softly. "Nobody gang bangs the girl of their dreams, so just let it go."

The buzzer sounded, and all the cell doors clicked open for breakfast. "Damn," was all Violet could say. She kicked her covers off and sat up. "I give up. Not being able to sleep must be part of my punishment.

Barbara climbed down from her bunk. "Morning, mamacita. You look like shit." She pulled her long, ebony hair into a bun and flashed Violet a bright smile.

Violet decided it would be better for both of them if she ignored that comment. She got up, stretched, and left the cell. Violet didn't wash her face or brush her teeth. She left her hair matted and nappy. She found that the worse she looked, the better off she was.

Walking over to the day room, she nodded her head at a couple of people who spoke to her, but that was as far as it went. She wasn't interested in trying to make any friends, plus Barbara had given her the low-down on their cozy little block. Half of the inmates and most of the guards were dikes, and Violet could never swing that way.

Violet could only stand being in the dayroom in the early morning because everyone else was eating or still asleep. She took a seat close to the TV but didn't really watch it.

I wonder if Tab was able to get in touch with Begonia. She had added Tabitha's number to her phone list but didn't have the heart to call her again. She was scared of what Tab might say. She looked over her shoulder at the phone sitting on the corner table and rolled her eyes. *If Begonia knows you are in here, then she'll come and see about you. Harassing Tabitha and her family ain't gonna get you nowhere for real.*

Officer Davis came into the day room and walked in front of the TV. "How come I never see you eating breakfast?"

Violet crossed her arms. "I don't like breakfast."

"Well, that can't be good for the baby."

"I truly don't care about what's good for the baby, Mike."

"Aw, man, don't talk like that. That's not cool."

Violet cocked her head to the side. "Why shouldn't I talk like that, Mike? You came in here, got in my way, and stuck your nose in my business."

"Look, calm down. I was only saying . . ."

"I know what the fuck you were saying." Violet leaned forward in her chair. "It's the same God damned thing everyone has been saying since I got here, but guess what? I don't want this baby. I didn't ask for this baby. I don't give a shit about this baby, and neither does the three motherfuckers who raped me. If you are so concerned about it, I'll give it to you as soon as I pop it out." She stood up so fast that her chair flipped over.

A female officer that Violet wasn't familiar with rushed to Mike's side. He put his hand up to stop her from taking further action, but Violet just gave her a blank stare.

Mike cleared his throat. He walked over toward Violet and picked up her chair. "You know, if you don't want to have the baby, you don't have to."

Violet opened her mouth to say something and then closed it again. The thought of not having the baby never really crossed her mind.

She walked back to her cell in a daze. I *could get rid of it. I wouldn't have to feel their hands on me or taste their sweat every time the baby moved.* She sat down on her bunk, brought her knees up to her chest, and wrapped her arms around them and cried. *This could really be over.*

Barbara ran into the cell, pulled her pants and panties down, and flopped down onto the toilet. "Girl, I swear this baby is sitting his little ass directly on my bladder. I've got to pee every ten minutes. I can barely eat." She rubbed her belly and sighed. "I can't wait to drop this load. I ain't seen my chocha in months. I know it looks like a hairy gorilla puta." She laughed and looked at Violet. "What's the matter with you, mamacita? You in pain or something?"

Violet wiped her eyes on her sleeve. "What do I have to do to get rid of this baby?"

"What do you mean get rid of it?"

Violet just looked at her

Barbara cocked her head to the side, waiting for an explanation. Her eyes bugged out of her face when she finalliy caught on. "Aww, sweetie, why you wanna do that?"

"Do you know how would I go about it?"

Barbara got up and washed her hands. She leaned against the sink. "If this is really what you want to do, sweetie, then you should try to go and see one of the nurses. I'm sure they know how to make that happen." Barbara's thick black eyebrows knitted together, and she looked at Violet with pity and sadness in her eyes.

"Why are you looking at me like that?" Violet asked as she unfolded her legs and stood up. "Not everyone got knocked up on a bed of roses by a man they loved. You don't know what happened to me. You don't have one fucking clue." Violet walked out of the cell before her temper got the best of her. She couldn't handle pity, especially from a psycho bitch that was just as knife happy as her sister.

Violet walked back to the day room. She saw Mike standing next to the water fountain, talking to Brandi. Taking a deep breath, she walked over to them both. "Excuse me." Her voice broke, and she cleared her throat. "I want to talk to someone, a nurse or somebody."

"What's the matter?" Brandi asked. Her voice was laced with honest concern.

Violet took another deep breath as fear wiggled up her spine. Her hands started to tremble, so she balled them into fists and stuck them in her pants pockets. "I need to talk to someone about getting an abortion."

They took her to the nurse, and everything was set up within the week.

Violet did her intake over the phone and received one counseling session by the prison's shrink. The day of the procedure, Violet was numb. They shackled her in her cell and escorted her outside to the bus. She was relieved to see Brandi and Mike standing by the gate.

"Both of you are going with me?"

Brandi smiled, and Mike nodded his head. Violet boarded the bus, put her head back, and closed her eyes.

"How long is it going to take us to get there?"

"About an hour or so," Mike said, sitting in a seat behind Violet. "The traffic is a mess in the morning, so it's gonna take a little longer than usual."

"You okay?" Brandi asked as she sat down beside Violet.

Violet shook her head. *I don't think I'm ever going to be okay again*, she thought as she looked out the window. The baby fluttered in her stomach, and Violet held her breath, willing the movement to stop. She could see Kyle's face, his eyes, and his smile. She remembered the way he smoothed her hair behind her ears and told her that she was beautiful.

She blinked back her tears and shook her head to clear her thoughts of Kyle. She turned to Brandi and forced a smile. "Do y'all do this a lot?"

"Do what?"

"You know, take people out of jail to get abortions."

"I wouldn't say it happens a lot, but it does happen."

"How long does it take?"

"It really depends on the clinic. Sometimes it takes a couple of hours, and sometimes we can be there all damn day."

Violet didn't care how long it took as long as it got done.

An hour later, they pulled up in front of the clinic. Protesters carrying picket signs of tiny caskets lined the pavement. They were shouting and carrying on.

"Murderers! Baby killers! Choose life. Your mother did!"

Brandi walked to the front of the bus, while Mike helped Violet up. "Are you ready for this?" he asked quietly.

"I'm about as ready as I'm going to be," Violet said as she walked to the front of the bus and stood behind Brandi.

Twelve men in red jackets walked out of the clinic. They formed two lines and locked arms, clearing a path to the door. Violet was rushed into the building and taken up service elevators that led right to the back of the clinic.

A short black nurse in white scrubs greeted them and led them to a small exam room. "I'm going to need you to change into this hospital gown and sit on this table. I'll be back when you are done so that I can take your vital signs."

Mike stood guard at the door while Brandi uncuffed Violet and helped her change. "You're not going to freak out on me again, are you?" Brandi asked as she held up the hospital gown. "'Cause I may have to knock your little ass out this time."

"I'm cool," Violet said as she slipped on the gown and hopped up on the table. "You're not going to have to knock me out. I promise.

"Okay," Brandi said with a small smile. She walked over to the door, and Violet panicked.

"Are you leaving? Where are you going?"

"Calm down, honey. I'm going to be right outside the door."

"Okay," Violet said, feeling a little silly. She stared at her hands until Brandi closed the door.

The room smelled like alcohol and disinfectant. The combination made Violet a little nauseous. The nurse came back in with a chart and some medical equipment. She asked Violet a couple of questions, poked and prodded her a bit, and then left.

Violet fought the urge to cry. She lay back on the table and waited for the doctor. When he finally came in, Violet was covered in goose bumps. Her heart was thumping against her ribs, and her blood was rushing in her ears. She couldn't make out a word he was saying.

The nurse instructed Violet to put her feet in the stirrups and scoot her butt down to the edge of the table. Violet's eyes followed the doctor as he washed his hands and took a seat between her legs. Violet stopped looking at him after he slipped on his gloves. Her skin began to crawl as soon as he placed his hands on her stomach. She focused on the ceiling tiles. She tried to count all of the tiny holes in each tile to take her mind off of what he was doing. Tears slid down the sides of her face into her ears.

The nurse offered Violet her hand, and Violet grabbed it and clung to it as if her life depended it on it.

"Shhhhhh." The nurse gently hushed Violet and wiped away her tears. "It's all going to be over soon."

Violet let those words sink inside of her. *It's all going to be over soon,* she thought over and over again. *It's all going to be over soon.* Violet heard the machine switch on and woosh like a vacuum cleaner. She felt a tugging sensation for a few minutes, and then nothing.

It was done.

The baby was gone, but Violet didn't feel any relief at all. She felt empty, hollow, and dirtier than she'd ever felt in her life.

The nurse helped her sit up and put on a pair of underwear with a pad inserted inside. She led Violet into a large recovery room with six beds divided by multi-colored curtains.

"Here, take this." She handed Violet two horse pills and a small cup of water. "You are going to begin cramping heavily, and these pills will help with the pain."

Violet downed the pills and lay down on the hospital bed. The nurse put a heating pad on Violet's stomach, pulled the curtain, and walked away.

I just want to die, Violet thought before she drifted off to sleep.

Chapter 44

Portia drove around for two hours, looking for Begonia.

"This sucks, Portia. Let's go back to the crib because I want to watch cartoons."

"Shut the fuck up, Babygirl. Ain't nobody going home until we find Begonia." Portia eyed Babygirl's outfit. She wore a pink Spandex mini dress with matching pink pumps. "Why the hell are you still wearing that?"

Babygirl rolled her eyes and slumped down in the passenger seat. "It ain't like I had a whole lot of time to change. Shit. I don't even know why we wasting so much time looking for this broad."

"Because she's like a sister to me."

Honey lit a cigarette in the back seat. "Babygirl, you know how Portia gets over family."

"Yeah, I know." Babygirl rolled her hazel eyes. "We are supposed to be like the Musketeers and shit."

Portia smiled. "That's right. One for all, and all for one!"

Honey flicked her ashes out the window and then tapped on Portia's shoulder. "Hey, Portia, I think that's Bee right there."

Portia pulled the car over and looked out the window. "Yeah, that's her."

"What are you going to tell her?" Honey asked.

"I'll make up something."

Babygirl sucked her teeth. "Why are you bitches making up stories anyway? Let's just make her get in the car."

"Bitch, you must be four different kinds of crazy if you think we can make Begonia do anything."

Portia got out of the car and leaned against it. "Where the hell did you get those fancy shoes, bitch?"

Begonia could tell Portia's voice from anywhere, but she didn't feel up to dealing with her right now. *Just stop, Bee. You know that she ain't gonna leave you alone if you ignore her.*

Begonia stopped walking. She pasted a smile on her face and turned around to talk to her friend. "I got them from your closet two weeks ago."

Portia took a good look at the shoes again and shook her head. "I'll be damned if those ain't my shoes."

Babygirl started laughing. "Yo, she's a cold-ass thief, man, I swear."

"Shut up, Babygirl," Honey said, flicking her butt onto the street and getting out of the car to stand next to Portia.

Begonia walked over to Portia's car. "What's up, Honey? What the hell do you want, Portia?"

Portia smiled. "What, no hug?"

"Get the fuck outta here with all that. T-Bird told me you were riding around looking for me. You found me, so what's up?"

"I need your help on a job."

"What kind of job?" Begonia asked, although she already knew. Her stomach clenched at the thought of tricking. She hated that shit with a passion, but she was running out of options.

Babygirl burst out laughing. "What the fuck she means what kind of job? What kind of work does this bitch think we do?"

Begonia frowned and bent over to see who was talking shit inside the car. Portia side-stepped to block Begonia's view, and Honey turned around and stuck her head in the car.

"Say one more motherfucking thing and I'm gonna beat the bullshit out of you, and I mean it."

Portia lit her cigarette. "A couple of execs from California are in town for a business meeting, and they want to have an orgy with a few hood rats."

Begonia's stomach flipped. "You buggin', Portia. I ain't doing no damn orgy." Begonia turned around and started to walk back across the street.

"Okay, so you don't need this money. Cool."

Begonia paused. "How much?"

"Ten grand."

Begonia wanted to walk away, but she couldn't. She needed that ten grand more than she needed air. She turned to face Portia. "One night."

Portia nodded. "One night."

Begonia walked around the car and got in the back.

Honey looked at Portia and shook her head before sliding into the back seat next to Begonia.

Begonia walked into Portia's house and sat down in the living room. *So now I'm gonna turn into a hardcore ho*, she thought as she put her feet up on the coffee table. *You are really following in Doreen's footsteps, Bee.*

Honey knocked Begonia's feet off the table and sat down next to her. Babygirl flopped down on the steps, and Portia stood by the door.

"Well, what's up?" Begonia asked. "Can a bitch get a drink?"

Honey crossed her legs. "As soon as a bitch turns twenty-one."

Begonia rolled her eyes. "Whatever. I'm old enough to turn tricks but not old enough to drink? Get the fuck out of here."

Babygirl started laughing, and Honey shot her an evil look.

"Hey, Peanut." Portia hollered into the kitchen. "Bring Begonia a fifth of vodka, please.

Peanut came out of the kitchen with a small bottle and Tabitha, Shanice, and Lisa.

"What the hell?" Begonia sat up in her chair. "Aw, naw, don't tell me you guys are tricking too?" She looked at Portia. "What the fuck? Do you actually work for the devil or something?"

Portia nodded her head,. "The fucking dental plan is amazing."

Shanice sat on the edge of the coffee table and faced Begonia. "We came here to talk to you."

"About what?"

Lisa motioned for Babygirl to move over on the steps, and she sat down beside her. "We know that you and Violet are in trouble, Bee."

Begonia looked around at all of them like they were crazy. "And how do you guys know that?"

"Come on now, Bee," Portia said softly. "You have a two hundred thousand dollar price tag on your head. The streets are whispering your name, sweetie pie. That's how I know. I also know that you've been playing stickup kid to the small sets all around Philly."

"I don't know what you're talking about."

Shanice's shoulders slumped. "Come on, Bee. Everybody in this room knows that you're the chick hitting up the corners."

"I ain't hitting up shit, and I don't have time for this." Begonia stood up. "I came over here to suck some dick for some quick cash. If that's not happening, then I gotta bounce, 'cause I don't have time for this bullshit here."

"Sit down, Bee," Lisa said from the steps.

"Fuck you, Lisa." Begonia headed for the door, but Shanice stood up and got in her way.

"Move, Shanice."

"No." Tears sprang to Shanice's eyes.

"I'm not going to ask you again."

"What are you gonna do, Begonia, huh? You gonna fuck me up?" Fat tears fell down Shanice's face. "Fuck me up then, but I ain't moving out of your way."

Begonia tried to shove Shanice out of her way, but Honey jumped up and grabbed her arms.

"Get the fuck off of me," Begonia screamed. She shimmied out of Honey's grasp and swung on her. Honey ducked, and Lisa leaped over the coffee table and tackled Begonia. They both fell on the couch.

"Get the fuck off of me," Begonia screamed.

Portia climbed over Lisa and grabbed Begonia's hair. "You are going to die, Begonia. You hear me? They are going to kill Violet and Daisy and then you. You need help, so stop acting so fucking retarded and let us help you. You cannot do this by yourself."

Begonia stopped struggling and collapsed against the sofa. Lisa let her go and slid down on the floor beside her. She wiped her eyes on her sleeve and patted Begonia's leg. "We are going to get through this together."

"How?" Begonia moaned. She looked up at Portia. "You got two hundred K? Is pussy paying that good? What about you, Lisa? We robbing McDonald's tonight? How are y'all going to help me?"

Babygirl stood up from the steps. "Well, first off, if you turn off the fucking waterworks and the all that damn drama, we can tell you how we plan to help."

"I thought I told you to shut the fuck up."

"Naw, Honey, damn. We trying to help this bitch, and she wanna fight and cry like a little-ass girl."

Portia shot Babygirl a look hot enough to melt ice cubes in the freezer, and Babygirl sat down and stared at her sneakers.

"Thank you. Damn." She climbed down off the couch and sat on the coffee table. "We're gonna set Rodney up."

"How in the hell are we going to do that?" Begonia asked softly.

Portia snatched the bottle out of Peanut's hand and took a quick swig. "I have a plan."

Chapter 45

Tabitha signed Erica into her daycare center, kissed her goodbye, and watched her run into her classroom to be with her friends. She zipped her jacket back up and put her purse back on her shoulder before walking back to her car. Although it was a pretty warm day, bright and sunny with little to no wind, Tabitha felt a chill down to her bones.

"Its okay, Tab. Everything is going to be okay." She had to have said that to herself a thousand times before leaving the house, and a thousand more times on the way to the daycare center, but she really didn't think it would be. Buckling her seatbelt, she took a big gulp from her tea to try to steady her nerves.

It wasn't working.

She drove home on auto pilot. Darren and Tony were already loading Erica's bed and dresser onto the UHaul truck parked in front of her mother's house.

"Hey, baby," Darren shouted when he spotted Tabitha walking up the steps.

"Hey, I'm gonna go put my purse up and come help you."

"Aw, baby, you don't have to do that. We got this."

"Are you sure?"

"Yeah, baby, relax. It's not like we have to pack up the whole house. We'll be done in no time."

Tony stuck his head out of the truck. "A brotha could use a fried egg or two and some bacon."

Tabitha laughed. "Are you hungry too, baby?"

"Now, you know I'm not going to turn down food."

"Okay, guys, I got the hint. Breakfast coming right up." Tabitha put her purse on the couch and hollered up the steps. "Mom, I'm back. Do you want something to eat? Because I'm about to cook." She didn't wait for a reply. Walking into the kitchen, she washed her hands and started to pull out everything she would need.

Shanice walked into the kitchen and sat down at the kitchen table. "I want some eggs."

Tabitha rolled her eyes. "Why aren't you in school?"

"Well, damn, good morning to you too."

"Don't start, Shanice. I'm really not able to take it this morning." She sprayed the frying pan with Pam and turned the flame on. "Go ask Momma if she wants bacon and eggs or something different."

"Momma Mabel's not here. She went to the church with my mom."

"And they just left you here?"

"They didn't know I was still here because I was sorta hanging out in the basement."

"Where's Lisa?"

"She's with Portia's girls, getting schooled on how to be a high class ho. She's going to be there all day. They're supposed to go shopping and junk later."

Tabitha dropped the eggs she was holding onto the floor. "Awwww, fuck!" She grabbed the dish towel off the sink and stooped down to clean up the mess. "You know what, Shanice? Nobody needs your shit right now, so why don't you just suck it up and go to school?"

"Because," Shanice said while bending down to help her sister, "you need my shit right now."

Tabitha's hands trembled as she picked the egg shells up and threw them in the trash can. She stood up, leaned against the counter, and looked at her hands. "I'm scared," she said barely over a whisper.

"I know." Shanice stood up and turned the flame down on the stove. She washed her hands and bumped Tabitha gently to the side with her hip.

"Everything is happening so fast, Shani. It's too fast. I mean, look, we're not gangstas. Lisa's not hard. She likes to act tough, but she's not tough for real. I think we may be in over our heads."

"So what are you saying, Tabitha? We can't back out. There isn't anybody else that can pull this off."

"I'm not saying we should back out. I'm just saying that it's all too much, and with the move and everything, I feel like I'm about to fall apart." Tabitha got more eggs out of the refrigerator while Shanice put the bacon on. "Maybe I should tell Darren that we need to call this off, you know, wait a little while longer before we move in together."

Shanice cracked the eggs into a bowl and threw the shells in the trash. "Don't do that."

"Don't do what?"

"You know what you're doing."

"What?"

"Don't try to use this mess as an excuse not to move in with Darren. Y'all are getting married in six months."

Tabitha sighed. "I'm not saying that I'm calling off the wedding or anything. I'm just saying that maybe we should wait a while, you know, until everything calms down."

"And then you will find another excuse to put it off."

"I'm not looking for excuses."

"Hell if you're not. You've been looking for excuses not to go through with this ever since Darren asked you to marry him. What the fuck are you afraid of?"

"Him. I'm afraid of him."

"Why?"

"What do you mean *why*? You don't know what it's like to live with a man. You don't have a clue."

"I know he's not Eric."

"What are you talking about?"

Shanice turned the burner off and faced her oldest sister. "He's not Eric, Tabitha. He's not going to hit you or rape you or leave you. He loves you, and you don't have to be afraid, because he's not Eric, and when you move with him, you are not going to lose us."

"What if I do, huh? What if he doesn't want y'all to come around?"

"He is not Eric, Tabitha. And nobody can keep me and Lisa away from you." She pulled Tabitha into a hug. "We are sisters, and nobody can change that."

Tabitha squeezed Lisa tight and then pulled away. "You're right. I'm being silly." She wiped her eyes and flagged Shanice away from the stove. "Move over. I'll finish this."

"You sure?"

"Hell yeah, I'm sure. I don't need those guys dying from food poisoning."

"I can cook my ass off."

"Now I know you're crazy."

Shanice laughed. "It is going to be okay, you know. Everything is going to work out."

"I hope you are right, Shani. I swear to God, I do."

Chapter 46

Begonia woke up with a banging headache. She opened her eyes and immediately closed them, because the bright light felt like sharp needles being pushed into her sockets. The night's events were fuzzy—there was a lot of talking and a lot of crying, followed by a lot of drinking.

"Morning, sunshine!" Portia said too damn loudly as she walked in.

"Shhhhhh." Begonia tried to sit up but fell back on the pillow, holding her head and moaning.

"Awwww, po' baby." Portia clicked the lights off and closed the blinds. She sat on the edge of bed and shook her head. "You really are just a baby, you know?"

Begonia stuck her middle finger up at Portia and tried to open her eyes again. *Sweet, sweet darkness,* she thought with a small smile. "Oh, thank you so much."

"You are welcome." Portia pulled a pill bottle out of her pocketbook and poured two pills into the cap and handed them to Begonia.

"What's this?" she said before popping them into her mouth and looking around for water.

Portia handed her a bottle of spring water from the nightstand. "It's Valium. You need to get some real sleep. I'll be back in a few hours." She got up and walked to the door.

"Damn, bitch. What you got, a job interview?"

Portia was dressed in a satin silver blouse and a black pencil skirt. "What the fuck I look like going to a job interview?" She smiled. "You know I work the missionary position. Naw, but really, I'm going to see the DA to call in a favor. It's time to put our plan in motion. You may want to wash your ass because if everything goes like it's supposed to, you will be meeting with his assistant tonight."

Richard Jamison had clawed his way out of one of the worst hoods in West Philadelphia. The youngest of nine children, his mother liked to tell everyone that he came out last but ended up first. He was the first to graduate high school and then college, first to own a car and then a home. Richard liked leading the pack. If there was an award, he would win it. If there was a record, he would break it. He learned early in life that everyone loved a winner, and so he decided to win everything.

Point blank.

The youngest district attorney in Philadelphia's history, his record was nearly flawless—his conviction rates the highest in the state. They called him the hammer because he showed no mercy. If you did the crime, Richard would not sleep until you did the time.

Brushing imaginary lint off of his Armani suit, he checked his reflection in the elevator door before he reached his floor. He stood six feet six inches and weighed 225 pounds of pure muscle. With his smooth caramel complexion, broad shoulders, and piercing dark brown eyes, Richard was so handsome that he made straight men stop and stare.

Richard stepped off the elevator and walked down the hall, nodding to his colleagues. No one stopped him for idle chit-chat because no one there particularly liked him. Richard didn't give a shit. He didn't plan to stay in the DA's office very long. Bigger and better things awaited this brother, and he knew it. Success was his only friend, and poverty was his only enemy.

He opened the door to his office, took off his coat, hung it on the rack, and then almost shit on himself. Richard Jamison had one weakness, and she was sitting in the corner of his office, reading the *Daily News*.

"What the fuck are you doing here, Portia?"

Portia folded her paper and tossed it on the floor. “Is that how you greet your friends, Ricky?”

Richard peeked out of his office window before closing the blinds, locking his door, and taking a seat at his desk. “You aren’t my friend, Portia. Now, what do you want, and what are you doing here?”

“Oh, I’m your friend, baby. What was it you whispered in my ear the last time you *came* over my house? Oh yeah, you said I was the best friend you ever had.” Portia walked over to Richard and sat on his desk directly in front of him.

“What are you playing at, Portia? What do you need, hush money?” Richard eyes slid up and down Portia’s profile. She might have dressed it up, but he knew that it was some Grade-A hood rat pussy beneath those fancy clothes. His dick got hard just remembering the way it felt to slide inside of her.

“Aw, Ricky, Ricky, Ricky, you know I wouldn’t fuck you for all the money in the world. I will, however, fuck you for a favor.” She hiked her skirt up to her hips, sat on his desk, and cocked her legs open.

Richard shook his head and looked away, but he couldn’t stop his hand from grabbing his dick, or his breaths from coming hot and heavy.

Portia raised her left leg onto his lap and dug the heel of her pump into his thigh. Richard put his hand in his mouth to stop himself from hollering out in pure ecstasy. Sweat broke out on Richard's brow as moans escaped out his mouth around his fist.

Portia arched her eyebrow. "I see that none of the high-classed bitches you screwing are giving it to you how you like it." She flicked her other heel off and kicked him in his face hard. His head snapped back, and his hand fell out of his mouth.

"What do you want, Portia?"

"I want to know if you tell all those pretty ladies you sport around town that you like it rough." She grabbed his tie and wrapped it around his fist. "Huh, Richard, do they know that you're a wimpy little masochist? Stand up."

Richard stood up without protest. It had been a long time since he'd been with a sadist. He knew he needed to stop sleeping with call girls before word got out and his career went up in smoke.

Portia unbuckled his pants and pulled his dick out. "Awww, Ricky, you really miss me, don't you?" She spit on her free hand and slathered it up and down Richards's shaft in swift motions, twisting and jerking the skin, causing ripples of pain and pleasure to shoot down his groin.

Richard put his hands on his desk around Portia to brace himself. "What do you want, girl?"

Portia slapped him so hard that his lip split open and blood dripped down on her blouse. "Did I say you could talk, Ricky?" She put the tip of his penis inside of her. Richard began to shiver.

"Did I say it was okay for you to open your fucking mouth?" She dug her nails in his ass and pushed him all the way inside of her. "For right now, big boy, I need you to listen." She tightened her walls against his swollen rod.

"Jesus," he breathed.

"I'm going to let that one slide, playboy," she said while loosening her hold on his ass. "Now, let's talk business," she whispered as she arched her back and let him move in and out of her on his own accord.

Portia's voice came out husky and jagged as Richard delivered hard, angry thrusts. "I have a word on a bust that will place you quite comfortably in the mayor's chair next election."

Richard wanted to ask her what she was talking about, but it was hard to think of anything outside of how wet she was, and she had not yet granted him permission to speak. She placed her hands up on his chest to slow him down and lifted his shin so she could look him in the eye.

"If you agree to help my friends, I will hand you the man that is responsible for providing every junkie in North Philly with crack rock." She placed her hands on his chest to slow his speed, and then she raised his chin so that she could look him in the eye. She tightened and released her walls so that her pussy felt like it was sucking him off.

Richard shivered.

"You have my permission to speak."

Richard's breath came out in a rush. "I'm going to need more information."

"Is that a yes?" Portia asked as she unlocked her legs from around his waist and scooted away from him.

He fell out of her with a growl. "Like I said, I need more information."

Portia took that as a yes. "Meet me at the Holiday Inn in one hour, and I'll give you all the information you need. Oh, and you might want to stop at a pharmacy for a first aid kit, because I intend to make you bleed."

Chapter 47

Violet spent two days in her cell after her procedure. She thought that she would feel better after they took the baby.

She was wrong.

Her celly, Barbara, tried her best to comfort her. She braided her hair and held her when she cried. She smuggled her in rolls and juice boxes from the cafeteria, but she knew that her presence disturbed Violet because she was so far into her own pregnancy, so she mostly stayed away.

Violet felt as if she left a chunk of her own soul in that exam room. On the third day, hunger pains forced her off of her bunk and out into the cafeteria. She picked up a tray and stood in line, ignoring everyone and everything that went on around her. She had never felt so alone in her life, and she didn't understand why she was living at all.

I never should have took his car, she thought. *I should have took one of his guns out of the closet and swallowed a few bullets*. Violet took her tray to an empty corner and scarfed down the food. It all looked like shit, but she ate so fast that she didn't taste a thing. Gagging, she braced her hands on the table and forced down the rest of the food in her mouth. Her eyes watered, but her throat cleared, and she continued shoveling food down her mouth to sate her hunger like she never choked.

Officer Mike walked over to her. "You know, that plate of food wasn't threatening to run away, was it?"

Violet didn't even look at him. She gulped down her glass of water, grabbed her tray, cleaned it off, and dumped it on the counter.

Mike watched her for a second before following after her. "Violet, I need to talk to you."

"About what?" Violet asked as she continued down the hall toward the yard.

Brandi walked past Mike and waved Violet back. "Come on, girl. You have a visitor."

Violet's heart leaped as Begonia sprang to her mind. *She's here. I can't believe she's here.* Violet almost ran over to Brandi and Mike. Her heart did the jitterbug in her chest. She shook her hands nervously as she followed behind the two guards. *Oh my God, what am I going to say to her? What is she going to say to me?* The switch was visible. Violet's brief moments of joy and excitement for seeing her sister morphed into terror at what her sister was there to say. Her palms began to sweat, and her heart's jitterbug turned into a jackhammer beating against her rib cage.

Mike walked past the place designated for visits. When Violet gave him a confused look, he just shrugged and motioned for her to continue following him.

They led her to a small room that looked like the interrogation room used on *Law and Order*. Three white men dressed in black suits sat at a small rectangular table in the middle of the room. The men varied in size and age, but they all seemed scary as hell to Violet. She tried to back out of the room and ran smack-dab into Mike's chest. She turned around to face him.

"Who are these guys, and what do they want with me?"

"They want to talk to you."

Violet looked at Brandi, and she nodded her head in agreement. "Well, I don't want to talk to them. Let me go back to my cell."

"I'm afraid we can't do that, Violet," said the oldest of the three. He was just a couple of inches taller than Violet. His ice blue eyes were cold under circular wire-rimmed glasses. Bald, his head shone under the light like it had recently been waxed, and his mustache and short cropped goatee were jet black and sprinkled with gray. He held out his hand for Violet to shake, but she recoiled back into Mike's chest as if she thought his hand was a poisonous snake about to strike.

"It's okay, Violet. None of these men are here to hurt you. They just want to talk to you. Go have a seat and hear what they have to say. Brandi and I will be right out here in the hall if you need us."

Feeling embarrassed, Violet took a seat and eyed the other two men in the room. They didn't look as scary as the old guy. The man sitting in front of the machine had fire red hair and looked like some sort of hippie-nerd crossbreed.

The third and biggest guy in the room was taller than Violet sitting down in his chair. He had a golden tan and dark hair and eyes. The older guy cleared his throat and introduced himself again, minus the handshake.

"Ms. Brown, my name is Edward Clements, and I am the Assistant District Attorney in Philadelphia. This is Bradley Thompson, a US Marshal, and Rodger Dunn from the Federal Bureau of Prisons. We are here to review your application for the Federal Witness Protection Program."

Violet's mouth dropped open. She looked from one man to the next in complete shock and confusion. "I didn't apply to any program."

Edward opened a manila folder and slid it over in front of Violet. "Do you know who this person is?"

Violet looked at the picture of Rodney and nodded her head.

Edward pulled the folder back over and thumbed through it. "Your sister, a Ms. Begonia Brown, is working with the DA's office to bring this man to justice. Your sister has implied that you have inside information on his organization, and that information will be helpful to our case. She's told us that you will turn state's evidence in exchange for a reduced sentence and acceptance in the program."

Violet's head spun. She blinked several times and cleared her throat, trying to process what was said. "Begonia told you guys that I would testify against Rodney. Are you serious? Does she know, I mean, do you guys even know what this man is capable of?"

Edward opened his mouth to respond, but the big guy held his hands up to cut him off. He turned to Violet. "Your sister said that you would be suspicious of us, and you have every right to be. However, she told us that Rodney put a bounty on not just your head, but on your sister's head as well. I am here to inform you that it would be in your best interest to cooperate. This man's arm has a long reach, and it wouldn't be the first time that he reached through the bars of an institution like this."

Violet couldn't care less about Rodney reaching through the prison bars to kill her. She wished for death every moment of every damn day, but she couldn't see her family paying such a high price for her mistakes. She took a deep breath and sat up straight in her chair.

"What do you need me to do?"

Chapter 48

Babygirl sat on the sofa Indian style, eating cereal and watching Begonia pace back and forth across the living room floor. "Why don't you sit the fuck down, yo? you making me dizzy."

"How the fuck can I sit down when no one's here? We were supposed to leave an hour ago, yet nobody's come back yet. We have a plan, and we agreed on a time to meet after we left the marshal's office."

"And you think walking back and forth in front of the TV is going to make everybody come home faster? Sit the hell down."

"Who are you talking to?"

Babygirl looked around the empty room. "Is there somebody here besides you?"

"I think you need to shut the fuck up and stop talking to me, 'cause I don't know you, I don't like you, and I don't have a problem with fuckin' you up."

"Aw, shit. Now that's what I'm talking about." Babygirl put her cereal bowl down and stood up. "I've wanted to kick your ass since I met—"

Begonia punched her in her face before she could finish her sentence. Babygirl fell back onto the couch with a smile. She wiped the blood off of her lip and got back up slowly. She jumped in the air and twisted around, kicking Begonia in the chest. Begonia fell back into the banister. "Let me find out that your little high yellow ass knows how to fight." She pulled her switchblade from her back pocket. "Let's play."

Portia walked in the door dressed in a black plastic jumpsuit and carrying a whip. "What the fuck is going on in here?"

Babygirl sat back down on the couch and picked up her cereal bowl. "Nothing. We were just waiting for everybody to come in."

Begonia closed her knife and put it back in her pocket. "What the fuck do you have on?"

"Our friend the DA likes to be dominated, and this get-up turns him on."

"I thought that was over with."

"That's why I stopped fucking with him in the first place, because it's never over with. Once he gets a taste of it, he needs it every day. He's sick, and I'm tired."

Begonia felt a pang of shame deep in her gut. "I'm so sorry, Portia."

Portia looked at her like she was crazy. "What are you sorry for? This is what I do, and I will do this and much, much more for my family."

"Portia, do you think they've talked to Violet yet?"

"Yeah, Ricky said they spoke to her today, and she's being transferred. Now, give me ten minutes. I need to get out of this hot shit and shower all of Ricky's blood and sweat off of me. When I come back down, we'll go over the plan again. In the meantime, you and Babygirl can count the money. Oh, and If I hear you guys fighting again, it's not going to be pretty. So try me if you want to."

Begonia looked at Babygirl and smiled. "I guess we'll finish this later?"

"You bet your ass we will," Babygirl said as she walked over to the safe by the minibar. She handed Begonia her knapsack and pulled out four large stacks of cash wrapped in plastic.

"What the hell do y'all wrap it up like that for?"

"Oh, so we're talking now?"

"Don't be an ass."

Babygirl smiled. She was really starting to likc Begonia. "I don't have any idea why Portia wraps her money up, and as long as she keeps my cereal stocked up, I don't really care."

"Are you trying to tell me that you trick for cereal?"

"Hell naw, I like cookies too."

Begonia could do nothing but stare. She reached into her bag and pulled out two rubber-banded knots of money. "I've counted this over and over again. It's twenty-five stacks."

Babygirl just nodded her head as she counted the money in Portia's stash.

She was almost finished when Portia came back downstairs dressed in sweats. "You know I really can't stand the sight of blood. I can't wait until all of this dumb shit is over so I can part ways with the good DA." She looked at the money on the table, opened the china closet door, and pulled out a silver .38 and stuck it in her waistband. "What has been counted?"

Begonia pointed to her money. "That's twenty-five K."

"Good," Portia said, pouring herself a glass of wine. "I've got about fifty thousand in that safe."

"I can't take all of your money."

Portia downed the glass and poured another. "That's funny, 'cause I would take all of your cash in a heartbeat." She grabbed another glass from the china closet and poured a corner for Begonia. "You know I've watched you and your sisters struggle for years. I've always wanted to help, but you would never let me."

"You wanted me to join this brothel."

"Yeah, I call that helping. Trust me, growing up in a whore house is way better than growing up in a crack house."

"Bullshit," Begonia said, taking a sip of the wine. She made a face and put the glass down.

"What's wrong with the wine?"

"Nothing, I'd just rather have vodka."

"Well," Portia said, emptying Begonia's glass into hers, "I'd rather you weren't fucked up when you go see Rodney tonight."

"Who gets fucked up off of one little shot of vodka?"

Portia cracked open a bottle of Smirnoff. "When have you ever stopped at one shot?"

Begonia eyed the gun hilt sticking out of Portia's sweatpants. "You plan on shooting somebody tonight?"

"No, I don't plan on it, but my money is on the table, and Peanut isn't here." Portia shrugged. "I'll shoot a motherfucker if I have to."

Babygirl tore into the last bundle of money. "What I want to know is what's wrong with living in a whore house."

Both Begonia and Portia looked at Babygirl like she was crazy. "Oh, y'all was just playing, huh?"

"Where the hell did you get this chick from, Portia?"

"Kmart. They were having a buy one, get one sale."

"Fuck both of y'all," Babygirl said, pushing the money into the center of the table. "There's sixty-two thousand here, Portia."

"Okay, cool. Put twelve thousand back in the safe and the rest in Bee's bag."

***

Lisa sat in the back of Peanut's car, thinking about Tony. They broke up about six months ago, but she still felt as though she was about to betray him. She still loved him. She would admit that to herself, but nobody else. She thought that he still loved her. *God knows he still hangs around like he does.*

Tony took the breakup hard. They had been through a lot together, so he didn't understand her decision. Lisa thought it was cut and dry. She couldn't see a future with a drug dealer. She wanted to get married and raise a family. She wanted to travel and see the world. How could she do any of that with someone who hugged the block as hard as Tony?

Lisa stared at the setting sun out of the car window. The sky was washed in pretty purple and pink hues. She'd left Tony because of drugs, and now she was going to sell herself to a kingpin to buy her friend some time. She looked down at her French manicure and sighed. What a difference a day makes.

She wondered what Tony would say seeing her dressed up like this. *He would probably shit on himself,* she thought, smiling. This was the first time she wore anything other than pants or shorts in about two years. Lisa even stopped wearing nightgowns to bed, preferring boxers, and now she wasn't going to get to wear either. In a few minutes, they were going to head to a lingerie shop on South Street to get her a bunch of skimpy, silly mess to sleep in with Rodney.

A shiver ran up her spine with that thought. She'd only slept with two men in her life: Tony and her stepfather. The thought of Rodney touching her made her skin crawl. *And just how are you going to get over that part, Genius? You want to play at being a prostitute like it's as normal as flipping burgers at McDonalds. How are you going to handle another evil man putting his hands all over you?*

Lisa had no answer for that. *I guess I'll cross that bridge when I get to it,* she thought with a small frown. She closed her eyes, sat back in her seat, and took a deep breath to focus her mind on the present.

Peanut and Honey were in the beer distributor, refilling Portia's stock. "What are they buying, all the damn beer in the store?"

Lisa was being left alone with her thoughts way too long. She began to rock back and forth slightly. Her nerves were getting the best of her. Even though it was her idea to sleep with Rodney, she couldn't believe it was about to go down.

"This is what you wanted to do, Lisa," she said to herself, half sad, half angry.

She had to spend half the night trying to convince everyone it was the only way. Lisa knew that Rodney wouldn't accept any of the other girls for the rate that they were asking, and she knew that she would demand top dollar because of Tony. Rodney had spent the better part of a year trying to seduce her away from Tony. He would tell her how fucked up it was that she had to serve french fries to fat fuckers all day and how if she was his lady, looking good and relaxing would be her only job.

"What grown woman wants to play at being a real life Barbie all damn day?"

Peanut and Honey came out of the beer distributor. Honey was carrying a brown paper bag, and Peanut was pushing a hand cart with five cases of beer stacked on it. Honey got in the car and popped the trunk.

"Damn, you really just going to sit there, huh?"

"You damn straight. What the fuck did I tell you in the store? I don't do manual labor, baby. Stop crying like a little bitch." Honey popped open a can of beer and handed it back to Lisa.

"Oh, no thank you. I don't drink like that."

Honey turned around in her seat to look Lisa in the eye. "Take it from a professional, baby. You gonna need a little buzz going to get through this night."

Lisa took the beer, sipped it, and then held it in her lap. Honey nodded at her and then turned around. She popped another can open for herself, chugged it, and then lit a cigarette. "Will the smoke bother you, sis?"

Lisa cleared her throat. "No, I'm all right."

"You ready for all this shit?"

"I'm about as ready as I'm going to be."

"You little bitches really got balls."

"Excuse me?"

"Oh, no disrespect, love. I'm just amazed at the lengths that y'all will go for each other." Honey took a few gulps of her beer. "I ain't never had nobody do nothing for me until I met Portia. You bitches bang for each other from the gate. I mean, for real, look at what you about to do for ol' girl. Y'all not even related."

"We're related," Lisa said as Peanut got into the car. Lisa took another swig of her beer. "We ain't blood, but we're damn sure related."

Honey took a long pull off her cigarette. "You sound like Portia."

Lisa smiled but said nothing. *Begonia may not be blood, but she is family,* she thought, *and family means everything.*

Honey had them in and out of the sex shop, and Lisa was now armed with enough silken, skimpy shit that would give an 85-year-old grandpa a stiffy.

By the time they pulled up in front of Portia's speakeasy, Lisa had finished her beer, and her buzz was in full gear. She felt a weird mix of nervousness, excitement, and fear. Everyone one knew that Rodney was a no-good nigga, but Lisa remembered the look in Tony's eyes when he came home after witnessing Rodney beat a 15-year-old boy to death for coming up short. Lisa knew that Rodney was a murderer without any remorse. He was a baby killer that would kill Begonia, Violet, and Daisy without blinking. That's why she was doing what she was doing. That's what she kept in the forefront of her mind. That's what was going to get her through.

Lisa walked into Portia's house and was relieved to see Tabitha and Shanice sitting at the living room table with Portia, Begonia, Babygirl, April, and Mookey.

Tabitha's mouth fell open at the sight of her.

"Oh my God," Shanice hollered out. "Bitch, you look fucking gorgeous!"

Lisa smiled, but Honey spoke out first. "I do good work, don't I?"

Lisa was dressed in a brown slinky shift that came down just above her knee. Her trademark braids were gone, replaced by a sleek wrap that hung down past her shoulders. She'd had her eyebrows waxed when they did her nails, and then Honey took her to the MAC counter at the mall to have the ladies there make her face up and teach her how to apply her own makeup. Lisa looked like a wet dream walking, and Tabitha and Shanice were amazed by the transformation.

Tabitha got up and rushed around the table to hug her little sister. Tears sprang to her eyes. "You look beautiful," she said while holding her sister tight.

"Thank you, Tab."

Shanice reached for Begonia's hand under the table and squeezed it tight. Begonia looked at her but said nothing. She didn't know what to say. It was still hard to believe that they were doing this. She had met every obstacle in her life by herself, so it was very odd to have so much support. Begonia was speechless.

Lisa took a deep, shuddering breath as she pulled away from her sister. "Stop crying, Tabby, because you are going to make me cry and ruin all this good makeup."

Begonia squeezed Shanice's hand quickly and then walked over to stand by Lisa.

Portia stood up, hefted the bag of money off the table, and passed it to Honey, who handed it to Begonia.

Portia looked at Lisa, who still had her hands wrapped around her older sister. "You clean up nice, youngin'. Are you ready for this?"

Lisa nodded her head.

"This is the last time you have to change your mind." Portia swept her hand over the heads of the girls at the table. "Any of my girls will trade places with you in a heartbeat, so I'm going to ask you this one last time. Do you want to go through with this? Because you don't have to."

Lisa shook her head and let go of her sister. "I'm not changing my mind, Portia. If fucking a dude is gonna buy my girl here some more time, then pass the condoms and the KY, 'cause I'm ready."

The girls at the table started cracking up. Portia looked at Begonia. "Ricky just called me and told me that the Assistant DA has met with Violet, and she is being transferred as we speak."

Begonia walked to the door. She was about to put her friend in harm's way. She really didn't have anything to say other than, "I'll see y'all later." With that, she walked out the door.

Shanice got up to hug Lisa before she left. "Please be careful." Tabitha joined in with the hug. "Call us as soon as you can."

Lisa said nothing. She just followed Begonia out.

Shanice buried her face in her hands and cried. Portia poured herself another glass of wine. "Don't worry, Shanice. Rodney's dick and ego is going to have a meeting, and then he's going to fall for this hook, line, and sinker."

Shanice wiped her eyes and shook her head. "I hope you're right, Portia."

Portia raised her glass to Shanice. "I don't know a lot of things, but I know pussy is a powerful thing."

***

Begonia walked into Rodney's house, took one look at the stiches on Big Mike's cheek, and smiled. "Nice tattoo."

Big Mike jumped off his stool, pulled his gun out, and stuck it in Begonia's face. "Oh, you real funny, bitch. How about I put a hole in your fucking cheek?"

Begonia laughed. "Aww, Big Mike, you are so sensitive, a real softy. Can't you tell when a girl is paying you a compliment?"

Honey walked in the door and pushed Mike's gun out of Begonia's face. "Put that away before you hurt somebody."

Mike lowered his gun just as Lisa walked in. Honey grabbed Mike's chin and turned his face toward her. "Mike, be a good guard dog and go fetch your master, because we have business to discuss with him."

The intercom on the wall by Mike's head buzzed, and Tweet's high-pitched voice came through loud and clear. "Rodney said have them searched and then bring them down."

Mike nodded his head at two young boys sitting on the couch. The boys sprang into action, pinning them to the wall and having a good time searching them thoroughly for weapons. "They're clean, Mike."

"A'ight, take them downstairs."

Begonia's stomach clenched as she walked down the basement steps. She expected to see plastic covering the floor stained with blood.

Begonia stood up straight and forced herself to walk over to the desk. She put the duffle bag on the table in front of Rodney.

Rodney smirked. "Word on the street is you've been a busy little bee." He pointed to the bag. "Is that all of my money?"

"No," Begonia said simply.

Rodney nodded to Amir, and Amir opened the bag and started to count the money. Rodney leaned back in his chair. "Come on, Begonia. You're a smart girl. Why would you come here without all of my money?"

Honey switched over to them and sat on the corner of the desk. "We're here because Portia wanted to make a deal with you."

"What makes you think that I'll deal with tricks?"

"Tricks make the world go round. Sex sells, and you're a businessman. Portia is invested in our girl here, and she's trying to protect her investment. There are seventy-five stacks in that bag. Portia's offering that and the use of one of her new girls for three weeks as collateral and to make it an even hundred K."

"A hundred K? Shit, that means your new booty is worth twenty-five K?"

Lisa walked over to the desk, and a slow smile spread over Rodney's face as he realized who she was. That smile threatened to stop Lisa's heart. Everything inside her told her to turn around and run as fast and as far away as she could.

Rodney stared at Lisa for a full two minutes before turning his attention back to Honey. "I'm listening."

"Portia says that she will give you another hundred K in three weeks and ten percent of whatever Begonia earns in the next six months."

Rodney raised his eyebrows and looked at Amir.

Amir zipped the bag back up and went back to stand against the wall. "It's seventy-five K."

Rodney smiled and looked at Lisa. "So, you a professional ho now?"

Lisa stuck her chin in the air. "I'm trying to pay for college, and flipping burgers ain't going to cut it."

Rodney looked at Honey. "I'm seriously considering the offer, Honey, but there is one small problem."

Honey cocked her eyebrow. "And that is?"

"Begonia here only has two weeks left."

Lisa swallowed hard, walked around Rodney's desk, and sat down on his lap. "That doesn't sound like such a big problem to me."

Rodney smiled and rested his hand on Lisa's thigh. "You might be right, Lisa."

Begonia locked eyes with Lisa and searched her friend's face but saw no signs of fear. She looked at Rodney. "Do we have a deal?"

Rodney smiled at her, an evil smile that never touched his eyes. "We sure do, ma'am. I have to say that I could've sworn you would be dead by now, what with all your activity in South Philly. I've got to tell you that you've got more heart than half the niggas in my camp." He squeezed Lisa's thigh and let his thumb travel up the hem of her dress. "You have three weeks."

Chapter 49

The intake procedure for the federal prison was practically the same thing Violet went through at the county, except she didn't freak out when they searched her the second time around. Violet kept her head down and her mouth shut as per the US Marshal's advice. He had spoken to her briefly in the hall after she took the lie detector test. He passed her a note that he said was from Begonia.

"Your sister is a remarkable young woman, Ms. Brown. I want you to know that we are going to do everything in our power to protect all of you."

It was a single sheet of notebook paper folded up into a neat square. It looked just like the notes they would pass around in class when they were kids. Violet felt a shiver up her spine when he shook her hand and passed the piece of paper to her. She asked Mike and Brandi if she could use the bathroom so she could read it.

Violet's hand trembled as she unfolded the paper.

Vy,

You are not alone. I'm doing everything I can, and I'll see you soon. I love you.

Bee

That was it. Three little sentences written in her sister's handwriting, and it changed everything. Violet no longer felt the need to end it all. It was replaced by a fierce sense of loyalty and love for her sisters. She had no clear idea of what Bee was doing, but she knew it couldn't possibly be easy. Violet smiled at the thought of her sister working with the police instead of against them.

The smile and the good feeling stayed with her as she walked to the prison library. For a short amount of time, all of the pain she felt lifted. No matter what happened, she knew that her sister didn't hate her and that she was not alone.

Violet looked around when she got to the library. There were already a few inmates in there, so she walked to the back and took a seat facing the wall. Someone had left a book on the table about the history of women in politics. Violet shrugged and picked it up. She would read anything as long as it was well written.

She was about two chapters in when a loud crash in the aisle closest to her caused her to look up. The older white inmate named Cheryl, who worked restocking books, was being backed into a corner by two younger girls. Cheryl's cart was overturned in the middle of the aisle.

Violet looked around, but the place was empty. Everyone must have cleared out when the two young thugs came in. Closing her book, she rose smoothly from the table and headed toward the exit.

"No, please don't," Cheryl moaned.

Violet stopped dead in her tracks. The desperation of Cheryl's cry tore at Violet's heart and touched that deep well of pain that she had inside. She knew beyond a shadow of a doubt that Cheryl was going to be raped today. She knew that kind of desperate plea, having made it herself. Violet turned around against her better judgment.

"Hey, Mrs. Cheryl, I loved the book you gave me on the Civil War. You were right. It wasn't boring." Violet walked over to them like she couldn't see what was going on.

"What the fuck is wrong with you?" said the short black girl. She had braids in her hair going straight back like Queen Latifah in *Set It Off*.

"Huh?" Violet asked, playing dumb. "I just wanted to tell Mrs. Cheryl about the book."

The second girl, who had Mrs. Cheryl pinned against the wall, released her and turned her attention toward Violet as well.

Queen Latifah looked Violet up and down with a sneer on her face. "Mrs. Cheryl is busy right now, so why don't you come back a little later? You guys can talk about all the fuckin' books in this place as soon as we're done here."

"Oh, she don't have to leave, Sammy. Look at how cute she is." She walked over to Violet and fingered the long braid that rested on her shoulder. "Look at all this pretty hair. You want to play with us, don't you, Barbie?"

"Get the fuck off of me," Violet said between clenched teeth.

"Oh hooo hooo," Sammy said as she came to stand on the other side of Violet. "Barbie has a little backbone."

Cheryl closed her shirt and ran from the library.

Oh, that's just rich, Violet thought, as she watched her go. *That's what I get for trying to be a hero.*

Sammy ran her hand up Violet's arm and down the middle of her chest. "You are a pretty little thing, aren't you?" Her breath smelled like stir fried shit.

Violet decided in that instant that if they wanted her, they would have to kill her first. She grabbed the big girl's hair, jerked her head back, and bit her in the face as hard as she could. Sammy punched Violet in the ribs so hard that the air rushed out of her lungs. She released the girl and fell to her knees.

Once Violet was down, the blows didn't stop coming. She was kicked and punched until everything went dark.

Diana banged on Portia's door like a madwoman.

T-Bird nervously looked around at the neighbors' houses. "Come on, Mrs. Diana. You don't have to knock that hard."

"Oh, shut up, T-Bird, before I start knocking on you." She turned around and started kicking on the door. "Open this door, or I swear I will break it down."

Honey opened the door and was surprised to see a tall, middle-aged white woman standing on the porch with T-Bird. Diana walked in the house without waiting for an invitation. She pushed past Honey and started screaming Begonia's name.

"Are you crazy, lady?" Honey asked, rubbing her shoulder.

"No, I am not crazy. I'm pissed off." Diana walked to the kitchen and back and then started up the stairs. "Begonia, I know you are in here, and I want you to come here and explain yourself this instant."

Babygirl came out in the hallway dressed in a pink nightie. "What in the world is going on?"

"Where's Begonia?"

"In the back room."

Honey rolled her eyes. "Babygirl!"

"What?"

Diana charged into the back room and ripped the covers off a sleeping Begonia.

"What in the hell . . ." Begonia said. She brought her hand up to her face to cover her eyes while she squinted at Diana. "Mom, what are you doing here?"

Diana threw her hands up in the air. "What do you mean what am I doing here? What are you doing here? You left home, dropped out of college, and quit your job to live in a whore house? Are you serious? Did you think I wasn't going to find out?"

Begonia got out of the bed and folded her arms under her chest. "How did you find out?"

T-Bird stuck his head in the room. "I'm sorry, Bee. She cornered me at the bus stop and threatened to tell my mom that I was hustling again."

"You can't be fucking serious, T?"

T-Bird shrugged. "What? You know how my mom is."

"Hello!" Diana screamed. Aam I not standing right here in a whore house? You watch your mouth, put your clothes on, and come home right now."

"Mom, I can't go home."

"Oh, yes you can, and yes you will. I've got a visit from Mrs. Briggs this morning, and she says that your sister Daisy is getting sick. She says that she is refusing to eat because you won't come and visit her anymore. I didn't know you were visiting her in the first place. There was also a message on the answering machine for you from a Mr. Thompson. What is he, one of your clients?"

"No, he's not a client."

Babygirl stood at the door. "Why is she calling that white woman Mom?"

"That's her foster mother," Honey said from behind her.

T-Bird frowned. "Yo, Bee, you sleeping with dudes? Who is this Thompson guy?"

"Shut up, T-Bird. Ain't nobody sleeping with nobody." Begonia closed the door in their faces and turned to Diana. "Mom, look . . ."

"Don't 'Mom, look' me, Begonia. Put your clothes on so we can go see your sister. You can tell me what the hell is going on around here on the way over there." Diana turned on her heels and stormed out of the room. She pushed by the girls on the steps and hollered over her shoulder. "You've got two minutes, Begonia. I'll be in the car."

Begonia tore off the nightgown that Portia let her borrow and slipped on a pair of jeans and a t-shirt. She put on her sneakers and walked out the bedroom door, ignoring the questions that everyone threw at her all at once.

She walked to Diana's beat-up old Lincoln Town Car and got into the passenger side. Buckling her seatbelt, she faced her foster mother and sighed. "What do you want to know?"

Diana started the car. "Everything, Begonia. I want to know everything. So why don't you just start at the beginning, and don't stop talking until you get to the end."

By the time they pulled up in front of Mrs. Briggs' house, Diana was in tears. She wiped her eyes and took a deep, shuddering breath. "Why won't you let me help you, Begonia?"

"Mom, you may live in my world, but you aren't really a part of it. I keep things from you to protect you, because I love you. I only told you a fraction of what I'm going through right now, and I can see your heart breaking. How do you think that makes me feel? Why would I come to you with my problems when I know you can't help me, and I know that it will hurt you?" Begonia got out of the car. "What sense does that make?"

Diana was speechless. She got out of the car and followed Begonia to Mrs. Briggs' door.

Begonia was tempted to pick the lock and walk right in, but she didn't want to upset Diana any more than she already had, so she rang the doorbell and waited.

Mrs. Briggs came to the door looking ragged. She was dressed in pajamas. Her hair was tangled, and her eyes bloodshot. She pulled Begonia into a fierce hug. "I didn't thank you were going to come."

"Why would you think that?" Begonia asked, pulling away from her. "Where's my sister?"

"She is in her room." Mrs. Briggs waved Diana in the house. "Thank you so much," she said, closing the door.

"I'll be down in a few minutes," Begonia told them as she headed up the steps. Diana tried to follow her, but Begonia stopped her. "I need to talk to my sister alone. Please wait down here with Mrs. Briggs. I promise that this won't take long."

Diana nodded and walked back down the steps. Her eyes were still glossy, like she was holding back tears. "Take all the time you need."

Begonia walked into her sister's bedroom and climbed into her bed. She took a moment to just watch her sister sleep. *God, help me. I can't do what I need to do if something happens to this little girl.* She picked up Daisy's small, sleeping form and laid her down on her chest. Daisy's feet hung past Begonia's knees.

"Wake up, munchkin."

Daisy opened her eyes, and the corners of her mouth turned up in a small smile. "Bee," she said softly and snaked her arms around Begonia's neck for a hug. "Where have you been?"

"I've been busy, little girl." Begonia fought the lump in her throat. Her little sister was covered in sweat and was weak. "Why haven't you been eating?"

"I don't want anything from them. I know they made you go away."

"Is that what you think?"

Daisy nodded her head.

"Come on, sit up." Begonia sat up and cradled Daisy in her arms. "No one can make me stay away from you. If I stay away for a while, it's because I have to. Do you understand?"

Daisy shook her head.

"Yes, you do."

"No, I don't, Bee. I don't want to be here anymore. I want to be with you and Violet and Mommy." Big fat tears fell down Daisy's cheeks, and Begonia wiped her eyes and pulled her in close.

"Aw, munchkin, don't cry. We all want to be together, but things don't always work out that way. I'm doing the best I can to make sure everyone is safe and happy, and maybe we can be together, but maybe we can't. I'm not going to lie to you." She held Daisy away from herself so that she could look in her eyes. "I have to go away for a little while. I'm going to need you to promise me that you'll be a good girl and listen to Mrs. Briggs. You have to eat all of your food and take all of your medicine so that you can stay strong and be healthy. Do you understand me?"

Daisy nodded her head.

"Good girl." Begonia scooted to the edge of the bed and stood up with Daisy in her arms. "You are getting big, girl. I don't know if we can keep calling you munchkin."

Daisy giggled against Begonia's neck, and Begonia smiled. "Now, that's what I like to hear. We're gonna go downstairs and get something to eat. There's a lady I'd like you to meet. Her name is Ms. Diana, and she's my foster mother."

"She's like Mrs. Briggs?"

"Yup, she's exactly like Mrs. Briggs, and she's going to help Mrs. Briggs take care of you. I don't want to hear about you not eating again, okay?"

"Okay."

Begonia kissed Daisy on her soft, wet cheeks. "I love you, li'l girl. Always remember that. I love you so much."

Chapter 50

The bathroom filled with steam as hot water cascaded down Lisa's form. *You can do this, Lisa,* she thought as she turned the water off and stepped out of the shower. She grabbed a thick towel out of the closet and wrapped herself in it. Running her hand across the mirror so she could look at her reflection, she bit her bottom lip and took the bobby pins out of her hair, letting it fall down to her shoulders. *I miss my braids.*

She squeezed Victoria's Secret Pear Glaze into the palm of her hand and slathered it onto her legs and arms while she was still wet. *You are not the first person to fuck for something other than love, Lisa. You have to keep your mind focused on the end game.* She toweled the excess lotion off and shimmied into a pair of purple lace panties. She slid a sheer black nightgown over her shoulders. It fell down to her manicured toes. Lisa put the towel in the bathroom hamper and her clothes in her duffle bag. Looking around the bathroom, making sure everything was in order, she thought, *You can't stay in here all night, Lisa.*

For the last couple of days, Rodney had been the perfect gentleman. He wasn't all over her like she imagined. He talked to her about his desire to travel and get out of the game. He was fascinated by the stock market and made modest investments, claiming that once he was legit, he was going to be a stockbroker. Lisa did her best to play her part. She listened to all of his stories. Smiled when she was supposed to, talked when she was supposed to. If he wanted to act like they were starting some sort of relationship, she was game.

She shook herself and put her hands on the door knob. She opened the door and stuck her head into the hall.

It was empty.

She sighed and walked quickly to Rodney's room at the front of the house. Lisa had been sleeping in the guestroom; however, Rodney made it crystal clear that he wanted her tonight.

She knocked on his door, then took a step back nervously. Goosebumps sprang up on her arms as she watched the door swing open slowly.

Rodney stood there, shirtless, with crisp white boxers and black jeans. The jeans were loose and unfastened. He had to hold them up with one hand. He stepped back a few paces to let Lisa in. "I thought you were going to be in the shower all night."

Lisa walked toward his king-sized bed and shrugged. 'What can I say? I like showers, and your water is hot and your pressure is strong. I really could have stayed in there all night."

"I would have had to come in there and get you," Rodney said, closing and locking the door.

Lisa sat down on the bed and crossed her legs. "I don't think I would have minded that." She leaned back, letting her breasts poke through the sheer nightgown. It was chilly in his room, so her nipples were erect and straining against the thin material. She arched her back for maximum effect.

Rodney walked over to her, rubbing the hard-on in his pants. "You are a beautiful little thing."

"You think so?"

He dropped to his knees in front of her and pushed her nightgown up her thighs. "Oh, I'm certain of it." He parted her legs and ran his tongue over her panties.

Lisa gripped the down comforter in a heady mix of fear and pleasure. He sucked the lace between surprisingly soft lips. His mustache and goatee grazed her skin, and her legs began to tremble under his fingertips. Lisa's head rolled back as he ripped the delicate lace seat of her panties and plunged his entire face into her wetness.

She looked up at the ceiling, confused. *I didn't know. Oh my God . . . I didn't expect it to feel . . .* Every stroke of his tongue made shockwaves of pleasure travel up her spine.

"You taste so good," he moaned while he tortured her with his mouth for a full five minutes.

Lisa's eyes glazed over. Heat rose from her mid-section and spread out over her entire body.

Rodney traced the outside of her hole with his thumb before sticking it inside of her. He sucked her clit between his teeth and started to gently nibble on it.

"Oh my God," Lisa hollered.

Rodney smiled as he watched her stomach muscles contract and felt her walls tighten on his thumb. Her entire body began to fold in on itself, but he didn't let her feel the full extent of her orgasm. He rose up off the floor, grabbing both of her feet. He brought her legs together and held them together by her ankles with one hand.

Lisa's chest heaved as the realization of what was about to happen slammed into her. Shame warred with ecstasy as he rubbed his hard cock against her swollen clit.

Lisa hissed like a cat. "I'm not supposed to like it," she said softly.

Rodney smiled. "And why is that?" he said while pushing inside of her.

Lisa couldn't answer him. Her ability to talk or think straight left as soon as he entered her.

He pushed inside of her until his hips pressed on the back of her thighs and she was filled with him. "Damn, girl. You too tight to be a ho for real."

Sweat dripped down his forehead as he pulled out slowly with a guttural moan. He repeated that motion until he could feel her adjust to his size, until he was slick with her juices. Until she stopped holding back, until she cried out freely, pushing her hips up to meet each thrust. Then he let her legs fall to her sides. He dropped down on top of her and slipped his hands under her back, gripping her shoulder and pulling her whole body down into his thrust.

Lisa screamed out until he covered her mouth with his, snaking his tongue in and out slowly until she returned his kiss, fiercely sucking on his tongue and lips. She tasted herself on his tongue, and it drove her insane.

Rodney began to speed up the pace. He rose up off of her, cupped her breasts, and pinned her to the bed.

Lisa began to tremble as a deep orgasm erupted inside of her. "Oh my God!" she screamed again.

Rodney pulled out of her, backed up, and jerked his dick until he came on the floor. He stumbled onto the bed beside Lisa and pulled her close to him. "Are you okay?" he asked softly.

Lisa nodded her head, but she wasn't okay, She was confused. *How can you feel so good and so bad at the same time*? she wondered as tears slid from the corners of her eyes.

***

Begonia sat in the visiting room, alternating between cracking her knuckles and biting her nails. Her leg started to shake, and she sat up straight in the chair, forcing herself to be still. *God, I need a cigarette,* she thought as she cracked her neck and rolled her shoulders. She hadn't slept well in the last couple days after she saw Daisy. She couldn't get over the guilt of leaving her there without saying goodbye. Daisy could have gotten really sick, and Begonia wouldn't have known anything about it.

She closed her eyes and exhaled. *This aint no time to have a pity party, Bee. Get the fuck over it and move on.* She looked around the visiting area at the few people gathered around to talk to the inmates and frowned. *Violet, how did you get here? You don't belong here. You belong in some sort of college studying and shit, and I belong in here.*

Violet came out the door and took a seat in the booth in front of her sister. She wore an orange jumpsuit. Her hair was pulled back into a sleek ponytail, and her facc looked like she'd been in a dogfight with some she-males.

They just sat there for a moment, staring at each other. Violet picked up the phone and waited for Begonia to pick up her end.

Begonia couldn't tear her eyes away from the bruises and cuts on her sister's face. She forced a smile. "Now don't you look pretty?"

Violet's eyes watered, but she returned her sister's smile. "I know, right. I'm going to be a model when I grow up."

Begonia laughed and wiped her own tears. "I can see that, you being a model and everything. You'd give Naomi Campbell a run for her money." She scrubbed her face with her sleeve. "We'll be rolling in the dough."

Violet's laughter quickly turned into loud sobs. She put her hand up on the window and put her head down. She was no longer able to look Begonia in the eye. "I'm so sorry, Bee," she said. "I am so sorry."

Begonia shook her head and touched the glass over her sister's hand. "Don't do that, Violet. Look up at me. Look at me right now."

Violet lifted her head as her tears flowed freely from her eyes. She bit her bottom lip and sank into her chair, but she met her sister's gaze, and she held it.

"Good," Begonia said, nodding. "You listen to me. I am not mad at you, Violet. I love you, and we are going to get through this. You hear me?"

Violet nodded.

"Good, then let me hear you repeat it."

Violet wiped her eyes and sat up in her chair. "We are going to get through it."

"Damn straight," Begonia said, smiling. "Now, tell me. How are you doing? I mean, um, how's the baby and everything?"

Violet grabbed the phone wire and wrapped it around her finger. "The baby is gone."

"What do you mean the baby is gone? You had it already?"

"No, I didn't have it. I got rid of it."

Begonia said nothing. She just sat there looking at her sister and letting the pain of it all wash over her.

"You got rid of it, or whoever decorated your face got rid of it for you?"

Violet let go of the phone cord and brought her hand up to her busted lip. "This?" She shook her head. "No, the baby was gone before I got here."

Begonia just nodded her head.

"You don't know what he did to me. What he let his friends do. I co-couldn't carry that b-ba . . ."

"Shhhhhh, don't, Vy. You don't have to explain it. It's done. We don't ever have to talk about it again."

"How's Daisy doing?"

"She's good. She's getting big." Begonia pulled Daisy's latest school picture out of her pocket and held it up to the glass.

"Oh my God, Bee, she's really getting big." Violet laughed. "She's starting to look like Doreen."

Begonia put the picture away and rolled her eyes. “Don’t remind me. She’s doing okay, though. She’s living in a foster home out Southwest Philly with some pretty cool people.”

“Oh yeah, and how many times have you broken in these cool people’s house?”

Begonia smirked. “Pretty much every night.”

Violet shook her head. “What about Doreen? How is our dear mother?”

“She pretty much gets her ass whooped daily in the crack houses she hangs in.”

“Same old Mom.”

“Yup, dear old Doreen. The glass pipe is still her best friend.” Begonia traced her sister’s hand through the glass. “We gonna talk about your face or what?”

Violet put her head down. “I got your note. That marshal guy, um, Mr. Thompson. He gave it to me before I was transferred.”

“Yeah, he’s a good dude. Now about your face?”

“Look, Bee, it’s a little rough in here, you know. This is a heavy duty prison facility. It’s not like I’m off in day camp or something.”

“Oh, okay, you’re right.” Begonia sniffed and leaned into the glass. “I got to go, Vy. I just came here to tell you that I love you. Tell you in person that I’m doing all I can to get you out of here. I don’t know how much we can trust Mr. Thompson or the DA, but they’re all we got.” Begonia stood up from her chair. "These bitches in here keep fuckin' with you. I get it. You are young, pretty, and smart, all unforgivable sins in the ping. Then one day, you wake up and realize that the grime of North Philly runs through your veins. You remember your name is Violet Brown, and you go to war!" Begonia hung the phone up and left the room.

Lisa sat in the center of Rodney's bed Indian style, dressed in nothing but his pajama top. She was tired, but she didn't want to lie down and go to sleep. Her body was still tingling from their last encounter. She'd been with him for week and a half, and he'd made love to her a dozen times in the last four days.

She was enjoying it.

Lisa felt as if she was the worst person on the planet. *What the hell is wrong with me? How can I like sleeping with a person that does what he does?* She leaned over and grabbed the phone off the nightstand and set it on the bed in front of her. She started to pick up the phone but stopped abruptly. Biting on her thumb, she looked at the bedroom door. She rolled her eyes and slid off the bed. Opening the door, she cleared her throat and hollered down the stairs.

"Yo, Rodney, are you using the phone?"

"Naw, babe, nobody's on the phone."

"Is it okay if I call my sister?"

"You can call whoever you want to."

Lisa climbed back onto the bed, picked up the phone, and dialed Tabitha's number.

Shanice answered the phone. "What's up?"

"Hello, um, can I speak to Tabitha?"

"She's not here. Who's calling?"

"Shanice, is that you?"

"Lisa, what the hell is going on? You was supposed to call a few days ago. Momma Mabel is freaking out. You have to call her as soon as you get off the phone with me."

"I will. I promise. What have y'all been telling her?"

"We told her that you were at some sort of McDonald's convention. We got a couple of people at the restaurant to back it up. What took you so long to call? Are you okay?"

"I'm okay."

"You don't sound okay, Lisa, what the fuck is going on over there? Is he hurting you?"

"No, Shanice, he's not hurting me. I'm okay. I swear."

"Well, why did it take you so long to call us?"

Lisa hit the flash button on the receiver to make sure no one was on the other line. Satisfied, she hit the flash button again and spoke quickly.

"Lisa. Hello, Lisa?"

"I'm here."

"Hey, what happened? Where did you go?"

"I had to make sure the line was clear."

"Is he hurting you?"

"No, I'm not hurt."

"Something is wrong. I can hear it in your voice. What is it, then? Wait, where is his girlfriend? Is she fucking with you?"

"No, he sent her and three of her friends to Jamaica or something for like a month. We've been, well, you know, screwing."

Shanice laughed. "Well, that's sort of the point."

"I know, but . . ."

"But what? Is he into all kinds of weird shit?"

"No, it's not that."

"He wants to put it up your butt, doesn't he?"

"No, Shanice."

"Don't tell me he wants you to put it up his butt?"

"No. Look, where's Tabitha? 'Cause I can't talk about this with you."

"I told you she's not here, so you might as well spill it."

Lisa sighed. She flashed the line again to make double sure it was clear, and then she told Shanice about the mind-blowing sex that she and Rodney were having. "I like it."

"What? You like what?"

"You know . . . it. I like it."

Shanice burst out laughing. "Is that why you sound like somebody pissed on your sunny day? News flash, my big little sister. Sex feels good."

"I know that, but—"

"No buts, Lisa. You are in a fucked up situation for a good cause. The fact that you are getting to cum on the regular is a fucking bonus. Don't feel bad about that shit."

"Yeah, but I'm so confused. How can I like it?"

"Does he have a big dick?"

Lisa giggled. "Yeah."

"And he knows how to use it. Girl, I'll be over as soon as Tab comes back. I can use a good nut."

Lisa laughed. "You better carry your ass home."

"Lisa, all jokes aside, you are one of the best people I know. There is nothing wrong with you. You are human. Sex feels good, and great sex feels spectacular. Nothing more, nothing less. Okay?"

"Okay."

"Call Momma Mabel."

"I'm gonna call her first thing in the morning. I promise."

"Good. Now go fuck him sideways for me."

Lisa hung up on her. She put the phone back on the nightstand. She lay back on the bed, feeling a little better.

Rodney came into the room and smiled at seeing Lisa stretched out on the bed. "You know I can get used to seeing you in my bed like that."

"Oh, yeah? And what about Carmen?"

"Maybe I can get her ass to stay in Jamaica." He slipped his shirt over his head. "Put some clothes on. We're goin' out to get something to eat."

Lisa's whole body jerked in fear, but she recovered before Rodney could notice her reaction. She slipped out of his night shirt and put it into the hamper. She hated going out with him. Philly is small, and she was afraid to run into the wrong people.

She pulled a pair of jeans on with a short-sleeve red blouse and black Mary Jane shoes. "Can't we just stay inside and order a pizza or something?"

"Naw, shawty, I've got to make a couple a rounds so that niggas can feel my presence, ya mean?"

"Yeah, I guess," Lisa mumbled.

Rodney walked over to Lisa and pulled her to him. "You got me goin' through cabin fever, holding a nigga hostage with that good pussy."

Lisa smiled and sat down on the bed while Rodney put on all of his jewelry. *Play your position, Lisa. Focus on the end game.* The butterflies in her stomach didn't leave her; they intensified when they walked out the door.

She walked to Rodney's car nervously. Amir walked behind her. His eyes were glued to her ass. He was high as hell off wet and giggling for no reason at all.

"Lisa!"

Lisa turned around at the sound of her name being screamed and pressed herself against the car.

Tony came running down the street. He stopped short in front of Lisa. "So it's true, huh? You stopped fuckin' with me for Rodney?"

Amir laughed. "I'm gonna need you to give this bitch at least six feet, my brotha." Amir lifted his shirt up, exposing his gun. "Or I can give you six feet. You know what I'm saying?"

Tony ignored Amir. "What about all that shit you said, huh? You said that you could never see yourself with a drug dealer. What happened, huh? You had a fuckin' epiphany or something?"

The pain on Tony's face split Lisa's heart in two. She didn't know what to say. She just stood there, shaking her head no and wishing she could disappear.

Rodney and Bunky came around the car. Bunky's gun was drawn and pointed directly at Tony's head. Rodney yanked Lisa around the car and pushed her back toward the house. "Go inside and stay there."

"Please don't hurt him. Tony, just go home, okay, 'cause you don't understand."

Nate grabbed Lisa and pulled her in the house.

"Wait. Let me talk to him. Get off of me." Lisa struggled to be free of Nate, but he hauled her off of her feet and carried her in the house.

"What the fuck don't I understand, huh? What, I wasn't pulling in enough cash for you?" Tony was breathing hard and shouting at the top of his lungs. "I can't believe I fell for your shit. You just wanted kingpin status. Then I got to hear it in the streets, though. Niggas laughing at me on the basketball courts and shit."

"I see why, nigga," Amir said, laughing. He lowered his gun and was holding his stomach, leaning against the car and cracking up. "You's a funny motherfucker, out here about to cry over some pussy."

Tony punched Amir in the jaw, knocking him out cold. "Laugh at that, you little bitch."

Bunky put his gun against his temple. "That was a mistake, youngin'. Looks like it's gonna be your last."

Tony put his hands up in the air, but Rodney pushed Bunky's arm down, lowering his gun. "I can't let you shoot a man right in front of my house, dawg."

Tony breathed a sigh of relief and started to lower his arms. Rodney snatched the gun out of Bunky's hand and hit Tony across the temple with it. Tony fell to his knees.

"It's okay for you to whoop his ass, though."

Bunky kicked Tony in the ribs, and then walked over to Amir and helped him up off the ground. They beat Tony until his blood stained the asphalt.

Chapter 51

Bradley Thompson sat on the edge of the queen-sized bed in the Holiday Inn Express downtown. He was watching local police detectives and DEA agents fit a young girl with a wire and explain the ins and outs of a narcotic sting. It was making him sick. He got up from the bed and walked over to the dresser. "You know, Begonia, it's not too late for you to back out of this. You don't have to go this far."

Begonia frowned up at him. She was wearing a pair of blue jeans and a navy blue Bart Simpson t-shirt. Her wiretap ran around her bra and up the strap. Her hair was cut in a bob that swung just below her chin, making her look much older than she was. "Have you seen my sister lately, Mr. Thompson?"

He shook his head.

"Well, she looks like warm dog shit. They took her innocence without blinking an eye or missing a step. She wanted to be a teacher—a high school history teacher. You almost never saw my sister without a book in her hand. Yeah, she was a sweet little girl, and they just came along and ripped out her soul." Begonia closed her eyes and took a deep breath. "She doesn't belong in a cage, Mr. Thompson. They do, and I aint backing out of shit."

A young black guy who looked to be about Begonia's age but had to be older based on the gun on his hip and the badge swinging around his neck came into the room and dropped a duffle bag on the bed. "That's two hundred grand in small bills." He turned to Begonia. "We are about to start running sound checks from the van outside. Keep talking normally. The van will be parked a half a block away from you when we get back to North Philly, so we need to test the ranges."

"You got it, youngin'." She smiled and turned to the senior agent in the room, an older white guy named Mark. "I'd like to go over everything you want me to do again."

Violet waited behind the shower wall with a white t-shirt rolled up in her hands like she was about to put it on. She held her breath when she heard the water stop running. Fear made her pulse jump, but it didn't make her leave. Sammy made every day a living hell for Violet, like she woke up in the morning with the sole purpose of fucking with her. Violet was determined to take it until she saw Begonia. Everything changed inside of her after that. She did not know how long she would be locked up, but she knew she was done with being fucked with.

Pressing her back into the tiles, Violet raised the t-shirt up in the air. Time seemed to slow down, and her sister's words echoed in her head. Begonia was constantly giving Violet fighting tips. *If a bitch needs another bitch to help her fight, Violet, then she can't fight at all. You get her alone, and then you make her regret that she ever saw your face.*

Violet smiled at the memory. The fear was gone. It had been replaced by white hot anger.

Sammy's feet slapped the wet floor like gunshots.

Come on, bitch, Violet thought as she looked around making sure the room was still clear. She knew she didn't have a lot of time, so she needed to be quick.

Violet wrapped the t-shirt around Sammy's head the moment she exited the stall. "Guess who?" Violet said as she yanked her head down and kneed her in gut.

Sammy hit the floor sputtering. Violet jumped on her back and ground her face into the cement. "My name is,Violet Brown," she said as she stuffed the t-shirt in her mouth to muffle her screams. She punched her in the ribs—they cracked on impact. Standing up, she kicked her in the stomach twice and once in the face. "I'm from North Philly." She flipped Sammy's limp form onto her back and spread her legs open. "And if you even look in my direction,"—Violet kicked her in her pussy as hard as she could—"I'll find you by yourself agian, sweet pea, and I'll fucking kill yóu."

Violet left Sammy on the bathroom floor, curled up in a ball, bleeding and crying. She walked to her cell, trying to figure out how she was going to corner Sammy's little friends. She knew it would take some time, but at the moment, time was on her side.

Portia sat in the DA's chair, doing the crossword puzzle from the daily newspaper. Honey was perched on his desk, filling her nails, and Babygirl was leafing through the law books on his shelf.

"Give me a four-letter word for warm greeting," Portia asked, tapping her pen on his desk.

"Hello," Babygirl said brightly

"That's five letters, nimrod." Honey shook her head. "We need to get her back in school, Portia."

"Fuck you, Honey. How many letters is that?"

Honey stuck her middle finger up at Babygirl just as Richard walked in his office.

He closed the door quickly behind him. "What the hell is going on? Portia, what are you doing here? I thought I told you—"

Portia held up her hand, and Richard stopped speaking in mid-sentence. She rose smoothly from her chair and walked around his desk. "My poor little Ricky can't seem to keep the hoes in line. Tsk, tsk, tsk." She shook her head and leaned against the desk next to Honey. "We just came by to talk to you, Ricky. You are not being very hospitable."

Richard's face look strained, like he was constipated and trying to pass a very large turd.

Babygirl looked up from the book she was holding. "Why are all these book written so funny?"

Honey snatched the book from her and tossed it from the desk. "Don't look at any more books, love. You might just hurt yourself."

Portia cleared her throat. "Sit down, Richard."

He walked over to his desk and took a seat.

"That's a good boy. In a few moments, I will let you speak, but first, I want you to listen up and listen good. Do you understand?"

Sweat trailed down Richard's forehead, and the log in his pants began to stiffen and grow.

Portia looked down at Richard's pants and smiled. "I'm gonna take that as a yes." She nodded her head to Babygirl, who pulled a VHS tape out of her pocketbook and placed it on the desk in front of Richard. Portia sat on Richard's lap and wiggled around a bit. "You see, Ricky, this tape contains video footage of all our little games—all of our beatings, suckings, fuckings, and druggings are all here—live and in color." Richard started to whimper, and Portia rubbed his shoulder. "Oh, don't cry, Ricky. It's okay. It's our little secret. Nobody has to know." Portia stood up, grabbed a tissue off the box on his desk, and wiped his eyes.

"My friend is about to walk into a real live drug dealer's house with a wiretap and a bag of money. I want you to make sure she walks out again. I'm gonna need her sisters released to her care, both of them. I'm gonna need you to make good on their relocation, Ricky. They all get new names and new lives, just like on TV, or everybody's gonna know about our little secret, and you can kiss your career and all of your dreams goodbye." Portia picked up the tape and walked to the door, nodding her head for Honey and Babygirl to follow. "Oh, you can talk now, Ricky."

But he had nothing to say. He just put his head down on his desk and continued to cry

Lisa was on her stomach with her head buried in the pillow. Rodney had her ass up in the air, driving in and out of her twat like he was drilling for oil, but it didn't feel good. The sight of Tony falling to the ground played over and over in her head. The look of betrayal on his face and the sound of heartbreak in his voice didn't leave her. She knew that Tony would never forgive her, and that knowledge was killing her.

Rodney squeezed her hips. "Oh, shit," he growled. "This is some good motherfucking pussy." He pulled out of her and released on her back. "I can't believe this is the last day I'll get to tap this ass." He smacked her on the ass before collapsing on the bed beside her.

Lisa scooted off of the bed and limped toward the bathroom.

"Where are you going?"

"I'm going to take a shower. Begonia should be here soon."

Rodney got up off the bed and ran up behind Lisa. "I don't know if I can let an ass this fine go." He wrapped his arms around her waist. "What if I decided to keep you with me forever?"

Bile rose up in Lisa's throat, and she had to swallow hard to keep from throwing up on the carpet. She forced herself to smile and turn to face Rodney, slipping her arms around his neck. "A deal is a deal, Rodney. Although I must admit, it is a sweet deal. Maybe we can strike it again next semester."

"Now, that does sound good." He squeezed her tightly and nuzzled her neck. "Go ahead and take your shower. I don't want you to be all sex-funky when your girl shows up with my cash."

Chapter 52

Ice slid through Begonia's veins as she became completely removed from her emotions. She took one last puff of her cigarette and flicked it in the street before ringing the bell and leaning against the door jamb. She looked up at the stars in the night sky, knowing that this would probably be the last time that she ever saw them again. That knowledge didn't stop her from walking in the door when Big Mike opened it. She dropped her bag and put her hands against the wall as Nate got up to pat her down. She nodded her head to him in greeting, and he smiled in return.

Most people said they would die for their family, but Begonia meant it. Her only concern going in was that Lisa made it out. She walked past Amir sitting at the dining room table on her way to the basement; however, Big Mike stopped her before she could open the door.

"Hold up there now, speedy. Where are you going? Nobody said for you to go down there. Have a seat on the sofa, and Rodney and ya girl will be down soon."

Begonia thought about slicing Mike's face open again, but she shrugged it off and sat on the sofa instead. She put the bag down between her feet, leaned over, and rested her arms on her knees. "You know, Mike that scar really does look good on you."

"Oh, really," Big Mike said, laughing. "You funny, Begonia. I always said that you was a funny little bitch." He stopped laughing abruptly. "I'm glad you like this scar, because I'm going to give you one just like it real soon."

"I'm really scared, Mike. You see me shakin', don't you?"

Mike rolled his eyes and flagged his hand at Begonia.

You're such a pussy, Begonia thought. *Why the fuck they put you on the door is beyond me.*

Lisa came down the steps first, dressed in a short black minidress and matching heels. Her hair was pinned up in a bun, but her eyes had a sadness that tore at Begonia's heart. Lisa carried a small gym bag of her own on her shoulder, although she dropped it when she spotted Begonia. She ran to her and hugged her tightly.

"Oh my God, Bee. I'm so glad this is over."

"It's not over yet, sweetie," Begonia whispered in her ear while returning her hug just as tightly. "As soon as Rodney gives the word, you walk out the door and head to Twenty-second Street. Don't wait for me, and don't look back."

Lisa didn't like the sound of that. She squeezed Begonia tighter as her stomach twisted in fear. She kissed Begonia on her cheek and walked over to the mirror by the front window and pretended to check her makeup.

Atta girl, Begonia thought as she sat back down. Stay *close to the exit*.

Rodney came down the steps, followed by Bunky. Rodney sat in the chair in front of Begonia, and Bunky stood off to his right. "Is that my money?" Rodney asked with a smile.

Begonia returned his smile. "Sure is."

"Let's have a peek."

Begonia opened the bag, revealing rubber-banded stacks of twenties, fives, tens, and hundreds.

"You know what?" Rodney said, smiling broadly, "You are my kind of bitch." He nodded to Bunky, who snatched the bag from between Begonia's legs and dumped it out on the table in front of Amir.

Begonia's heart was doing the electric slide in her chest. She sat up straight and looked Rodney in the eye. "So we square, right, and my girl is free to go?"

Rodney looked at Amir but spoke to Begonia. "If you have all my money, ya girl is free to go. However, I would like to have a little talk with you."

"It's all here," Amir said simply.

Rodney shrugged and waved Lisa over to him. Lisa glanced at Begonia before walking over to Rodney. Her palms were sweating, and goosebumps rose up on her skin. She stopped in front of him, and he turned to Amir.

"Toss me a stack."

Amir grabbed a knot of money off the table and chucked it to Rodney, who then handed it to Lisa. "This is a gift. I want you to know that I'm here for you. Call me whenever you need me."

Lisa took the money and bent over to kiss Rodney softly on the lips. "Goodbye," she said. Stuffing the money in her bag, she hefted it on her shoulder and walked out the door.

As soon as the door closed behind Lisa, Begonia's heart settled into a normal rhythm. "You mind if I smoke?"

Rodney sat back and smiled. "It's your lungs."

Cute, Begonia thought as she pulled a soft pack of Newports from her pocket and knocked it on her fist. Nate walked over and lit her cigarette for her and handed her an ashtray.

"Thanks," Begonia said, taking a long drag. "What would you like to chat about?"

Rodney rubbed his chin. "You impressed me, shawty."

"How'd I do that?"

"First of all, you're sitting here talking to me. You should be dead."

"I'm not following you."

Rodney got up and walked over to his minibar. "You want a drink?"

Begonia shook her head.

Rodney poured himself three fingers of bourbon. "The last time I saw you, I said that girl would be dead in a week." He pointed at Bunky. "Ask him. I said that young trick can't even tell when she's in over her head." He sat back down. "Look at ya now, sitting in a den of killers, smoking a Newport." He shook his head, and a deadly glint came to his eyes. "I need to know how you managed that."

Begonia flicked her cigarette in the ashtray, got up, stretched, and walked over to the table. She picked up a stack of hundreds and fanned through the cash with her thumb. "You know, Rodney, it wasn't easy." She tossed the money back on the pile. "But seeing you shoot a motherfucker right in front of me was one hell of a motivator."

"I had to kill Kyle. He had become a liability, a very expensive mistake. I thought you would appreciate that after what he did to your sister. You know, they say you never really recover from a gang rape."

"Is that right?" Begonia asked, leaning against the wall that led to the kitchen. She let the comment about her sister slide off of her like water. Her survival instincts were on high alert. Rodney had just hung himself with that confession, and the boys in blue should be coming in any minute now.

Taking a step back, she scanned every possible exit.

"Yeah, that's right," Rodney said, putting his glass down on the table. "I need to know where you got all of this money."

Begonia opened her mouth to respond, but the battering ram exploded through the door, and DEA agents swarmed into the house.

The party turned into a shit storm in the space of five seconds. Big Mike was knocked unconscious, and Rodney hit the floor and covered his head like a little bitch. Nate shot an officer in the forehead and received two in the chest. Begonia didn't know what happened to Bunky and Amir because she'd turned around and dove through the kitchen door just as a bullet blasted through her.

She was stretched out on the kitchen floor, leaking blood and struggling to get a pack of cigarettes out of her pocket. As soon as she got a Newport free, she put it in her mouth and then realized she had no way to light it. "Oh, this day is just getting better and better."

Police officers swept through the kitchen dressed in full body armor with their guns drawn.

Begonia looked up at the cops "Which one of you fuckers shot me?"

Mr. Thompson busted through the line of police and dropped down on the floor at Begonia's side. "Dear God, I am so sorry. I never should have gone along with this."

"Bradley, please shut the fuck up and light my cigarette. I'm sure I won't die from a hole in the arm."

Epilogue

Eight months later . . .

"If you don't hold still, I swear I'll jab this hairpin straight through your skull," Lisa said while she tried to secure Tabitha's wedding veil.

"Okay, I'll try to stop moving around, but you do realize I'm about to get married today. Why am I the only one freaking out?"

"Because you're the only one who can't tell that you are being blessed." Lisa smoothed out Tabitha's gown and smiled. Tears sprang to her eyes. "Look how beautiful you are. Everybody doesn't get to love someone who's good for them and to them. I am so happy for you." Tabitha stood up and hugged Lisa just as Shanice walked into the room.

"I swear I can't leave you two together for five minutes without y'all crying all over each other. Sheesh! Get it together because I've got a surprise for you both." Shanice stepped to the side, and Violet walked in the door, followed by Begonia. Lisa and Tabitha rushed them.

Begonia was the first to pull away from their embrace, although she hung on Lisa's shoulder. "We can't stay for the ceremony, but I couldn't miss this day."

Tabitha let go of Violet and fanned her face. "Where's Daisy?"

Violet smiled. "She's in the other room with your mother, playing with Erica."

"How did you guys get here?" Lisa asked, wiping her tears.

"Oh, we got a ride." She walked to the door. "Hey, Tony, get your ass in here, or I swear I'm gonna stab you again."

Tony walked in the door dressed in a black tuxedo, and Lisa thought her heart was going to stop. She didn't know what to do or what to say.

"Tony . . . I . . ."

Tony walked up to Lisa and wrapped his arms around her. "Begonia told me everything, and I have the knife marks to prove it. I know why you did what you did, and I think you are very brave. It's okay, Lisa. It's okay."

Lisa felt a weight lift from her shoulders that she didn't know was there.

Violet hugged everybody again. Tears ran freely down her face. "We have to go, but I just wanted you all to know that I am so grateful for what you've done. You guys saved me from hell. Pulled me right from the flames. Thank you so much."